# CELEBRISI'S JOURNEY

# CELEBRISI'S JOURNEY

A Novel by David Rounds

 **J. P. TARCHER, INC.**
LOS ANGELES

DISTRIBUTED BY
HOUGHTON MIFFLIN COMPANY
BOSTON

Library of Congress Cataloging in Publication Data

Rounds, David
   Celebrisi's journey.

   Revision of: 1976 ed.
   I. Title.
PS3568.0887C4   1982       813'.54       81–50011
ISBN 0–87477–202–8               AACR2

Requests for such permissions should be addressed to:

J. P. Tarcher, Inc.
9110 Sunset Blvd.
Los Angeles, CA 90069

Library of Congress Catalog Card No.: 81–50011

Design by Valerie Daley

MANUFACTURED IN THE UNITED STATES OF AMERICA
P 10 9 8 7 6 5 4 3 2 1
*First Edition*

# AUTHOR'S NOTE

Gold Mountain Monastery, at 1731 Fifteenth Street in San Francisco, is a real place where the orthodox tradition of Buddhism is transmitted to the West under the direction of the Venerable Abbot Hsuan Hua. It is there and, subsequently, at the City of Ten Thousand Buddhas at Talmage, California, that the author has been a student since 1971. All the other institutions and, without exception, all the individuals portrayed in this novel are fictitious, and any resemblances to people living or dead or to specific institutions past or present are mere coincidence.

*Celebrisi's Journey* was first published, in an earlier version, by the Buddhist Text Translation Society of San Francisco, and the author gratefully acknowledges the Society's support of the book and its permission to publish the present volume.

If there is any merit in this work, the author dedicates it to the enlightenment of all beings.

*City of Ten Thousand Buddhas*
*Talmage, California*
*Anniversary of the Buddha's Birth, May 11, 1981*

# 1

# THE MONSIGNOR STUNT

Now I am to tell you how I came to this great place, and who I was before I came, if such a thing can be known. For the last two weeks, my son Vin has been visiting us here at the monastery. I've been doing my best since he came to explain what the religious life has meant to his father, who he hadn't seen in eleven years, and what it can mean to anyone. I won't say he hasn't understood; we have done our best to understand each other. He came all the way from New Jersey just for that, after begging his mother and stepfather for more than two years to send him, though he is only just fifteen. I think he is beginning to see why we live here in the way we do. But he hasn't been able to connect our life here with his own distant memory of his father, or with the life that I once lived and that he has always known.

It all began with the stunts. I've told Vin about them, but that hasn't been enough for him. I have to remember for his sake how the things that happened seemed to me back then, when I still knew nothing of what they were. I have to try to tell him how I changed in the language I knew when I was changing. I won't be able to do that completely, and Vin and all of you who are here to listen with him will have to pardon me for not always remembering everything faithfully. That year is very clear to me, but my mind is different now. I don't even talk the way I did when Vin last knew me.

I was and still am a very ordinary man. There was nothing on the surface then to distinguish me from any other working person around me. I went into the service after high school like everybody else, and after the service I got married like everybody else. I lived with my wife Margherita and our little boy Vincent, Vin for short, in a two-family house off Bergenline Avenue in West New York, New Jersey, which is where I was born. Joseph Richard Celebrisi was my name, Joey to my friends, and I had a job more or less like my friends had, operating a forklift truck on the night shift in a truck freight terminal in Jersey City. I took care of my family, like they did; I had clean habits. But I never gave up the stunts.

We'd done stunts since high school: myself, and Jimmy DiLorenzo, who'd been my best friend since kindergarten, and Steve Palcewski from Hoboken, who Jimmy had met in the high-school baseball circuit. At first the stunts were nothing but practical jokes meant to stand something solemn and self-important on its head. Later, when we'd come back from the service, they became intense and elaborate. Once we wired the Jersey City Armory so that all the lights went dead during the Army National Guard exercises. Another night we took apart the Revolutionary War cannon squatting like a black frog in the park along Boulevard East and reassembled it inside the mayor's office, to point at him the next morning when he came in. Another time we dressed up as policemen and kidnapped a crook named Herbie the Walnut, who was boss of the Bergen County mob, and we sent him up in a hot-air balloon over Newark Bay. He drifted down after a while and was rescued by a Japanese freighter carrying Toyotas. Margherita, Vin's mother, was convinced that the mob would track us down and pack us in concrete and toss us off the end of a garbage barge. But I believed we'd never get caught at the stunts. How could anybody trace us? It was impossible, because what we were doing in the stunts had nothing to do with who we normally were.

The whole point of the stunts, the way I'd come to see it, was to forget who I was and become someone else. Instead of my usual respectable working-person self, who would never do anything crazy to jeopardize his family, here I'd be concentrating everything on closing a trunk line in the armory before the night patrol was due, or pretending to a mobster that I was the police, sinking myself up to the hilt into being somebody I wasn't; who was I, then, at that moment? "Who's Celebrisi?" I'd ask myself. For a few minutes, I wouldn't know. And the thought that the truth about Celebrisi was a mystery, even to myself, would fill my mind with delight.

I never spoke to anyone about it, not even to Margherita. I didn't think there was anything special to tell. Everybody already knew that Joey was a wiseacre who didn't take seriously the things that people were supposed to take seriously. What filled my friends' minds left my mind empty. Hockey and football and who was getting married and who'd offended whom and the peaceniks demonstrating against the Vietnam War and the Cubans moving in along Palisade Avenue—from my point of view, the less I knew about such things the better, because out of my ignorance came ridiculous remarks that made everybody laugh. My own mind, after all, was lined with things that weren't any less ordinary: fixing up cars and tinkering with old electric motors, going to my job and working in my yard, playing with my kid and minding my own business, and now and then hiding out with Jimmy and Steve for a strategy session on the next stunt. If there wasn't much meaning in the things I did, there wasn't much meaning in anything else I knew that people did, either, and it never occurred to me that there might be something else to do, until the monsignor stunt broke my life open.

The monsignor stunt was Jimmy's idea. "Maybe they're right: the new monsignor isn't normal," he said; I remember we were discussing it in the garage where Jimmy worked, on Kennedy Boulevard. It was the beginning of July, eleven years ago.

He was taking a muffler off a beat-up old Nash, a 1957, which was the last year they made them. The new monsignor hadn't been in the parish a month and had already irritated practically everybody. He was young and slim and a bit soft in the face, with dark hair he wore in waves a bit too long. He blinked when he looked down on you, and people said he talked like a book, which is not a compliment in the kind of neighborhood that I grew up in. People there liked to look up to a monk or a priest, but only because they expected him to be a better person than they were, a person who led a purer kind of life; they weren't likely to forgive him if he put on airs and made a claim to their respect without deserving it. I believe the new monsignor would have been accepted if he had been given more of a chance, and if Jimmy and Steve and I hadn't interfered. But his appearance was against him. Carmella, Margherita's sister, who lived downstairs from us and could be counted on to hear and repeat every rumor, said she'd heard the new monsignor took a scrub brush to himself twice a day and changed his clothes, probably so he could get the smell of decent working people off him. It was also being said that he didn't even drink wine or beer. Just who did he think he was?

The straw that broke the camel's back was the Fleetwood limousine. The priest who'd come before him, the old Irish monsignor, who had just retired and who wasn't liked very much either, had used to make parish calls in a dove grey Fleetwood Cadillac; I remember you could just catch a glimpse of his black hat brim in the oval back window. Now that the old priest had left, people naturally assumed that whatever new priest was sent would have the decency to sell the limousine. No. The new monsignor fired the chauffeur and drove the thing himself. Everyone became very indignant. Someone started the rumor that the monsignor wrote poetry, and immediately everybody believed it. People will tolerate a lot from a priest, but you have to draw the line somewhere. The whole town wrote him off.

"Maybe he is a deviant, and maybe he isn't; now, how are you going to prove it?" is what Jimmy said.

"Follow him at night," Steve told him. "You couldn't lose that limousine."

"That isn't the point," Jimmy said. His idea was that it didn't matter what the poor priest's personal disposition actually was. There could be something wrong with him, although it wasn't very likely; he was just shy, maybe, and read too many books, or he'd grown up in a rich family and didn't belong with working people, or maybe he was secretly crazy. But if anyone in any other position wanted to look right, so that people would stop talking about him, he'd just let himself be seen going out with a decent-looking woman, and everybody would start talking about somebody else. The new monsignor, though, was in a very ruinous situation. He was a priest; how could he go out with a woman? Even if he did, it would have to be done on the quiet, and what use would that be? He was stuck. He couldn't repair his reputation. The stunt was to repair it for him.

We went over to Manhattan to a used-clothing loft where the theater actors go, and we dressed me up as a priest, since I was the only one with a slight enough build to pass for the monsignor. I got a wig with the proper waves, putty for the right shape of soft dimpled chin, and a pair of three-inch elevator shoes. Jimmy was always a genius for coming up with the proper raw materials. As for him and Steve, they dressed up as women. At first Steve claimed he couldn't possibly do it because of what his wife would say if she found out, but we badgered him into it. "How can anyone find out?" we said. Jimmy and I could always talk faster than he could. Besides, we needed two women, because it wouldn't be right for a priest to be going out with just one woman. We didn't want to do anything to endanger the new monsignor's record in regard to his vows.

Originally we'd planned our first appearance for a baseball game, but the wig and the elevator shoes wouldn't have passed the test in the glare. We had to settle for bars. Every Thursday night for a month, the three of us made the rounds of the dimmest night spots in Jersey City. It wasn't two weeks before Carmella said she'd heard that the new monsignor must be all right, because people were saying that he'd been seen with a woman. "With two women is what I heard," I told her. Carmella thought that wasn't very likely, but the next week there she was on the back stairs to say that I was right, it was two.

The stunt had worked. We'd planned to stop right there. But good stunts weren't easy to come by, and we weren't ready to let it go. We began inventing decorations. Jimmy and Steve dressed up as seminarians, and the three of us rented a rowboat and went fishing in the Hudson River off the Weehawken piers. I caught a catfish with a face like a demon out of hell. The next day we decided to row across the river to Manhattan. Steve said we were crazy, but we didn't pay any attention to him. Halfway across the river, we were spotted by the WCBS traffic helicopter on duty over the West Side Highway. The reporter flew over us, and we heard ourselves described over Jimmy's pocket radio. The reporter kept referring to us and joking about us with his anchor man. We docked alongside a luxury ocean liner at the Forty-Second Street pier, which was packed with shouting tourists and baggage and taxicabs. The radio news show had sent out a reporter to ask us what priests might be doing crossing the Hudson in a rowboat. Someone tried to take a picture of us. With our hats in our faces, the front page of the *Jersey Journal* had us right up top in the morning.

Was this really the new monsignor from West New York? People weren't sure any more. They argued in the bars and the beauty parlors about whether the priest in the photo in the *Journal* was too heavy-set to be the monsignor, or maybe it was him and he just looked heavy-set because of the camera angle? We were a success. The monsignor was a success. The whole parish flocked to St. Mary's of the Fields to hear this mystery man say Mass and give his sermons, which were full of little jokes and educated quotations and exhortations to be thoughtful of our fellow man.

Steve resigned. He said he wasn't doing another stunt for a good long while, if ever. But Jimmy and I couldn't resist another decoration, although it wasn't for the same reasons. What he wanted was what we'd always wanted from the stunts: another chance for something unusual, anything that would flavor the ordinariness of our lives. But for me the monsignor stunt was different from the others. None of the parts I had ever played in stunts before, even the act of cop, had prepared me for the change that was worked just by wearing a priest's clothes. On the street, on the bus, in the roughest tavern, the presence of a priest changed the air. People treated me with a special respect, as if I was a different order of a man. Half the time I didn't pay for my fare or my drinks. I felt sometimes that I was stealing. I'd always thought of the priesthood as just another kind of job, with its own uniform and special fringe benefits; the part of not having a family or much of your own property or private life had never struck me as important. But stashing the costume at Jimmy's garage and walking into my house after the stunt, with a sleeping four-year-old and a wife in front of the television set, I felt I had left behind another kind of existence. It fascinated me that someone could change the way he lived so completely. The new monsignor, I thought, or any priest, just by turning in his ordinary clothes for the Roman collar, had turned in his ordinary self to do a permanent stunt with real life.

Two nights later, the two of us stole the new monsignor's Fleetwood limousine from its parking place in front of the parish residence. We put the car on the lift in Jimmy's garage, made cutouts in the muffler, and jacked up the rear suspension—the kind of thing you see in high-school parking lots. We propped me up on cushions behind the steering wheel as the new monsignor. We powdered Jimmy's hair white and put him in the back seat in priest's clothes too, as the old monsignor, making sure that his black hatbrim showed clear in the oval back window. We roared down Bergenline Avenue at nine thirty the next morning.

Bergenline is the main street of West New York, full of gift shops and beauty parlors, bargain stores and supermarkets, pizza joints and newsstands where bets are placed. Our plan was to barge five blocks through the traffic, turn off, ditch the limousine, and disappear. It didn't happen. Our audience turned our heads. People poured out of the stores; kids ran up and pounded on the windows; the town was wound up like a top for the monsignor's next act, and here it was. When I'd driven the five blocks we'd planned, I didn't even ask Jimmy; I just swung the limousine around and drove back down the avenue again. We went up and down Bergenline nine times. The cutouts made a racket they must have heard in Secaucus on the far side of the Jersey Swamp. Jimmy gave benedictions through the oval back window. I had it nearly up to sixty and did the cleanest racing changes of my life. Who was going to flag down a monsignor? The cops just stared.

I believe we could have got clean away even then. But neither of us knew what we were doing or who we were anymore. I drove that Fleetwood all around West New York; I probably would have tried to drive it across the bottom of the Hudson River and up the sides of the Empire State Building if anyone had asked me. To us, this was the finest stunt of all.

Someone finally went and jimmied the police commissioner out from behind his desk, and when we went down Jackson Street, which is narrow, there was the commissioner parked broadside to our path in his personal car. He took his cap off his head and walked up reverentially to the new monsignor and the old monsignor, until he saw it wasn't any monsignor at all but Joey Celebrisi, who lived in one of those two-family houses off Bergenline Avenue, and Jimmy DiLorenzo, the night mechanic at the Shell station on Kennedy Boulevard. He went instantly red, and shouting burst out of him.

I didn't hear a word he said. Getting out of that car, looking around, I was absorbed in that stunt feeling of being somebody else, only it seemed a hundred times stronger than before, as if the feeling had been supercharged along with the limousine. I didn't exactly know where I was. Jackson Street was around me, and the people and the cars and the police commissioner puffing there and waving his arms, but the place of my thinking mind had been jacked up out of my head and was spreading upward into the air. As I stood there, my mind seemed to rise along the wooden houses and up the high brick walls of the knitting mills. Below me, all the people in the street moved silently and slowly; they could have been under a charm.

The street was filled with a golden light. It was like the last warm hour of sunlight of a summer evening, but far brighter; for a moment it half-blinded my eyes. I felt that my mind had filled the street to join the light, to be the same as it. I thought I had always lived in it without my knowing, and not only myself but everyone in West New York, everyone I had known and would ever know. Our thoughts moved together in the light like motes of dust that float in the sun. The light connected us; in it we were one. It struck me that what I had thought at the end of the other stunts was true: I had never actually known who I was. That fixed and separate person his friends called Joey was a mistake; he was a falsehood. He was someone else, and we all were someone else, something larger that moved beneath the ordinary days in happiness and light.

Suddenly the new monsignor himself was walking up beside his limousine. I hadn't noticed him before, but now he was staring at me very intently. I wondered if he also saw the golden light. As soon as I thought that, I believed it. I decided he was staring at me because he wanted to find out just who this other person was who knew. I told myself that it must be showing somehow on my face. I wanted to laugh with happiness, but I didn't exactly know where my body was to do the laughing. Shouldn't I know where my body is, though? Shouldn't I find it? While I had these thoughts, they seemed to sweep together down into my head. I was standing there on the ground. The light faded. Everything was as it always had been.

The monsignor was looking coolly around. Everybody including the police commissioner had shut up to watch him. The monsignor bent down for a look at the cutouts and the jacked-up suspension on his limousine. Then he straightened up and said, "Commissioner Lacerra, I want you to know how very much I regret this incident. As you may have heard, the parish has been anxious to sell this limousine for quite a while, but we were unable to secure a buyer until these two gentlemen"—he meant Jimmy and myself—"until these two gentlemen managed to locate a fancy automobile buff who wanted the car if it was modified in this manner. These gentlemen out of Christian charity offered to do the work, solely for the cost of the parts."

At first I thought maybe I'd missed something, but it was obvious that everyone there was thunderstruck at what the monsignor was saying. He pretended that he didn't notice. He had more to say in his sermon-giving voice about the temptation and distraction and source of discord that we all knew the limousine had been in the parish, not just to these young people— he nodded toward us—but to everyone, clergy and layman alike. Everyone murmured at that; he'd hit the right note. Therefore he, the monsignor, would insist that the new owner drive the limousine only under proper and seemly conditions. He moreover would insist that he, the monsignor, be held wholly responsible for this regrettable incident, as he understood that no one was injured? And there was no damage to property?

He let it be known that he was finished. The commissioner didn't say anything. What could he have said? The monsignor opened a rear door of the limousine for us, ushered us inside, got in behind the wheel himself, and waited without a motion or a sound until the commissioner turned his car around and the crowd moved off the road. Then he started up the engine, said "Mary Mother of God" when he heard the blat of those cutouts, and drove us away.

Still without saying anything, and with a small amused smile on his face as he drove, the monsignor sat politely through the noise of our thanking him and praising him for rescuing us. It was the first time I had seen him close at hand. He had the perfectly right features of the man in the magazine advertisement: square dimpled chin, straight nose, wavy dark hair, broad forehead. Only his eyes seemed like they might be a good priest's, with a look in them half of good humor and half of thoughtfulness. I wondered if his handsome face embarrassed him. If he was vain about anything, I thought, it would have to be his bookish speech.

When we had quieted down, he introduced himself—his name was Bolignioni—and then he asked us our names in turn, saying he'd been very curious to meet us. "I have something to thank you for," he said. "You let my parishioners know that I exist and also that we celebrate the Mass at their parish church, which they seemed to have forgotten. I presume it was you that put on those other performances as well?" We admitted that it was. "I must say you have a most peculiar way of propagating the faith," he said mildly. "Have you done it before?"

His treating it as something serious that aroused his curiosity made it look ridiculous. We were too uncomfortable to say anything.

"Why did you do it?" he asked.

Finally I answered, "There were some rumors going around, Father. We wanted to get rid of them. You know."

"No, I don't know," he said. "What were they?"

"I wouldn't want to say, Father. If people don't know something, then they invent it, that's all. We're real sorry if we embarrassed you."

"Did you embarrass me?" he said.

Neither of us would say.

"At any rate," he went on, with zest in his voice, "I wouldn't want to have missed that police commissioner; he was wonderful. It isn't every day you can have fun like that in these clothes I'm wearing. And this absurd limousine. Here I've been driving it for months because I thought it was expected of me. What's it worth, do you know? Do you think I could trade it in for a Peugeot?"

We stopped at Jimmy's garage, and while Jimmy and I changed our clothes and put the limousine back to normal, the monsignor cross-examined us about cars, as if he was quite interested in them, and he asked us about our families. Our embarrassment wore off. He couldn't have been much older than us—we were in our late twenties then—and we could see that he wanted to be treated as just another person. I was itching to ask him about the golden light, but I didn't want to talk about it with Jimmy there, since Jimmy had looked at me strangely once when I'd mentioned that the stunts made me feel I might be someone else. The monsignor dropped Jimmy off at his bus stop and took me home. As I was getting out of the car, he gave me a sharp look, the same look he had given me earlier, when the street was flowing with light. "It seems we have something to talk about, Joey," the monsignor said. "Come and see me."

"Okay, thank you, Father." I watched him drive off and thought to myself, What a stroke of luck! He did notice what was happening with me. Here's a friendly, educated guy; he's going to explain the whole thing. That we were completely misinterpreting each other never occurred to me.

It wasn't that I thought the light would have a religious explanation. I'd been raised a Catholic, the same as nearly everyone else in West New York, and I'd gone to parochial school until the fourth grade, but I'd never developed any faith. My father, who had no use for the Church, had instructed me very carefully that whatever they said in church was nothing but a lot of baloney—he'd made me promise not to tell my mother or my sister. It was our secret among the males. But the new monsignor was the only educated man I knew, and besides, I thought, as a priest he was a stunt man with his life; when he'd taken his vows he'd vowed to change himself far more deeply into someone else than I could hope to do with my shallow playacting. If he thought the ordinary things of life were the last word, why wasn't he out there with a job and a family and payments to meet on the car and the clothes dryer? He must have known there was something else beneath.

I thought maybe that was the reason my father had paid so much attention to steering me away from the Church: he'd probably been afraid I'd end up in a seminary. He needn't have been afraid; the idea of God had never interested me. But when I was five or six or seven, I used to tell him and my mother about things happening in my mind, and that may have alarmed them. I'd told them about feeling sometimes that my life was a dream in which I'd taken the wrong road and couldn't find the way back to where I'd been. Other times I'd think that the solid objects around me were unreal and that if I stared at them long enough, they would dissolve and disappear, to leave me in the midst of another world. My parents told me 'no' kindly; this was the world right here, and there wasn't any other. It was no dream. I'd believed them and forgotten about it. But in my mid-twenties, when we began doing elaborate stunts, I'd remembered. Yet even then the idea that the surface of my life might not be real was no more than an idea to me, just an intriguing feeling that came from the stunts and from my mild boredom with ordinary things, until, getting out of the monsignor's limousine in Jackson Street, I caught a glimpse of that other world beneath the surface with my own eyes.

Margherita didn't know about these thoughts. She didn't know that we were still doing the stunts. At first, before we were married, she'd taken the stunts to be just practical jokes—they weren't much more than that then—and she'd laughed along with the rest of us. My stunting fitted in with my habit of wisecracking and with my slightly irresponsible attitude, my refusal to take many things seriously; it all probably attracted her. In high school she was a bit of a wiseacre herself. Without being particular friends ourselves at the time, we were both part of a crowd that liked doing the more or less innocent crazy things that kids like to do in high school, such as packing as many people as possible into a jeep or a phone booth, or leaving a baby alligator in a fishbowl on the principal's desk, or painting his private bathroom chartreuse from floor to ceiling—in fact, Margherita chose the color.

Her parents thought she needed to settle down, and so they

weren't very happy about me when we got married. They were Neapolitan in origin, like my family, and Margherita grew up in West New York, just as I had, but her people were better class than mine were. My father was a clerk at the local post office, while Margherita's father was a plumbing contractor with two employees; and his brother, Margherita's uncle, owned the fuel-oil delivery business in town. Margherita had been popular in high school, and her people thought she could have done a lot better job of finding a husband afterwards.

We laughed at them for it. Everybody our age thought we were the perfect couple, probably because we cracked jokes together for their benefit. If they read in the paper that a gaudy pink dye had inexplicably transformed the Hackensack River, or if the radio announcement that the German Oktoberfest would be held this year in September turned out to be unauthorized and false, we let our friends assume we'd had something to do with it, even if we hadn't. But I think Margherita expected all along that I would eventually change, the way she had begun to change. She was more and more nervous during the stunts, and several times she dropped out at the last minute on the grounds that she wasn't feeling well. Her job during the cannon stunt, which was by far the most complicated one we'd tried up to that time, was to watch for cops while we were dismantling the cannon and loading it into the truck; but when we started for the municipal building, she looked so sick and frightened that we dropped her off at home, and we put the cannon back together in the mayor's office without a guard. Later we found out that she was already pregnant with Vin.

She told me we'd have to cut the stunts out, because they were too dangerous and too irresponsible with the baby coming. One time or another, she said, we were going to get caught. I didn't argue with her. I knew her interests had already moved onto daily things, and how could I say she was wrong? Everyone we knew was slowing down. We decided to use the money her uncle had given us as a wedding present to buy into a house with Carmella and her husband, Arthur, instead of trying to set me up in a small-appliance repair business. Starting a business was too risky, and we wanted a place with a yard where the baby could play. I didn't mind letting the notion of the business go. I had already realized that at bottom it didn't interest me any more than anything else did. I found the good job at the truck terminal. Margherita sank into the life of housewife and mother, and her wisecracking nature slowly leached out of her. I played with my kid and let my life drift. Once a year or so, Jimmy and Steve and I did a stunt on the sly.

I knew I wouldn't be able to hide the monsignor stunt from Margherita. We'd been caught, just as she'd predicted, and West New York is a small town. I was just as glad. I was bursting to tell everyone about the vision of the light. I couldn't remember ever feeling so elated with vigor and excitement. When the monsignor dropped me off at home, I sailed upstairs and banged through the front door and called out, "Hey, Margherita, did you hear what happened? Hey, I bet they got it on the news, did you have it on? Where's Vin, he's got to hear what his daddy's been doing."

Margherita didn't say a word to me; she didn't condescend to look at me. She is a small person, like myself, and when she was angry, her voice and body would tremble as if the emotion was too strong for her to hold down; that would mortify her, and she wouldn't speak. She just went into the kitchen where she'd been keeping the dinner hot—I was half an hour late—and she slapped down the plate in front of me like a waiter who thinks his restaurant is too high class for your kind of person. I tried to calm her down a little. "Look, Margherita, I know you don't think too much of my doing another stunt, but I guess you heard I did, and it was really tremendous this time, it went very smooth without a hitch, and listen, something very interesting happened; I mean very interesting."

Not a peep came from her; not a word. She was shifting her food around on her plate with her fork and pushing her hair away from her forehead.

"You want to hear about it, Margherita?" I said. "Maybe you'd consider this is something you'd want to hear about?"

Nothing. After a minute or two—I'd become a little irritated—I told her the vegetables were cold; could she heat them up for me? She got up, took my plate, and scraped whatever it was into the garbage. I yelled at her for that, but she just sat down and stared at her plate again. Right then the coffee began boiling over on the stove. I reached over and grabbed her wrist and asked her could she hear? Had she gone deaf? She looked up at me finally, with her dark eyes black, and she was shaking so that her head was almost nodding and the fork in her hand was ringing against her water glass. She hissed at me that I should get my hands off her. I was amazed; I'd never heard her speak that way. "What's come over you?" I asked her. "What's come over you?"

I let go of her and turned the burner off. She was muttering, half to me, half not, which was her way of saying something without saying it: "He wants to know what's come over me. With him acting the way he acted, he wants to know this."

I told myself I was in too good a mood today to let her ruin it, so she was just going to have to listen. "You're not understanding this," I told her. "It was a perfectly all right thing we did. You could say we were trying to help the monsignor. He rescued us from the cops, Margherita. He put the finishing touches on the stunt himself. He thanked us. There aren't going to be any charges brought, there isn't anything going to come of this. The most they can slap me with is reckless driving and maybe cop my license for thirty days, sixty days, and what's that? Eat your dinner. It's nothing."

She looked like she was ready to throw her dinner at me. "Listen, Margherita. I wish you'd rest easy about this. I want you to know what happened in my mind. Everything changed while the stunt was going on. Everything around us suddenly looked beautiful and light; I don't know if I can describe it. It was a hundred times better than any of the other stunts——"

She interrupted me, almost yelling at me: "That's right,

because the other times you didn't have those sluts along to get your kicks with."

That silenced me. It had never crossed my mind that she would think I'd been unfaithful to her.

"You had to do this in public," Margherita was saying, with her face tight and hardened, "and everybody knows about it, everybody sees just what you think of me."

"Listen, Margherita." I felt ashamed to tell her what the truth was.

"I'm not listening to you."

"Yeah, but listen: the women were Jimmy and Steve. They were just Jimmy and Steve dressed up and made up. The stunt was nothing but the three of us, except for the monsignor there at the end."

I could see I'd lost my chance to tell her about what I'd seen. It would have to wait. She was crying now.

"You promised me, Joey. You promised me you were ready to settle down."

I went around behind her place and put my arms around her shoulders. "I'm real sorry about this, Margherita. It was just a perfect opportunity. The stunts didn't have anything to do with women or anything like that. We never meant to hurt anybody by the stunts, you know that. I never would have done it if I'd thought it would hurt you."

"Have you done other stunts, Joey? Without telling me?"

"Yeah, I guess, one or two. I didn't think anything would happen from them. I see now. I won't do them anymore." I meant it then, although I don't think she believed me.

"What's going to happen to you?" she was saying. "Carmella heard, she told me what you did this morning, embarrassing the priest like that and getting into trouble."

"I don't want you to worry, Margherita. The monsignor's going to keep us in the clear. He wasn't embarrassed. He said I should come see him. There won't be any problem."

"He can't do anything, Joey. He's not anybody who can stop anything."

"Yes, he is. You calm down now; you calm down. He's going to clear up everything that happened."

It didn't turn out that way. Two days later, the archdiocese transferred the monsignor out of the parish. I went over to the parish residence to find out where he'd been sent to, but nobody seemed to know. That same afternoon the police commissioner, the detective captain, a sergeant, and five patrolmen came roaring up to our house in three squad cars with sirens going full blast. They all trooped upstairs with loud feet, and when he'd got his breath back the commissioner handed me a warrant for arrest on charges of breaking and entering and willful destruction of property. Somebody had broken into the parish garage and had spray painted foul language all over the monsignor's limousine. Jimmy was already in custody in the back seat of one of the squad cars. He and I had both been at our jobs during the entire night that the garage had been broken into, so there was no basis for the charges against us. But they set bail at ten thousand dollars each and kept us in the city lockup for nine days.

I'd never seen Margherita so depressed as she was during those visiting hours. I kept telling her nothing would come of a false charge, because the union protects your job in such cases, and I made promises and promises and promises that the stunts were finished whether we wanted it or not, because of the publicity. We sat there in the day room arguing while the old guard at his desk worked on a model sailing ship. I tried to ignore him and to explain to Margherita that it wasn't a question of my still being a high-school wiseacre at twenty-eight. I told her that what had kept me at the stunts was the chance to experiment with the idea of being someone else.

She couldn't see why I wanted to be someone else, unless it was because I was unhappy with her as a wife.

"That doesn't have anything to do with it," I told her. "I never think about being unhappy at home. It's just that I don't believe the things that people normally do are particularly interesting, and I thought it was fun to break up the pattern sometimes. I've already told you I know the stunts are over, so I don't see what you're worrying about."

She sat there biting her lip and staring at her hands.

"I'm trying to tell you that it isn't anything personal, Margherita. I was working on some ideas I've been having, and the stunts seemed like a good way to work on them, that's all. When I do something very different, like in a stunt, then I feel like it could be possible to be someone else—this is what I've been wanting to tell you about. If a person can be someone else, maybe it's because people's different personalities aren't completely real; can you see what this could mean? Right there at the end of the monsignor stunt, when the police commissioner stopped us, I had the wonderful feeling that people are the same as each other, not actually the same but not separate somehow, and there was a wonderful light everywhere that connected everyone together——"

I stopped; she was shaking her head and crying. I was completely surprised.

"There's no reason to cry over this, Margherita. It was a very happy thing to see this. Even if I do have to stay in the lockup a few days, that's not anything that matters if the charges are dropped."

"People are saying there's something wrong with you, Joey," she said finally, "and I don't know, maybe something did happen somehow."

"Wrong with me, what do you mean wrong with me? I'm not any different than I was before. Who's saying this?"

"I don't know, different people."

"Who's saying it, then? Carmella? Is it Carmella?"

"Her and other people, Joey, because you can't seem to see how it looked to people, driving up and down in that stupid limousine."

"It was just for a laugh, Margherita. Maybe it was a little extreme, I guess I could say it was, but maybe I never would have run into the light I told you about if I hadn't taken a stunt that far. It's too bad if we got the monsignor into trouble with the archdiocese, though I don't know if we did—but I have the feeling he knows about the light, Margherita. It was beautiful to see it; I never saw anything anywhere near so beautiful. I don't care that the stunts are finished. As far as I'm concerned they were just a method to show me what I saw."

"Can't you hear how this sounds?" she said. "It just sounds so crazy."

"It's not crazy, Margherita. I saw this light. I saw it."

She was holding her fingers to her temples and shaking her head. "I don't know what you saw."

"Okay, Margherita. We don't have to talk about it now. Tell me what Vin did today."

I dropped the subject after that. I decided I'd have to wait until after I was out of the lockup and things had calmed down. I hadn't expected Margherita to be frightened by what I'd seen, and I couldn't understand why people would think I'd gone off the deep end just for driving a supercharged Cadillac down Bergenline Avenue. It was true we'd lost our heads for a few minutes, but no more than fifty thousand other people lost their heads at Yankee Stadium every Sunday watching high-priced idiots bang their heads against each other over a football. What were people so worried about? I felt a little indignant, especially after none of our friends came to visit me in the lockup over the weekend, when they were obviously free to come. But I decided not to let it bother me; it was too much trouble to worry about it. I could turn the whole thing into a joke quick enough once I was out of there.

It was another matter for Margherita not to visit me. After the words we'd had, she skipped a day, and when she did come she brought Vin and didn't stay for very long. We played with Vin and kept clear of what had happened. During the last three days I was in jail, she didn't come at all. I persuaded the old guard to call the house, but he said he couldn't get an answer. I thought maybe she'd had an accident, she was sick in the hospital, some people had persuaded

her I actually was a mental case and she'd decided to avoid
me, she'd moved back in with her parents and was petitioning
for a divorce—every kind of panicked thought crowded into
my head. I tried to persuade the guard to call her parents or
her sister Carmella, but no, he couldn't do it, he took a risk
calling up my own house as it was.

We had a lawyer named Bohanian. Margherita's uncle had
found him for us. The court finally decided to hold what they
called a preliminary hearing on the evidence; of course, there
wasn't any evidence. Margherita wasn't in court. No one came
except Jimmy's kid sister. Bohanian saw his job as proclaiming
some beautifully arranged sentences the point of which, as I
noticed after a while, was to subtly insult his pals the judge and
the police and the assistant district attorney and the marshal and
the ancient reporter from the *Hudson Dispatch*. They were all
winking and chuckling and smiling there together, busily creat-
ing a mysterious atmosphere for the defendants and the audience. The hearing took hours, with recesses and a lunch break
and different cases going on all at once, and the judge, whose
name was Schlemmer, ordering the windows closed then opened then closed, and everybody up front at the bench snickering with each other. Schlemmer finally did us the favor of
ruling that there were no grounds for the charges. Then he
delivered us a lecture on proper respect for the law and the
established institutions of society and said the nine days we'd
spent in jail were far too few as far as he was concerned. Bohanian told us that he'd tried to keep the costs down but that he'd
have to charge us two hundred and fifty dollars.

I walked home and barged upstairs. No one was there. As
I stood wondering where to look for Margherita, children's
voices sounded from downstairs in Carmella's and Arthur's part
of the house; I thought I heard Vin's voice. I went down and
knocked on their kitchen door and walked in without waiting
for an answer. There was Carmella at the kitchen sink with
Vin and her own four-year-old Michael sitting behind her on
the floor, debating what piece belonged where in a puzzle.

Vin got up and ran over to me when he saw me. "How you doing, kiddo?" I asked him as I picked him up. "Where's your mommy?"

He glanced doubtfully at Carmella, who was keeping busy at her dishes. "Aunt Carmella says it's a secret," Vin said.

"Oh, a secret, huh? Are you having a good time with Mikie while Mommy's doing her secret?"

"Mm-hm," Vin said, nodding at me. "I'm going to stay and play with Mikie while Mommy goes to work."

"Okay, that's good. Well, don't tell anybody." I put Vin down and said to Carmella, "Where's she working, Carmella?"

Carmella splashed the water around in her pots with her back to me. "I don't know where she is exactly," she murmured.

I walked over and said angrily, so that the children looked up—my quick temper was at its worst with that woman—"You going to tell me where she's working, Carmella?"

She looked around at me finally; I could see she was frightened.

"There's nothing to be afraid of, there's nothing wrong with me. Just tell me what I'm asking you."

She said softly, half-swallowing her words, "She didn't want me to tell you till she'd had a chance to talk to you, because Lyle's is a very respectable place——"

I knew what Lyle's she meant: it was a high-priced beauty salon over the city line in Guttenberg. "See you later, kids. Thanks for everything, Carmella."

I left her shaking her head and complaining to herself, "I can't be to blame if he forces it out of me."

For some reason, of all the things I thought Margherita might be doing while I was in jail, the obvious thing of her taking a job had never dawned on me. It wasn't that a lot of women we knew didn't go to a job. Before Vin was born, Margherita had worked herself, in another beauty salon; she had studied cosmetology in high school. But she hadn't consulted me this time; she hadn't even told me. She'd just left me in jail like she'd given me up for worthless, like she couldn't trust me to bring home a paycheck anymore. That she wanted to hide it from me infuriated me. She had obviously persuaded herself that I was unbalanced and couldn't be trusted.

Without any certain idea of what I was going to do, but with a thousand agitated thoughts streaming through my mind, I took the bus up Bergenline Avenue to the beauty salon. It was crowded with Greek statuettes and tall vases of permanent flowers and a fountain and large lamps with drooping shades made of colored cut glass. At the end of two rows of women reading magazines in white ironwork chairs, I found Margherita at the receptionist's desk, almost hidden by a tropical-fish tank. I asked her would she mind coming out and talking to me a minute?

It was the same as before: she didn't say anything at all. She shook her head a half inch and looked down at her appointment book, as if I was a man she didn't know who was trying to bother her on the bus. I asked her would she please? Would she tell me what was going on? I was shouting at her under my breath, and I could feel the women in the ironwork chairs prick up their ears and begin staring at us over their magazines. I took hold of Margherita by the arm and yelled in a whisper: "You're coming out and talking with me, you do as I tell you."

She had her fists doubled up on either side of the blotter on her desk, and she wouldn't look at me. All she said was, "Get home."

I began yelling at her out loud. "What is this, I'm not good enough for you anymore? Vin isn't good enough for you? I'm so on the skids you can't even talk to me, you're afraid I might find out where you've gone, you don't even care what happened in court today, because the case was dismissed, if it's all right to tell you this, since as far as I can tell you're the one who's saying to everyone that I've gone off the deep end——" In a minute her boss, Lyle Rosen the hairdresser, a pint-sized man around fifty with a moustache and gold-rimmed glasses and perfectly clean fingernails, rushed in from the back, gripped my arm with a numbing-tight hold, walked me down through the statuettes, staring women, and plastic flowers, and shoved me stumbling out onto the sidewalk. Right away I was back at the door, yanking and banging, but he'd locked it, and I yelled at the top of my lungs, "You come home, you're coming home or you'll regret this, Margherita!"

I took the bus home and sat down in front of the television. My anger slowly quieted, and I felt exhausted and drained. A feeling of shame and hopelessness fell on me. She was obviously right to try to hide where she was working; I'd made exactly the kind of scene she'd probably been afraid I'd make. I could hardly believe I'd done it. What did I think I was doing by letting myself loose like I'd done? No wonder she'd taken a job. No wonder she thought something had gone wrong with me. How was I ever going to tell her about the light and persuade her it was real if she thought I was unstable? I wandered fretting about the house, waiting for her to come home, rehearsing in my mind how I could apologize.

I didn't get a chance to talk with her then. She had our car, and I had to leave to catch a bus to my job at the terminal before she came home. When I got there, the shop steward told me that he and my supervisor had already met about my case. They'd agreed that management would dock me for the days lost, but leave it at that, since the charges in court had been dropped. Feeling nervous and a little weak, I punched in and started up my forklift.

The freight terminal was a building the size of two city blocks. It was completely open inside, like a gigantic barn. All along the four walls were garage-style doors that the trucks backed up to, to be loaded or unloaded. The lighter freight the dockmen moved around along a track in bright orange carts, and the larger and heavier freight and the awkward pieces, such as steam pipes and drums of solvent, were handled by the forklifts—we called them hi-los. The work was nothing but unloading each incoming truck and distributing the different pieces to the proper outgoing trucks in as little time as possible. The dockmen kept track on their clipboards, and they had to signal on a display board if they needed a hi-lo at their dock, because you couldn't have heard a loudspeaker clearly over the revving of the truck engines and the clanging and the thumping of the freight and the crashing of the carts on their track.

One corner of the terminal was screened off by a cage; here was where we put damaged or mislabeled freight. Some nights they'd race the hi-los there, when the section supervisor in charge of the cage went to hide out in the washroom to read Superman comics. The champion of the races was a heavy-set Irishman named Mickey Greenan, who always wore a baseball cap backward on his head and who handled the hi-lo with a skill that nobody could match. He was a surgeon with those prongs; he could have parted your hair with them. He was also a union officer and very bitter against management. That night, he backed his hi-lo up to mine and challenged me to a race. I hadn't ever raced; I'd never thought it was right to cheat that much on the job, and I was afraid of getting caught. I told him no.

Ha, ha, ha, for him this was extremely funny, considering that business with the monsignor, he said, like he always thought I was superstraight and regular, since I wouldn't ever race, and now this, he said, and hey, he said, a lot of the guys are saying it must have been you, too, those priests who rowed across the river and got into the papers? And those women you were with, who might they have been? And off he went to move some freight.

I felt the same nervous anger at him that I had felt at Margherita that afternoon. What right did he have to go around snickering to everyone about the mess I'd made of things, like he obviously was doing? I'd only just calmed down enough to get back to work when Greenan zipped past me again: " 'Scuse me, Monsignor." A little while later he was back: "How's about that race, Father?" He kept going out of his way to torment me about his race, till finally I yelled at him that I'd do it, if he'd only shut up and leave me alone.

I didn't have time to think twice. Greenan had hardly

finished shooting around announcing the race to his buddies when the section supervisor of the mislabeled-freight cage drifted by with a stack of Superman comic books under his arm. In a minute we were up to the starting mark. We each had a crate of four hundred-fifty-pound drums of solvent on our prongs; drums are harder to race with than solid freight, because the liquid tends to shift your balance on turns. We were doing ten laps around the course for a dollar a yard at the finish line. Greenan gave me the inside lane to start and a quarter lap as a handicap. I'd never raced before, and he assumed he'd win without any trouble. But I kept to the inside, and he couldn't pull ahead of me. By the fourth lap he began side checking me—swinging up beside me and trying to shove me off the course.

The course had four sides. On two sides it ran between banks of empty loading carts. That's where Greenan was side checking me. On the other two sides, the race course followed straight along the walls at the corner of the building. At any particular moment, some of the doors along the walls would be open to the backs of trucks. So the first rule of hi-lo racing was never to side check your opponent on the two sides of the course that followed along the walls. If someone was shoved off course there, he might charge right through an open door onto the back of a truck and wreck the freight on it. Then there'd be hell to pay.

I broke the rule. I didn't forget about it; but we hadn't raced two laps when I figured out that I'd been had. Here I'd been feeling terrible about what I'd done, about embarrassing Margherita at her job and maybe getting her fired for all I knew, and getting the monsignor into trouble probably, and now losing all that pay, and what was I doing now but getting involved in another crazy escapade that didn't even interest me and that might get me fired? With that, I thought, I'm supposed to obey rules made up by a joker like Greenan? I kept count, and every time he side checked me legally, into the loading carts, I side checked him illegally, toward the walls of the building. He fell behind a bit, and I could hear him there, cursing me at the top of his lungs. It never occurred to me to just drive out of the race. I was sold on the angry thought of beating him at his own game and collecting five or ten dollars to show him what I thought of him.

On the last lap he got his revenge. When you have a crate of drums up front on your prongs, the hi-lo makes a very good battering ram. What Greenan must have planned was to ram me from behind, just before a turn, and send me barreling through an open door into the back of a trailer. That would have meant some damage that I would have been blamed for. But one or two laps before the end, the truck pulled out that Greenan must have planned to ram me onto, so there was nothing outside the open door now but the asphalt parking lot outside the terminal, five feet below. I believe Greenan didn't notice that the truck had left; he probably was concentrating on getting his hi-lo right up behind mine. Or perhaps anger had turned his head like it had turned mine; I don't know. But at the last turn of the race, he rammed me square, and I went sailing through the open door into the night.

As soon as I was clear of the walls, I jumped off the hi-lo, landed on the pavement below, and rolled aside to get out of the way. I wasn't fast enough. The crate of drums slid off the hi-lo prongs and crashed onto my right leg, pinning me to the ground. The prongs stuck into the asphalt like a fork into a potato. The hi-lo shivered a bit, and then it started falling slowly down toward me.

I tugged and scratched; I heaved in a frenzy at that crate of drums, trying to get it off my leg in time to drag myself away before the hi-lo could land on me. It seemed to take years. I raised myself up on my free foot in a sort of crouch, with the other leg all twisted and numb under the crate. I had the crazy idea I could lift the heavy crate off of me. I heaved, and up it came. I thought I was doing it myself; it was a miracle. Later Margherita told me that Greenan and some others had jumped down after me, and they had done the lifting. But I didn't see them, all straining as I was, and as the crate of drums came up off my leg, I felt a tremendous energy sweeping through my body and up through my mind. It felt like an electric charge had been set off in my body, and I thought that its power had let me lift the crate off my leg. But unlike an electric shock, it brought no heat and no pain. Instead, my body felt suddenly cool and light, as if I had set down a heavy weight that I'd been carrying for a long time. As I looked around me, I thought that I and everything I saw, the trucks parked in the lot, the men running across the asphalt or standing over me or leaning down to rip my pants leg, the hi-lo on its back beside us, and the roof of the terminal against the dark sky, belonged together to something else, something hidden that I couldn't name. I thought to myself, I'm here. I don't remember anything more.

# 2

# ENERGY

I was in and out of surgery for two days while they patched up my shinbone with steel pins and some kind of plastic. They never found all the old pieces. At first, Margherita and my parents were the only ones who visited me in the hospital. I asked Margherita where our friends were; hadn't she told them what had happened? She kept putting off an answer. Finally she said that Jimmy had called up to ask if it was true they were keeping me in the psycho ward; he said if it was true, he wanted her to know that he was real sorry. She told him that it wasn't true, and after a while he did come over to the hospital to see me, but he treated me with a kind of sorrowful respect, and he got up to go almost as soon as he'd sat down. I asked him would he wait a minute? Would he mind telling me what was going on?

He winced slightly and pulled on his right ear, a habit of his that usually meant the conversation had brushed against the subject of his wife's giving him a hard time.

"Cynthia?" I prompted him. "So what's Cynthia saying?"

"Well, you know, she didn't actually want me to come over to visit you, Joey, that's all. She doesn't know I'm here, see."

"Oh, that's nice," I said. "She doesn't want you to come over because of what?"

"She wants to pin the blame on you for everything, see what I mean," he said.

I started feeling hot, with him sitting there pulling on his ear and clearing his throat, but I told myself to keep my temper, since losing it while I was lying in traction would probably be fairly uncomfortable. Besides, how could I blame him for keeping peace with his wife this way, if that was how he had to do it? We'd known each other too long to hold a grudge against each other.

"Just call people up when she's out shopping and tell them you saw with your own eyes that Joey's head was sitting right there on his neck and his hands were still stuck on the ends of his arms, and believe it or not he answers to his name and talks in sentences anybody could understand, will you do that for me?" I asked him.

He pleased me by laughing. "Yeah, sure, Joey. I got to go, hey. Cynthia thinks I went out for the evening sports page."

Jimmy did as he'd promised. Our friend Richard came around the next evening, when Margherita was there visiting. Richard was an uncle of Carmella's husband Arthur, although they were about the same age. He was one of the few people I knew who didn't care for gossip and the only person I knew who had nothing to say against the Cubans' moving into West New York. In fact, he hired them; he was a supervisor at one of the knitting mills. He said they worked harder than anyone else except, of course, the Germans. That made people mad, but he just shrugged and smiled and said it was true. I liked him for it.

He had a kind nature as well as a frank one, and I could see after a few minutes that it was out of kindness that he had come to see me.

"How long are they saying you'll be laid up?" he asked me.

"Three months, probably, till I can walk without a limp. I already put in for disability pay."

"There'll probably be something you could have at the mill by then," he said. He meant a job at the knitting mill where he worked.

"You think they're going to fire me at the terminal, do you?" I asked him.

"For racing like that?" He turned to Margherita and smiled, then shrugged his shoulders. "Firing is what I would have to recommend if it was my report to write."

"It was partly my fault, though, Richard," Margherita said. She'd already apologized to me for not telling me she'd gotten a job and then not talking to me at the beauty salon. "He probably wouldn't have done it if I hadn't gotten him all upset."

"I know, sure," Richard said. "Just because something happens once doesn't mean it'll happen again. We all know Joey's got plenty of sense underneath. Just be glad you weren't let go at the beauty salon, too, Margherita."

"No, Mr. Rosen's a friend of my father's—they know each other from the Elks," she said. "He called my father with the job, just because he'd heard we were having some trouble."

Richard nodded. "Good." It was the kind of thing he liked to hear. He was one of those people who almost never went across the river to Manhattan, and he often said we were lucky to have been born in a small town.

But lying there staring at the bed sheets and mulling over what had happened, I could see that the closeness of West New York, which Richard liked, was an obstacle for me. Richard and probably most people we knew were ready to forgive me for the ruckus I'd made, and Margherita had already forgiven me, at least for the hi-lo race and the scene in the beauty salon, because she believed she shared in the blame. Their forgiveness, though, was for doing something different from what they would do, and it was given on the condition that I wouldn't act any different from them from here on.

It wasn't that I thought there was something to be defended in hi-lo racing or in yelling at Margherita in a beauty salon. Although it had never landed me in nearly so much trouble before, I already knew perfectly well that my hasty temper had never done me any good—though sometimes I'd enjoyed it anyway. No, the problem was that I wasn't in any position now to tell my friends about the vision of the light. I'd lost all my bargaining power. How could I discuss my new ideas with them if they all were convinced that I'd flown off the handle? They'd obviously dismiss the light as somehow coming from Joey's being upset and overexcited, or else they'd get upset themselves hearing about it, the way Margherita had done when I'd told her about it in the lockup. I'd have to hide everything from them until they'd accepted me again.

But I didn't want to hide what had happened to me. I didn't want to think about my ideas in secret. I wanted everyone to know about the electric energy I'd felt sweeping through me during the accident as I was trying to lift the crate of drums off my leg. I wanted to see what Richard thought of it, what Jimmy thought of it, what Richard's wife Angela thought of it, because she was a very intelligent woman. Did they suppose the energy was the same as the light I'd seen in Jackson Street, the same frequency, except that I'd felt it this time instead of seeing it? Had they ever felt such a thing? Did they ever have the idea that our ordinary personalities might be hiding something else from us? And Margherita: it was painful to keep the ideas that interested me from my own wife, but I hadn't dared yet to bring up the subject with her again. I knew she wasn't ready to listen. It was true we'd more or less been reconciled, but it had been on her terms.

"I know we can get back on track again, Joey," she'd said once we'd apologized to each other, "especially now that you're going to get a rest. Everything's going to calm down again, I just know it will."

"Sure, Margherita, I know it will, too." But I didn't believe what I'd said as strongly as she did. The idea of going back on the track again made me uneasy, if it meant swallowing what had happened and never mentioning it again. I told myself to wait and be patient, though I knew that was going to be hard for me.

The doctors let me out of the hospital on crutches after two weeks, in time for our monthly dinner and canasta party. We took turns as host, every third Tuesday of the month—Tuesdays had been my night off. That month it was Richard and Angela's turn, which everybody always waited for because Angela was a superior Italian cook. When Margherita called at the last minute to say that we were coming, Angela told her we should certainly come ahead, although they'd already invited another couple to fill out the canasta hands. That irritated me. "They're going to find out it won't be so easy to dispense with me," I said to Margherita when she hung up the phone and told me about it.

"Joey, that's ridiculous," she said. "You didn't know yourself that you were getting out till this morning."

"Yeah, you're right. Where's Vin, I've got to go sweeten up my mood for this."

"He's in the yard," Margherita said. "But we don't have to go. I can call her back and say you've decided you'd better not go out yet."

"No, I feel okay. I want to go show them I'm still human."

"I wish you'd stop talking like that. You make it sound like they're our enemies instead of our friends, when everybody's been just terrific to me."

"Yeah, I know, you're right." I labored down the stairs with my crutches and heavy cast and went outside to push Vin on his swing while Margherita made herself ready for the party. What she had said was true: our friends and families had showered her with favors and phone calls and invitations to dinner while I'd been in jail and then in the hospital. I knew I should feel grateful to them—in fact, for her sake I did. My thoughts lightened, as they always did in Vin's company. Probably I was wrong to resent my friends for disapproving of what I'd done and for not wanting to hear about what had happened in my mind. Maybe they'd want to listen after all, if I just got the job done of being good old Joey for a while.

They were all there when we arrived: Richard and Angela, who was plump from her own cooking and very pretty; Louie and Thelma—he was a dispatcher at the freight terminal, and she was working on their fifth child, though she wasn't yet thirty; Tommy and Patti—she was my cousin on my father's side, and they both worked at the school district, he as a custodian and she as a typist, since they had no children; and the new couple, Bill and Mary Jo. Bill was an Irish guy from Richard's job, and Mary Jo was a sister of Thelma's brother-in-law. Richard introduced us. Bill said he'd heard all about me.

"Yeah, but none of it's true," I said, which made them laugh. "Everybody has to sign their name, Bill and Mary Jo first." Leaning over on my crutches, I lifted up my cast, which was covered with Vin's scribbles, to prop it on a chair. I'd brought a marking pen along with me. They all signed in turn.

"I didn't have time to go get any Pepsi for you, Joey. I'm sorry," Angela said as she signed.

I was the only one of the men who didn't drink beer; it had always given me a headache. "That's all right," I said. "I'm on bread and water for my sins right now. Except bread includes sfogliatelli, Angela." They all laughed again. Sfogliatelli are a special Italian pastry stuffed with ricotta cheese and served hot; Angela always made them for dessert on canasta nights. "Hey, I'm stuck. Will someone put my leg down for me?"

Good, I thought; I've started off right with them. The men sat around while I rattled off stories about the people I'd shared my hospital room with—the German vegetarian who'd done calisthenics while recovering from an appendectomy, the Puerto Rican grandfather who always had at least ten visitors, and the Italian kid laid up from a motorcycle accident who refused to turn down the jangle of his radio until the German and I ganged up on him by wheeling our beds next to his and singing "America, the Beautiful" and "Deutschland, Deutschland, über Alles," which the German taught me, in competition with the rock stars on the radio. The head nurse had swept in and silenced all of us.

At dinner the conversation among the men turned to football; the season had just begun. They were discussing the prospects for the Giants team. It turned out that Bill, the new guy, was even more fanatical a student of the subject than Louie, who always knew all the scores and names and important plays. Each time Louie brought up a name on the lineup, Bill said: "Six foot four and a half, two hundred and sixty pounds," or whatever the particular player's specifications were. After a while I asked Bill why he didn't know how much the players' heads weighed, but the joke annoyed him instead of amusing him. He looked at me as if I'd lumbered with my ignorance onto sacred ground. There was an uncomfortable silence until Richard said heartily, "Everybody have some more gnocchi," or whatever the dinner was that night.

It could have been partly because I was tired—the accident and the surgery had drained me, and my leg itched and ached under the cast—but with that failed joke I fell into a discontented silence. If they relied on football for something worth talking about, I thought, let them talk about it. Bill was right; why should I interfere, any more than I should interfere with the women, who were talking about being pregnant? What was I doing there with them, anyway, if I was bored by what interested them and if they didn't want to hear about what interested me? It was exhausting to pretend all the time that I was one of them.

The thought surprised me, but I saw that it was true. Of course I could make them laugh with my stories and ridiculous remarks—I always had been good at throwing words around. Even this guy Bill had been laughing before. I liked them to laugh; it flattered me, and it passed the time. But that was all I could do with them. I was acting in a play, and parts had been written for everyone except myself. Good old Joey was the clown act who filled in the gaps when the rest of them needed some relief. I was tired of being their clown, and it seemed to me that I'd been tired of it, without realizing it, for a long time.

We sat down to canasta. I played without much interest, although usually I enjoyed the game. I kept wishing the light or the energy I had felt during the accident would return to brighten my thoughts. The light and the energy had brought such a natural delight, like the sound of running water on a hot summer day. If the light were to shine there inside Angela's living room, wouldn't they all have to see it, or feel it? Even thinking of it, I felt a sudden touch of happiness. I noticed that Richard was watching me as I sat there smiling to myself, and I wanted to jokingly scold him: Play your own part, Richard, you don't have to be the prompter for everyone else, too. I'm just trying to work up some electricity, because the clown has to put out a lot of effort, in case you didn't know. It amused me to rehearse the line in my mind, but I knew I couldn't speak it. I would have to explain everything to him before he could know what it meant.

Thinking these things, I kept losing track of the play. They had to remind me it was my turn. Finally I said that the new woman, Mary Jo, who was sitting out the game with Margherita, should maybe take my hand, because I was obviously not paying attention very well; I guessed I was tired. "Oh, yeah, sure, that's fine, Joey," Richard said. Everybody had a comment. "Yeah, sure, after an accident like that; sure, it takes a while to get going again; sure."

Later, when the cards were over and everyone was standing in the hall ready to go home, Angela brought out a couple of the sfogliatelli wrapped in aluminum foil and gave them to Margherita. "I always make a couple extra ones for Bethie and Marie"—who were their kids—"but they aren't going to mind going without for once," she said. Margherita started biting her lip, and everyone looked on nodding and murmuring. One of the women squeezed Margherita's arm.

Suddenly I thought to myself: Okay, Celebrisi, here's your chance. Don't say anything they might consider unusual, just lay some groundwork by getting their confidence back. "That's real nice of you, Angela," I said. "You don't have to worry about Margherita, though. Once I start getting around a bit better, I'm going to be cleaning up the house and taking care of Vin so long as I'm on disability—seeing as how she's working now and all." I hadn't actually told Margherita that; the thought had just struck me at that moment.

"That's real nice, Joey," everybody said. "Sure, you keep yourself busy."

"Just don't give her any pants to wear," Bill said.

"That's right, that's right," the other men said, and everybody laughed.

"Besides," I said, "I've been feeling pretty bad about getting sucked into that stupid race at the terminal and also about barging into the beauty salon where Margherita has her job—though actually, I don't know what you heard about it, because the rumor mill's been saying I hit Margherita in the face and knocked over the tropical-fish tank they have in there, but all I actually did was yell at her for a minute or two. I was mad at her, which was wrong of me, since I was the one who'd messed up and not her, but at least when you're mad at someone it's better to yell it out of your system than to beat it out of their system, am I right?" Everybody was falling all over themselves to agree with that, especially the women. "How's about it, Margherita? Did you rather I'd broken your nose instead of your eardrums?"

It was as if I'd opened a window in the direction of a spring breeze. Everybody was standing around talking all at once and recalling this or that time they'd gotten furious. I'd brought it off; I'd begun the job of rescuing my reputation with them. We should have gone home right then. But their sympathy turned my head. I thought I'd been wrong to think of myself as their clown; I'd just been tired and depressed. They were my friends; what reason did I have to think they wouldn't want to hear about what happened? Margherita hadn't wanted to hear, but that had been when I was in jail, and of course she'd been upset then. These people weren't upset; why shouldn't I share what I felt with them? I was the one who'd been making myself into an outsider.

There was a silence once everyone had finished recalling the times they'd lost their tempers. I told them, "The other thing, now, maybe you think those routines we did with the new monsignor in the parish were a little bit crazy, but——"

"Oh, yeah, I heard about that," Bill said. "That actually was you, then?"

"It was a laugh, just meant for a laugh, a once-in-a-life-time thing, so let's forget about it," Richard said.

"Yeah, sure, forget it," the men were saying. "Who cares?"

"No, okay," I said, "but there was something real in the things we did, besides just the fun and games. The way I felt in my mind while I was doing it, it was something very unusual, something you wouldn't ordinarily run into."

"Let's go home, Joey, all right? Joey?" Margherita said, tugging at my elbow.

"No, I want to explain it to them. It's simple. If you change the way you act and you move into somebody else's type of shoes, your mind isn't going to have all the usual things to do, and so you have a whole lot of extra energy all of a sudden." It had only just occurred to me to explain it that way, but it made sense. I told myself that of course it would be easier to understand if I talked it over with people. "So once there's this extra energy, it naturally starts building up, and you can feel it like a kind of electric charge."

They couldn't seem to see it yet. They were shifting their feet and looking at me with worried expressions on their faces. "Joey please, will you please?" Margherita pleaded.

Richard began loudly asking Mary Jo about their kids; they had just gotten over the measles.

"Okay, Margherita," I was saying, "I know I don't explain it very well, but just give me this much, Angela: if there could be this kind of energy——"

People were clearing their throats and saying it was late, they had to go. I didn't want them to. "Listen, there's nothing wrong in this, since if there is, then why does it feel so beautiful, because that's what I haven't told you yet."

"Joey, stop it, stop it," Margherita was saying.

"All right," I said, "I will stop, but if I'm right in this, then you people should be worried about what you're missing. I just thought my friends might want to know about it."

They weren't listening now. They were ignoring me and saying good night to each other and going out the door.

"I was going to keep it to myself," I said angrily to the people who were still there. "You can just pretend I didn't mention it and forget about it."

They looked up at me for a second; there was a silence. "It's all right, Joey," Richard said. "Rest up, and you'll feel fine soon."

"Yeah, I'll feel just wonderful. Come on, Margherita." I stumped my way out to the car without saying good night to any of them.

Of course I apologized to Margherita the next evening over dinner; what else could I do? "I told myself they wouldn't want to hear about it, I told myself a dozen times," I said to her. "But I guess I couldn't make myself believe it. I believe it now."

"It's just they don't understand, Joey. They don't know what to think."

"I don't know what to think either. I just felt that maybe if we could discuss it, but I'm not even allowed to discuss it. I wish the monsignor hadn't gone."

"The monsignor? I don't know what you're still thinking of *him* for," she said, sawing vigorously at her lamb chop. "Can't we just let bygones be bygones and for Heaven's sake forget about it, like Richard said?"

"Yeah, Richard," I said wearily. "Richard's great. Richard's wonderful."

"You've always said he's about the best person you know, and if you can't trust him, who are you going to trust, Joey?"

I pushed the food around on my plate. "I guess I don't know, Margherita. If he saw the light I told you about, he'd probably take care of it by writing up a report on his eye doctor. Maybe you're right, I should just stop thinking about it, I don't know."

"You should, Joey. You'll feel like your old self again as soon as your leg stops bothering you. Go on and eat your dinner. I've got those sfogliatelli in the oven."

"I know, I can smell them."

"It's lucky I can't cook like her. I'd never be able to control myself."

She didn't say so, but I could see that she was relieved that our friends had backed her up by thinking my ideas weren't worth talking about. I resented her for it, but she also had me partly persuaded she was right, especially because neither the energy nor the light showed any sign of returning. I admitted to myself that it was in extreme situations—the stunt and the accident— that I'd encountered them, and there didn't seem to be much likelihood of my being involved in an extreme of any variety at any time again soon. Maybe it was just something physical and unimportant that had to do with being under stress, something familiar to mountain climbers and to sailors for long distances in small boats. Maybe I'd just imagined that it had any real beauty or any meaning. Margherita and the others were right: it was stupid to get so sidetracked by a couple of odd experiences that after all had lasted only a total of three or four minutes out of my life.

Sometimes these thoughts made me feel relieved, because they showed me the way to allow myself to forget what had happened. At other times, the idea that I would never feel the energy or see the light again, and the thought that I was mired in being good old Joey for the rest of my life, filled me with a sadness and a bitterness that surprised me by their strength. I still had no way to explain to myself why those three or four minutes meant so much to me.

The news came that I'd been fired from my job, just as Richard had predicted. Mickey Greenan, the man I'd hi-lo raced with, came over to the house to tell me about it. He said the company management hadn't technically fired me, since they couldn't actually prove I was racing—the supervisor had been reading comics in the washroom, and everybody else who knew had clammed up; but they wanted me out to make an example, so they laid me off with the excuse that there were too many hi-lo men on the floor. Greenan yanked his backwards baseball cap farther down on his head and announced to me that they had another thing coming if they thought they were getting away with this, since it was in violation of seniority rights and no-speedup agreements and everything else. He was personally going to take it to grievance for me. All I had to do, Joey pal, was sign these papers here. I signed them and more or less forgot about it. With disability pay and Margherita's salary, more money was coming in than before, so for the time being we didn't have to worry about keeping up. I just wanted to rest and let the time pass until somehow my thoughts could be resolved.

After another two weeks, the doctors replaced my heavy cast with a much lighter and smaller one, and they told me my therapy was to walk. I used to go out twice every day with a cane in one hand and Vin's hand in the other. We'd head down the back streets together, or we'd take a bus to North Hudson Park in North Bergen or pick around the Hoboken piers. It was autumn then. Day after day there was clear air and a blue sky, and everything was bright in the sun, even the faded bricks of the old mills. I taught Vin the names of the cars as we walked. We discussed what the different trucks were carrying. He was pretty certain then that truck driving was in his future, because the drivers got to sit up so high off the road.

One day we were walking on the grounds of Stevens Institute, a technical college in Hoboken. Between the old physics building there and the piers on the Hudson River nearby was an acre or two of very large old trees. We walked under a roof of high branches and leaves. A wind came up off the Hudson, and the leaves, pale green and tan and bright yellow with the fall, trembled and flipped back and forth all through the branches over us with a long hiss. Vin and I stood staring up as the dying leaves rained down on us. All of a sudden the electric energy that had swept through me during the accident began rising up my spine. It was much milder than before, but it continued longer, flowing slowly and quietly upwards to gather just under the center of my scalp. It was as if the top of my head was a dam that held back the current of a cool stream. The energy piled up until I thought it would be strong enough to push my mind open, so that my thoughts would fly out with it into the air, the way they had flown out with the light in Jackson Street. I thought the energy would pour out everywhere and make everything tremble, not just the leaves but the ground and the buildings and Vin, too, and myself; everything would tremble into the autumn sunlight and dissolve away into a hiss. I thought I might lose myself and not be able to find myself afterwards. The monsignor had brought me back to myself that first time, but what would bring my thoughts back now, if they were lost in the energy and the air? How would I keep an eye on Vin? I felt afraid, and I tried to stop the energy from building up by standing still and looking at the ground. I tried to think the energy down into my body. It seemed to work. The current slowly sank down my spine and was absorbed. After a minute or two, the wind from the river died down. The leaves were still.

Riding home on the bus, I felt sad that I'd sent the energy away so quickly. I'd been wishing for a whole month that it would return. Why should I think that it would take away my thoughts or change me more than I wanted to change? There shouldn't be any reason to be afraid. Yet from the very beginning I'd felt it would change me, though I couldn't have said why or how. I only knew that it was somehow drawing me away from my old life. For that I was grateful, since my old life was of less and less interest to me. But I was also nervous, because I knew that I had no idea what new life the energy was leading me to.

That night I dreamed that I was wading in a brook; it was a summer evening. There was a homemade dam just a little downstream, so that the water was held up in a clear pool around me. The current flowed past me up to my waist in some places, sometimes just up to my knees. There were trees leaning over the banks, and smooth pebbles were on the bottom. Though it was dark out, I could see down through the water, and there some fish perhaps a foot long were swimming back and forth and nibbling at my legs, as they will sometimes in streams. Their scales were full of bright streaks of green and yellow and tan like the leaves in Hoboken; I remember noticing that in the dream.

The fish were talking, and I could understand them. There weren't any actual spoken words. What they said just sounded up to me, in a kind of high-pitched singing. They were telling me about the energy piling up in my mind and waiting to pour out; they told me what would happen if I calmed down and wasn't afraid and let it pour, and how I would see new things. They said I was changing in the way I'd changed a thousand times before, times I had forgotten; they said I didn't have to be afraid. If I was patient and didn't get angry, they said, I would find a new place. Don't rush, but don't hold back. Kindness and gentleness washed up to me from their singing and from their nibbling on my skin and from the flashes of the colors of their scales. It spread up through the current of the stream and up into the trees and the air. Everything was solved. I woke up and fell asleep and dreamed it again, and then again.

For days afterward I had that feeling you can get from a strong dream, of another life soaking through your own. I thought the fish had told me exactly what was in store for me, but I couldn't remember what that was. But I believed what I had dreamed. I told myself: See, it's right for you to feel the energy. Your thoughts won't be lost; something new is going to be found. Next time the energy comes, or the light, let it pour where it wants. Nothing happened for another week, but I held onto the memory of the fish in the dream and tried to follow their instruction of patience.

Then one afternoon near a drinking fountain in North Hudson Park, Vin slipped on the wet pavement and scraped his knee. It wasn't much of a wound, although it probably stung, but I made a big production of it, ripping my handkerchief in strips, soaking one strip in the fountain to wash his knee, and wrapping the other strips around for a bandage, telling him how we both had bad legs now. Like other kids, he'd suddenly forget sometimes that he'd been crying, and he'd start staring at what I was doing, with his face all wet. It was that way with the bandage; we became very absorbed in it.

While I was concentrating on knotting it up a final time,

suddenly the energy was there in my scalp again, in a mild current, like a silent buzzing. It flowed in a straight thin line underneath my skin from the bridge of my nose back across the top of my head and down to the nape of my neck. I told myself to be quiet and remember the dream; let it happen. When we got up to walk again, the silent buzzing began to spread down the sides of my head and into my shoulders and then all the way down my body, just underneath my skin, as if it was traveling along my nerves. As it built up strength, it began radiating outward from my body, it seemed from all my pores, just as if it was a kind of light. I felt larger. I tried to keep my thoughts on the fish in the dream in order to stay calm. The energy grew; I felt I was burning. But no heat or pain was in the fire. Instead it cooled me from the heat of the warm day. The energy seemed to burn away my physical boundaries till I couldn't feel my clothes or tell one part of my body from the other or tell where my skin bordered on the air.

I was convinced that the energy must be the same as the golden light, and as it radiated from my skin, I thought I would see the light there in the park. But the autumn sunlight was unchanged. Yet just like the cars and the people in Jackson Street, everything in the park seemed to be moving slower and to grow quieter—the children running in the grass and their mothers and their dogs and the wind—so that all hardly moved and their voices dimmed out to a trace; you might have thought that the park was under water. But the water was as empty and as peaceful as space, and perfectly clear and still. The same stillness was in myself. I knew where I was, and my thoughts ran on in their usual place, but below my mind, my body felt continuous with the quietness of the air. Everything seemed resolved. Within me and outside, there was no tension, no opposition, no plans, and no fear.

I looked down at Vin, thinking I'd ask him if he felt anything strange. Walking there next to me, with his little feet zipping out in front, one, then the other, trotting for a second to keep pace, he seemed perfect to me: the only child in the park. Everything around him had receded behind, as if it was only stage scenery. Then I noticed that if I looked at something else than him, a bench, the grass, even a piece of paper, then it too would silently bloom, like a lamp turned on in a room in the late afternoon. When it did bloom, though, all the while that it was perfect, I could see how caught it was being itself; how the drinking fountain was completely shut into being a stone fountain, so that it could never be the little black girl drinking from it or the water dripping down it at the sides.

Suddenly this seemed like a terrible thing to me, that none of the people and things could change. I felt myself, too, stuck like the little girl and the fountain, hammered down by spikes in my ankles and my shoulders, a machine that couldn't do any other thing than what it had always done. Again and again I felt a wave of desire to change from what I was. I wanted to drop everything in my life so that I could turn my body and all my thoughts and feelings into the energy pouring out of me. I wanted to pour into the stillness around me and never return.

It was concentration of my mind that must be bringing on the energy; coming home on the bus from the park that day, it suddenly struck me that this was the common element. Concentrating on Vin's bandage by the fountain, or on lifting the crate of drums off my legs the night of the accident, on watching the leaves fall at Stevens Institute, or on the crucial moves of a stunt: for those moments, without planning it, I had brought all my thoughts to one point, putting aside all the disorganized affairs of my life; it was then that the energy rose up inside me. To test the idea, I stared at a photograph of a tree in one of the bus advertisements, trying to think of nothing else. After a few minutes, the energy began burning quietly at the top of my scalp. As soon as I got home I called up the energy again, listening to water drip from the tap, and later again, watching the gas flame flit on the range.

For the next month and a half, all through the fall while my leg regained its strength, I practiced concentrating my mind.

When Margherita was at work and Vin and I weren't walking, I spent my time working on the car or cleaning up the house or building a shortwave radio for Arthur, who had come over from Italy when he was sixteen and still wanted the music from the other side. I learned how to cook and to look after all the details of raising a child. I understood why women get into the state where all they talk about is children. Cleaning Vin and touching him and watching him and hearing him filled my mind till I believe that even now, if I had the skill, I could make a plaster cast of him from memory as he was then, down to the last wrinkle. We had a washing machine completely paid for, but I took to washing his clothes by hand, and Margherita's clothes and mine too: anything to concentrate my mind and bring on the energy.

During that time, the energy was never again as strong as it had been at first; I never saw it again as light, and my thoughts didn't leave my body as they had at the end of the monsignor stunt. But the energy was there every day, whenever the house was quiet and my mind at rest. Noise and distraction, irritation or strong emotion put an end to it immediately. It would come back only when the house and my thoughts had calmed again. Then, when I concentrated on what I was doing, it would rise along my spine or linger at my scalp and burn away the residue of any fatigue or ill humor, and it left behind it, when it was gone, vigor and peacefulness.

I no longer thought of it as a kind of electricity, because it was far cooler and softer than the shocks I sometimes got from tinkering with electric motors and radios. It brought refreshment rather than pain, and a lasting clarity in my thoughts instead of the brief numbness of a shock. Nor was it a fire, though it felt as if it was burning on my skin. In a way it was more like water, though it had no substance, and like the fragrant breeze of a summer evening, in that it brought delight; and like clear space, in that it was empty. Like space, it flowed through me and all the things around me and contained them and myself in its invisible light.

From the very beginning, though, I had felt it was alive—not a being in itself, but a force that came from life, instead of from the purely physical world. In the early days after the monsignor stunt, I had sometimes wondered if the light was something supernatural that was kindly visiting me. But now I was convinced that it came from myself, from my own body and my mind. It was the basic energy of my human life. I had felt that it connected everyone because it obviously had to be present in everyone. Normally it was scattered through the events of a person's body and his days, but when he concentrated his attention, some of its currents were drawn from their separate channels and brought together into a single stream. When the stream flowed strongly enough, it rose above the threshold of feeling and became a sensation of its own.

Far from seeming supernatural to me now, the energy seemed of all things the most natural. It was partly because the simple sensation of it was so wonderfully comfortable and delightful. But there was something else about it that I found far harder to explain to myself: unlike any other thing I had known in my life, except perhaps Vin's uncalculated childish feelings, the energy felt true. It was alive, but it had no motive, no desire, no self. Like light, it was empty. It came from somewhere beneath the ordinary selfish personality. Now there returned to me all the feelings I had had in the past about my life being false: the childhood suspicion that I was trapped in a dream, the guess during the stunts that I could just as easily be someone else, the idea that I was acting with my friends in a play that they believed was real. I couldn't believe along with them any longer, now that I'd finally met something that came from a real world outside the play. I didn't think that the energy was necessarily itself that real world; I had no way of beginning to imagine what a real world might be. I only felt that by coming from somewhere true, the energy confirmed my guess that there must be a waking life hidden beyond our deep dream.

I didn't go play canasta with our friends again. How could I play a game in the midst of a play, when something true had shown its face? I had no appetite for talking to my friends the way I had before, pretending that nothing had been happening to me. I had the obligation of a husband to Margherita, and I loved her, though more out of habit, perhaps, than either of us would care to discuss; I loved my boy. As to the rest of the people in West New York, if their terms were that I speak my old part and ask no questions, raise no doubts, then there was no point in going on with it. I'd been in the army, and I knew perfectly well that West New York was not the only city on the face of the earth and Jersey not the only state, although among the people I knew it was not considered polite to say so.

Margherita kept asking me when I was going to be ready to go out and see people again and when I was going to start looking for another job. For a while I put her off by saying I was waiting till my leg was back to normal. But eventually I told her frankly what I was feeling, although I knew there was no way I could explain it to her, because I couldn't explain it to myself.

"What I need is someone who knows about the energy, someone who knows how to use it and what it's for," I said to her one evening after Vin was asleep. "That's why I wish the monsignor hadn't gone."

Margherita shook her head. "I just don't see why you think he would know anything."

"Because he's an educated man, and he was very friendly to me, Margherita. You don't trust him because he's a priest, probably, that's all. Anyway, he's gone."

"Richard's an educated man, and he's worried about you, Joey; I know this."

"Richard went to night school to study production management, and what's that have to do with these things? Besides, I've tried to tell Richard about the energy, and that's exactly what's worried him."

"Yes, and that's why you should be worried, too," she said. "You should be, Joey, and some days you are, don't think you can hide it from me."

"Okay, some days I am, because it bothers me that nobody

wants to hear about what interests me, and it bothers me that I don't have anybody to teach me what it means. But most of the times I'm really absorbed in it, Margherita. I've never had anything that really interested me before."

She laughed a little bitterly. "You're so absorbed in it you hardly talk to me any more."

"That's completely an exaggeration," I said.

"Yes, but sometimes it feels that way, in case you want to know."

"I do want to know, and okay, I'm sorry, but you always fight me on this Margherita. You don't like to know the things that are on my mind. If you'd only try concentrating your thoughts, like I've already asked you to do a number of times, because if you felt the energy just once, you'd turn a hundred and eighty degrees around on this thing, I promise you."

"I have tried sometimes, Joey, but there's too much on my mind, with you and Vin and the job and getting dinner and everything. You have all this free time now. If you went back to work, you'd probably forget all about it."

"Don't hope for that, Margherita. I'm telling you not to hope for that. It means too much to me."

She bit her lip and picked lint off her skirt, but she didn't say anything.

"The thing is, anyway," I said, "it's very easy to concentrate when you have a laboring-type job, including cleaning house, but I can see why you have trouble with it at your job, what with talking to people all day and answering the phone and making appointments—the phone never fails to break up my concentration when it rings here, I can tell you. This is one of the reasons I've been thinking of changing our routine, Margherita. I've been thinking we ought to move to the country."

She looked up at me with alarm in her eyes.

"Yeah, I know it's not an idea you'll take to right off," I said. "But if we were in a peaceful place, it would be a lot easier for both of us to concentrate, if there weren't so many people around, and you wouldn't have to go to a job."

"But I like my job, Joey. You know this. I like talking to people, I like all our friends to be around."

"That's just why you can't concentrate. But okay, you can get another job, I don't care. We don't have to go very far, and our friends can come out on the weekends; everybody will like that, Margherita. It's just that I can't stand people looking at me funny half the time. You like them to be around, but I'd like to be quiet by myself for a while."

She didn't answer, but at least she hadn't said no. I knew it would take a good while for her to get used to just the idea of moving away. Jimmy found me some road maps of northwest Jersey and northeastern Pennsylvania, and I took out subscriptions to a couple of the local papers there to study the want ads. I told Margherita what I was doing, but it only seemed to worry her. I remembered that the fish in the dream had warned me to be patient, and I tried to wait for the right time.

One thing she'd said was true enough: on some days I was very uneasy. Usually in the mornings, before I got out of bed, I would try to call up the energy by staring quietly at the shapes of sunlight on the ceiling, in order to begin the day with a hopeful mind; but once a week or so, irritated thoughts would be there when I woke, and the energy would not come. Sometimes I would calm down and rescue the day. Other times, I wouldn't be able to stop thinking about what I knew everybody must be saying about me. I'd think of them talking about how I was avoiding them, how I was staying home and doing women's jobs; how it looked like poor Joey had somehow gone off the deep end.

Then I'd think they all were right; something horrible had happened to me, something frightening. It wasn't my old life that was unreal, it was the energy. How could the monsignor or anyone else possibly know about it? It was my own mental sickness, and it was stealing my mind. It was taking me over bit by bit until I would never be able to be a normal person again. If I didn't stop it, I was going to end up in a mental ward. A kind of panicked jumpiness would come over me. I'd have to bite down hard on my lip and try to put the mop or the broom or the shortwave radio away calmly and go over to Jimmy's house to talk about cars, or sit away the rest of the day in front of the television quiz shows, hoping I could quiet down before Margherita came home. But then slowly it would disappear. My mind would be calm; the energy would return. I'd tell myself there was no need to worry, although the attacks of uneasiness made me anxious to leave West New York for a more peaceful place before too much longer.

One morning near the end of October, when I had been feeling jumpy and uneasy for a couple of days, Greenan and two of the paid officers from the union local came over to talk to me. I was on my hands and knees putting down wax on the floor of the hall. Usually I liked waxing floors, because I had to concentrate on laying the wax down evenly, but that day I was thinking very uncomfortably that what the energy had really done to me was to trap me at home to do the job of a woman. I'd finished Arthur's radio, and I had it bawling Italian music at me, to shout down my thoughts; and so I didn't hear Greenan and his union friends on the stairs. The three men barged through, calling out for me, and the first one walked into the mop, which was sticking out of a pail of dirty water by the door. Splosh, the pailful slopped down the hall over the wet wax to where I was kneeling. With my pants all dripping, I leaped up in fright, the way people will do when they're caught at something they don't want to be seen doing. Immediately I was yelling at the three men at the top of my voice. "Who are you coming in here wrecking my place like you own it? I'm in here peaceful by myself not bothering anybody, and you've got to come in and mess things up like this——"

Greenan and his friends didn't know what to make of it. Here was a madman in bare feet and a flowered apron and an old felt hat on his head and his hands full of rags; they decided to joke their way out of it. "Hey, listen, Joey," Greenan said, "we ought to get you into grievance work yourself. You'd have them shaking so hard they'd sign anything."

"You get out of here! You get out of here!" I was yelling, and I was shivering as if the spilled water had given me a chill.

"Okay, Joey, okay." They backed out, their soaked shoes sloshing in the water. "We just wanted to tell you we got shot down on your grievance, so maybe you'd okay an appeal?"

"No, I don't want an appeal, why should I want to work in that garbage dump full of you creeps?" I was crying with confusion and rage. Greenan came back in, challenging me to repeat that, but the union men yelled at him, and one got hold of his arm. After a minute they went away.

I sat there on the upturned pail, trying to keep still. I felt shaken, as if I had vomited. Greenan's voice was down there on the street; they were obviously talking about me. I began imagining his union friends telling their wives about me and their wives having concerned faces, and Greenan telling his buddies at the terminal, and them shrugging their shoulders and laughing. "Joey's just crazy; he's crazy." Pictures shot up in my mind of different people saying that, with sad or amused or bewildered or scornful expressions on their faces. The pictures flashed at me one after the other very fast, as if a reel of film was being yanked through my head.

If they see how I clean up, I thought, then they won't be saying that, and I began wandering through the house, putting things in different places and moving lamps and knickknacks around without keeping track of what I was doing. I was arguing in my thoughts with the supervisor of the hi-lo racing corner about how he shouldn't let the racing go on the way he did, and then Greenan was in the argument and the police commissioner and Bohanian the lawyer and Schlemmer the judge, all arguing at once till my mind was full of shouting. More and more people crowded into the argument, each one criticizing me for what I'd been doing—my father, my mother, Margherita, the monsignor, Richard and Angela, all making sober observations about how serious this was and how Joey ought to reform; my head was stuffed with their blabbing. I thought it would pack itself in till the sides of my mind would crack open under the pressure and all my thoughts would burst out like hornets from a torn nest. I wanted to run downstairs, to where Carmella was with Mikie and Vin, so that her talking would put something else into my mind, but the idea of doing it wouldn't stay still long enough for me to remember what it was that I'd decided to do. As I wandered around the house, what I saw with my eyes became mixed with the pictures in my mind, till I forgot there was a difference, and the blabbing filled up the rooms.

Slowly it quieted down, as one by one the people left. It seemed like they stepped backwards out the windows and the doors of the room that I was in. I couldn't remember if they all had actually been there in the room or if the room was my mind. I tried to think which, but immediately I forgot what I was thinking about. Broken bits of pictures and stray words were wandering upward in the air, just out of reach along the walls, not staying long enough for me to look at them or listen to them. They floated past and up through the ceiling. They came up faster and each one fainter, blowing all around in a garbled mist full of colors and vague sounds.

After a while they were gone. I looked around; there were no thoughts. The room was empty, and it had no ceiling or walls. There were no sounds anywhere and no shapes and no light, and I lost my body in the darkness. There was nothing at all except a small place of knowing that there was nothing. Suddenly I knew that that place, too, would be taken. A feeling of damp chill began to grow at me from everywhere around me; it seemed to fill up the darkness. I knew that when it reached me it would swallow that last place in myself, so that I would never know anything again. I was terrified till I was nothing but terror.

Suddenly I felt something else, something warm. I tried to find where it was, so I could go to it and escape. The thought came that the warmth was on my face; it was around my head. At first I didn't know what that meant. Then suddenly it hit me that I must be a person. I wasn't sure about it, but I scrambled at it— anything to escape. I tried to think of everything I knew about being a person: a body, and other people, hard things to touch, being in one place at a time. Pictures and voices slowly began to rise out of the darkness, more and more of them coming faster and faster, spilling over themselves like the water of a fountain, so that the air was alive with a shower of bright colors and sounds. Then I noticed the shapes were all outside me, and I was among them. Margherita was there. We were sitting on the floor of our kitchen, and she was holding my head in her arms.

I held onto her for a long while. The chill left; the dark emptiness was gone.

"Joey? Joey, are you all right?"

I waited another few moments, then sat back by myself, nodding.

"Carmella called me at work, she heard you shouting at those men."

"Those"——It took me a second to get my voice. "What men?"

"They came up here, she said you sounded terrible——"

It came back to me then, how it had started.

"Union guys. The grievance didn't make it."

"The grievance?" She was squatting behind me and embracing me again, with her face next to mine. "Joey, what happened? What happened to you? You were sitting here just shouting and shouting like somebody was attacking you, and you didn't even hear me talk to you, you didn't even hear me."

"I felt you, Margherita." I held onto her arm, which was bent around in front of me, with the watch on it and the fine hairs and the smooth skin; I thought it was something I never wanted to let go of.

"Why didn't you hear me, Joey?"

"I don't know, Margherita. A lot of blabbing thoughts came in and took over my head, and I couldn't hear anything. I didn't know where I was."

"How could this happen? I don't understand how this happens."

"I don't understand either. How am I supposed to understand?"

"Okay, Joey. It's okay now."

She came around and squatted down in front of me, look-ing very concerned, and dressed very spiffily for work, in a blue-grey blouse and dark blue skirt, with her hair carefully fixed. I felt proud of her. "You look real fine, Margherita."

"Can't you tell me anything, Joey?"

"I don't know, except it was the opposite of what's happened before. I got angry, which was a mistake, and I lost myself more than I ever have with the energy, and all my thoughts emptied out, and there was nothing but a cold darkness."

"Why do you do it, then? Joey, why do you do this?"

"I didn't do it on purpose, Margherita. I told you, this wasn't the energy. It was something else. The energy fills every-thing up, but this time there was nothing there at all, and it was dark, not light. The energy always feels really comfortable, Margherita, but this was frightening. I've got to find someone to help me. I don't want to make this kind of mistake again."

She was sitting on the floor in front of me, leaning against me. "I wish you'd just forget about this, Joey. I wish you'd just forget about it. You don't know what it was like to hear you shouting like that."

"If I could find somebody to tell me how to do it right, though, Margherita—if I could find the monsignor or some-body who could tell the both of us what the energy is and how to keep clear of this other thing—I don't know what it was, this darkness."

"And what if you can't find anybody? Who's going to know about this, Joey?"

"I have to go look."

"Where are you going to look, though? Nobody's going to know, because it's just so crazy."

"It's not crazy, Margherita. You just have to know how to use it, and I don't know. I have to go find somebody."

She was looking at the floor and shaking her head. I think it was then that she first began to move away from me in her mind.

# 3

# FATHER JEREMY'S VALLEY

Richard came around to see me the next evening. Margherita had called him to tell him what had happened. I'd been guarded before when I'd talked to him about the energy, but I told him about it frankly now. I didn't care anymore what he or any of them thought of me. It was obvious I needed someone to teach me, and there was no reason not to admit that I didn't understand what I was doing.

Richard didn't say whether he thought I was crazy, but he was ready to help me. He sat polishing his glasses and listening to me in silence, and when I was done he said, "If you think that this priest can help you, why don't you go talk to him?"

"I don't know where he is; otherwise I already would have."

"Did you ask down at the archdiocese?"

"No, I didn't. Would they know, do you think?"

"Of course they'd know. He's a diocesan priest, isn't he?"

I shook my head and laughed. "I never thought of this."

"So, well, try it," he said.

"I just don't know how to go get things the way you do," I said. "There's certainly got to be some advantages to believing everything's completely real." I'd already told him that I thought the life we all lead with our ordinary personalities was in some way a kind of dreaming. "I don't pay attention to things sometimes, that's the trouble."

He was looking at me a little oddly, as if he meant to say something, but he said nothing.

"You've never had any doubts that everything is set up the way it seems to be set up?" I asked him. I waved my hand around the living room, with the television and the sofa set, which we were still paying for, the glass-doored china case, and Margherita's Siamese cat on the throw rug on the floor. "This is all there is to it, and we're stuck with it?" I said.

He looked at me steadily, but for the first time since I'd known him I felt he wasn't being frank with me when he answered, "We do what we have to do."

"Sure, I know you believe in doing right, and so do I, except you're better at it than most people. But you didn't answer my question."

He said after a moment, "I don't ask that question."

As I watched him there, the thought struck me with a kind of shock that he was afraid. He didn't want to think of the possibility that everything he had committed himself to was not real. I suddenly realized that to say good old Joey was a fake was to charge them all with their own habitual lives also being fakes. I hadn't actually meant to do that. It wasn't unpleasant at all for me to think of my usual habits as false, since I was bored with them and since I'd seen something else I thought was real. But to them it was a challenge—a ridiculous one, if their faith in ordinary life was complete, and an upsetting one, if in even one percent of their hearts they felt the challenge was true.

I didn't press Richard any further. There was no need now. I was full of hope that I could find the monsignor and that he'd have an explanation for me that I could bring back to Margherita and Richard and all the rest of them.

The next day I took the tube to the archdiocese headquarters in Newark to see if the people there knew where the monsignor was. Inside, thin young priests surrounded by paneled walls sat behind desks under chandeliers. One after another they told me that there was no priest by that name in this archdiocese.

"Okay, but he was here four months ago."

"I don't know about that. For that you'll have to ask Father So-and-so, second floor, turn to your left."

The elevator had thick wooden doors with large crosses carved in them. I rode from floor to floor with priests who carried briefcases and wore wire-rimmed glasses and discussed business. Father So-and-so on the second floor didn't know. Finally a young sister on the top floor went into a back room and came out grinning and waving a file folder above her head. "Believe it or not," she said, "I found the man, which could be classified as a miracle. He joined the Carmelite Fathers and is living in a monastery near Sussex, Massachusetts."

The monsignor had become a monk.

"You got to be kidding."

"Nope," she said.

I wrote him a letter. "Dear Father Jeremy"—this was the Carmelite name he'd taken—"You said I should come see you, and now I hope you'll let me. There's something I have to ask you. By the way, they sold the parish limo."

He wrote back right away on a postcard: "You're welcome to come. What day do you propose?" There was a postscript that said, "It was all for naught. I never got my Peugeot."

I charged upstairs from the mailbox to show the postcard to Margherita. It was a Saturday, and she was working in the kitchen. "What'd I tell you?" I said when she'd read it. "He knows something about the energy. He's going to help us, you watch."

"What's a Peugeot?" she said sullenly.

"A Peugeot? It's one of those French cars—Vin knows it. Hey, Vin?" I stuck my head into the living room, where he was watching a cartoon. "You remember when we went up to Englewood to look for Jaguars, and there was a Peugeot on Walnut Street? A 404 Injection, right?"

"Yup," Vin said.

"He's a smart kid, he'd like the monsignor," I told Margherita.

"A *monk*, though, Joey," she said, handing the postcard back to me.

"So, a monk, they walk and eat and talk, there's nothing to be disturbed about. Look, if he says I'm full of baloney, that'll be something to back you up, and I won't have a leg to stand on in this thing, did you think of it that way?"

"I guess so, Joey. I don't know," she said wearily.

"You don't know, so don't worry so much. I'll probably be three or four days getting up there and back, so you'll have me out of your hair for a while. You probably forgot what a relief it was to have the house to yourself in the evenings, Margherita."

I wasn't going to let myself get angry at her. I'd been thinking more and more that losing my temper at Greenan and his union friends was what had opened my mind to the dark emptiness that day in the kitchen. Anger scattered my thoughts; it was the opposite of concentration. Probably it had invariably led me into mistakes in the past, but I'd never made the connection until I'd begun to look at my own mind.

The following Monday there was another postcard from the monsignor—from Father Jeremy. A brother at his monastery, named Stephen, was visiting his parents in Hackensack, which isn't far from West New York. Father Jeremy suggested that Brother Stephen might drive me to the monastery on his way back. I called him. "If Father Jeremy says this is okay, I take you," said Brother Stephen in a very noticeable accent which I took to be German. "You don't mind paying the tolls, of course," the brother added.

The next Friday morning I took the bus to Hackensack, feeling pretty hopeful. At the last minute before I left, Margherita got very worried and asked me to wait a little longer. "Maybe if you rest a bit more you'll feel more relaxed," she said, "and then there won't be anything to ask him about."

"This is going to be relaxing, Margherita. I need some air.

Anyway, I'm feeling good now. Since what happened the other day, I've decided that losing my temper is absolutely out, so I'm being real careful. See how you've already gained something from all this? Cheer up, will you?" I left her standing by the breakfast table, biting her lip.

Vin was already downstairs with Carmella and Mikie. I barged into her kitchen and picked Vin up and said, "Daddy's taking a little trip. If I find some new kinds of cars, we can go back and look together, okay?" After a few minutes I put him down, and I left West New York. I didn't see him again for eleven years.

The street where Brother Stephen's parents lived was lined with narrow three-story houses with peaked roofs and large banks of front steps—the kind of working people's street with old trees where they'd rather see a tornado strike than a black person getting out of a decent-looking car with the classified section of the newspaper in his hand. Brother Stephen was at the door; he didn't invite me in. He was a broad-shouldered man over six feet tall, with very light blond hair, even on his eyelashes. He wore long brown robes and a gold cross that swung on a chain from his rope cincture. He couldn't have been more than twenty-one. "You are Father Jeremy's friend?" he said.

"Yes, Brother, that's right."

"We are going." He led me to a broken-down old Ford Mustang parked in the driveway, and after stalling it a couple of times, he got it started and said, "Please pay me for the tolls now. It is three dollars and twenty-five cents."

"Yeah, okay, but look, Brother, I've been looking at the road map"—I'd had it out twenty times in the past week, to daydream over it—"and if you'll let me show you"—I opened the map and showed him how we could get to Massachusetts through New York State instead of Connecticut and avoid most of the tolls on a route that was shorter.

"There are many hills this way," he said.

"I'll drive that part if you don't like them," I told him.

He frowned a minute. Then suddenly his face flushed very red, and he jammed the car in gear and roared out of the place. I thought to myself: Well, one oddball deserves another; this is going to be an interesting trip. But he went up into New York State as I'd suggested, and he didn't say a word the whole morning.

We stopped for lunch at a turnpike cafeteria. "Please eat," Brother Stephen said as we went through the line. "I am paying for you." He must have seen how much that surprised me, so he added, muttering it, "This toll matter was very stupid of me."

"Hey, no," I said, "I'm sorry I forced myself on you."

"Forced?" he said. "I have Father Jeremy to thank for sending you."

"Yeah?" I didn't know what to make of him. Over the food he completely loosened up and breezed on about this and that, how his sister was pregnant again and his parents were moving to a mobile-home park in Florida, meanwhile stuffing himself with beef and potatoes and flashing smiles that made him look three or four years younger, a clean-cut kid just turned eighteen.

Later on in his car we began talking again, and I asked him how he happened to have become a brother—not expecting much of an answer. But he seemed to want to talk about himself, and he told me his story. He said he'd come over from Europe when he was fifteen and had gone to a high school in Hackensack. In his senior year he took up steady with a girl, but after graduation she wouldn't marry him. "She said I am such a tight-fisted German."

"You aren't particularly, Brother," I told him. "You've just got careful instincts is all."

"I am *Swedish*," he said, but instead of being offended, he laughed very loudly and delightedly, which made him take his eyes off the road and nearly sideswipe somebody. He wasn't a very good driver.

Of course the girl was right about him, he said. He had the peculiarity of always being afraid that things would be taken from him. When he'd go up to the blackboard in class or out to recess, for example, he'd take his books along with him, thinking someone might steal them. Naturally, soon enough a group of wiseacres took to hiding his briefcase or pencils or hat, just for the laugh of seeing him frantic over it. After a while, he was handcuffing his briefcase to his wrist wherever he went. Once he had graduated, he went to work in a shoe factory. His problem was no better for having left high school; it got steadily worse. He didn't take lunch to his job at the factory, since who could tell if his lunch pail might disappear? He mounted a series of elaborate locks on the doors and windows of his parents' house, the kind they mount on the entrances to commercial establishments. He had to check and recheck the locks five times over to make sure they were fast before he could go off to work or get to sleep at night.

"I wanted to reform, believe me I did," Brother Stephen told me. "I said to my girlfriend, 'Please, give me a chance.' But I couldn't change. I would lie there in bed and think about that back door. Was I sure it was locked? Certainly I was sure; I'd checked it only ten minutes back. But I wasn't sure, and I'd drag myself up out of bed and check the back door and also check all the other ones just in case. 'Christ in Heaven, aren't you asleep?' my mother would call out—I drove her to blasphemy.

"I knew it was all foolishness. But I couldn't silence my doubting and my fears. Many times I asked myself, What is it that gives me this? It is someone controlling me, perhaps? I wondered if I had a devil. Could it be? I began to go to Mass; I prayed to God. 'If this is a devil, take it away, please, God.' I confessed my sins, all of them, every one; I made up new ones to confess and then confessed that. But I never mentioned the locks to the confessor. I couldn't bear the idea of a venerable father laughing at me the way my girlfriend had laughed when I told her about the devil. She sat down on the front steps and laughed till she cried and walked away down the street laughing till she was out of sight. Nothing helped. I put on more locks and more; I believed I was damned. There was no sleep. My head burned. At last my parents had me committed to an insane asylum.

"It was a hospital of the Sisters of Mercy, may God bless all of them. A priest came around hearing confession. Many sinners are saved in such hospitals. I thought to myself, This father has heard very many insanities; perhaps he will not laugh at mine. I told him about my lock-devil. 'You cannot help, Father,' I said. 'I am damned.'

" 'No one is damned if he repents,' the father replied.

'I reproached him: 'But I have repented of everything, and the devil is still here.'

" 'Have you repented of this devil?' the father asked.

" 'I can't repent of him! That's for him to do!'

" 'He is your devil, my son. You have accepted him as yours. It's a sin to accept a devil and to turn away from God, your family, and yourself for the sake of such a thing.'

"I was astonished at what he said, even angry. 'How can you say that the devil is my sin?' I asked him. 'He's not mine. I don't want him.'

" 'If you don't want him,' this quick-minded father said, 'give him to God to deal with. Commit yourself to God and tell God you're sorry.'

"I was even more astonished, and I burst into tears.

" 'Tell God you're sorry,' the father said, 'and he will forgive you.' And he said the absolution."

It was so simple it was laughable: the Swede could actually become someone else than the lock-fanatic of Van Steuben Street. He sat there on his hospital bed in a daze at the idea; he'd just consign the devil and the locks to God. It hit him that he was exhausted; he slept for two days. When he woke up, he thought the devil had gone. God had taken it. Relief spread through him, he said, like the scent of a rose. They let him out of the hospital and he walked the twelve miles home, feeling like he didn't weigh anything, like the whole city didn't weigh a pound, like everything in it was ready to float away and disappear at the touch of a feather; he wouldn't have cared. When he reached his house, he dismantled all the locks and opened wide all the doors and windows in the place. When his mother came in, she nearly had a heart attack.

"So now that you were fixed up like the girl wanted," I asked him, "you decided not to get married after all?"

"Fixed up, I was?" He laughed his delighted loud laugh. "I had to sleep, and how could I sleep without locks? Yes, I had given the devil to God, but perhaps God had given him back. I was waking one night, two nights, three nights. Every sound on the street, every creak in the house was a knife in my heart. Without locks, I thought my friends from high school, the mob, the police, the devil himself would break in and kill us and destroy everything. Near morning, of the third night, I began mounting locks on the doors again. My mother sobbed, my father in his bedclothes was shouting and hit me. It was as if I heard nothing and felt nothing. They called for the strait-jacket, but by the time they came with it, it was not needed. The locks were back on, and I was sitting among the tools, weeping like a frightened child.

"The wise father at the hospital scolded me. 'You cannot take all the locks off at once, my son. The miracles of God only seem to come suddenly. In truth they are his response to much prayer. Can you take off just one of the locks?'

"For a month I had no lock on the side door to the yard. I believed I would die, but I prayed that God would let me ascend to heaven after purgatory, where I would do penance for not having taken off the other locks. I went back to work at the shoe factory; I slept, though not well. One day the father at the hospital told me, "Take the lock off the back door, my son.' Now he was certainly consigning me to death, but I obeyed him. It was only important to me now that I die with the name of Christ on my lips. When the father at last told me to take the third lock off, too, the one on the front door, he said, 'You will indeed die someday, as we all will. Do you see that it doesn't matter when you die, but instead whether your soul is true while you live?'

"I took off the third lock and prayed harder. One early morning I woke up very suddenly. Someone was in the room with me. Though it was light, I did not dare open my eyes. I prayed fervently and gave my soul to God. The person in my room hit me and said something that seemed to be in a foreign language. As I waited to die, this thought struck me like a thunderbolt: I am happy. I had never been happy before, and the feeling astonished me. I prayed and prayed, and I forgot about the intruder in the room until she pulled at the covers and I opened my eyes. It was my sister's two-year-old child trying to climb onto my bed.

"Why should I die like I was, a frightened and miserable mental patient, when it would be happiness to die close to God and prepared for heaven? I said to the father at the hospital that I would spend whatever time I had left praying and purifying my soul. I told him that I wanted nothing else. He cautioned me to practice moderation. But he brought me to a Carmelite father. As soon as I met that monk, who owned nothing and thought of nothing but God, I knew that I had found what I wanted for myself. In six months I had taken the vows."

Listening to him, I remembered how changed I had felt playing a priest in the monsignor stunt. It was obvious that Brother Stephen had outdone even a priest; he had given away everything, even his name. He had said it himself: he owned nothing, and he lived according to a discipline which, the way I'd heard about it, ordered every detail of his days. His stunt was total; he had reinvented his entire life.

His story made me a little nervous. I was going to see Father Jeremy for advice, but I didn't want this kind of advice. I wanted to keep some things: my independence, my family, the ordinary comforts. I wasn't interested in giving up everything, especially to exchange it for God, since God meant nothing to me. I wondered if Father Jeremy had set this ride up just to introduce me to the legitimate ways of changing myself the Church could offer me. I told myself he was going to have to be disappointed. I wasn't about to take a role in another play that I didn't believe in.

I wondered if Brother Stephen had really solved his problem. His vows seemed too extreme to me: he'd adopted a rigid life that just remounted the locks on himself. "Have your vows worked, though, Brother?" I asked him. "If you don't mind my asking? Don't you get the urge sometimes to lock up your cell at the monastery, for example?"

He laughed again. "Sure, I am sometimes afraid. I think perhaps another brother will take my cross. I thought you would cost me something by riding with me today. Suddenly I was thinking the car and the toll money belonged to me. It is hard to be at my old home, where all the insanities happened. Even at the monastery, I can forget that everything I have, including my life, belongs to God. But the vows remind me. They tell me who I have promised myself to be. When I think of them, then I am no longer afraid. Anyone can come in and take anything they wish, take it all, take my life, because how can they take what is already God's? My vows are my friends. They have set me free."

We left the Taconic Parkway in the late afternoon and drove northeast into the Berkshire Hills, low and round, orange and crimson from the turning maples, with a yellow sprinkling of birches and oak. The fields were still green—it was the beginning of November; on both sides of the road, black and white dairy cows sat munching on the grass near red barns with round-topped silos. Signs saying Apple Cider with dried paint dripping from the letters leaned against the mailboxes. White wooden farmhouses stood right against the highway, with brick chimneys running up their sides. Narrow roads wound up into the hills. To me it was a storybook, a picture from a magazine. It never would have crossed my mind that such places existed outside of cigarette advertisements or the drawings in school textbooks. "How long does this go on, Brother Stephen?"

"What? Does what go on?"

"These places. These farms."

"Yes, I do not know. Massachusetts, Vermont, New Hampshire, part of Maine also. All very nice. I have been. Nicer than Hackensack."

"So what about the rest of Maine?"

"What? There are forests."

I wanted to pump him about all the places he knew, but he didn't want to talk now. I watched him there, bent over the wheel with his lips moving slightly and his brown robe flopping over the gearshift, crawling along at thirty miles an hour through the hills. On the upgrades he wouldn't bother to shift down, and the transmission would rattle and groan. He never noticed. He was getting ready to begin his life again. As we crossed the hills toward his monastery, I thought I could feel tension in him seep out the widows and dissolve among the farms.

Suddenly I thought, What makes me decide his vows hadn't worked for him? How do I know what goes on in his monastery? Or what goes on in that farmhouse there, where someone's just turning on a lamp against the evening? Or what goes on up that side road there, in Massachusetts now, in Vermont, in New Hampshire, in any of the states I've never been to? With his vows the brother had challenged his own madness, even what he believed was his own death, and he had won. He had been afraid to lose anything, and instead of running from it he had faced his fear and walked right through it by giving up everything. He was a hero in his own inner war. Then who was I to say his discipline was too severe? His discipline was the road he had taken without turning back; I couldn't compare with him, because I hadn't found a road for myself. Here I'd been complaining to Margherita about our friends, how they can't accept what's happening to me because they don't know anywhere else than Jersey, and how they don't understand what different kinds of people there are; yet I'd been just as suspicious of Brother Stephen. But look: on the map on the seat in the dim light, all those lanes and highways scribbled like twigs over the page; and outside, the miles, the hills, the entire world turning over toward the night; couldn't Margherita and Vin and I find our own place, too, where we could change, the same as Brother Stephen had found his?

He bumped us over a driveway and stopped the car by stalling it. Up ahead in the dark was a lit doorway in a three-story building shaped like a barn; faint glimmers of light showed in rows of small windows. Other dim buildings sailed on the outskirts in the night. "That way," Brother Stephen said, pointing to the lit doorway, and he disappeared. I went to the doorway and opened it. An old brother who'd lost most of his teeth stood up suddenly in the hall, startling me. "Come." He led me down a corridor lit by a single bulb to a small room with a cot in it. "Mass is said in the chapel at midnight and at six and eight in the morning. You are welcome here. Good night." He was gone before I could open my mouth to ask where Father Jeremy was and furthermore when and where dinner was. There wasn't a sound in the building or outside in the night. It didn't seem like a good start to knock on someone's door or shout down the corridor. I reminded myself that there were other places than Jersey and that I was certainly in one of those places. During the night I dreamed of monks chanting.

A white mist filled the morning. The air was clear for only the first four feet above the ground, so that I couldn't see the red monastery buildings above their first-floor windows. The buildings stood around a duck pond; a stream spread out into it quietly. Over the water, and down from the cloudy undersurface of the mist, drops of sparkling condensation hung like strings of beads in the light. I wandered around the place, trying to figure out where everybody was, with my hungry stomach growling in the silence.

Suddenly the chanting I'd heard in my sleep burst out of the white air. The chapel was right in front of me; its faint steeple seemed to be gliding backward in the mist, as if the chapel wanted to hide itself from someone who didn't believe. I went inside, where they were celebrating the High Mass. The chanters stood on the far side of the altar, behind a heavy ironwork screen, and through it I could make out sections of their robes and patches of their faces and held-up hands. The congregation of a dozen other monks and some local people were murmuring some of the ritual, and then, without warning, the chanters' voices leapt out again at full strength and rolled through the little building like a charge of blasting gel set off in the air. It was sung all in unison, so that it sounded infinitely deep, but without an interior; that music seemed to me as cool and clear as the energy, as if they had tried to represent it in sound. After each chant, I thought I sensed a feeling of rest in the chapel. I thought each blast of music must be loosening another layer of tension in the monk's minds. For a moment, I would have sworn that no one in the chapel had anything against anybody.

The mass was over. From behind the screen the chanting fathers filed out in a single line down the center aisle. Suddenly, as the fathers passed me, the energy began buzzing silently under my scalp. It took me by surprise; I hadn't been trying to concentrate. Instead of rising up my spine as it usually did, it brushed against my face like a faint wind that came from the direction of the monks, as if it was theirs. I started wondering just what was going on in the place. When the fathers filed out the door, the energy faded out as suddenly as it had come.

I waited in the chapel near the door, in case Father Jeremy might come in. I hadn't seen him there at the Mass, but I thought maybe he might have seen me. For a while I stared idly at a fat little lady kneeling straight as a ramrod on a prayer stool in a side chapel and offering up Hail Mary's to the Virgin. I'd noticed the woman before during the Mass: she'd limped forward to receive the host with the help of a cane. She probably had a bad case of arthritis. Her cane rested now against a pew. Kneeling there with no coughing, no shuffling, not one bit of shifting to ease the joints, without moving anything but her lips, she prayed for what must have been twenty minutes. She probably forgets she's the fat little lady with arthritis while she's down there muttering, I thought to myself. No wonder she goes at it. Faith is her stunt, and prayer is her method of concentration; it's obvious, once you think of it. If she prays hard enough, she'll forget she's there, and she'll call up enough energy to burn away her aches, the way the energy had often burned away my tiredness at the end of the day. In fact, I thought, she's probably blazing with the energy right now while I'm watching her.

In a flash I was down on a prayer stool myself muttering Hail Marys to test the idea. I didn't believe in the Virgin, but, I thought, so what? I concentrated my mind on the words of the prayer, which no one forgets after a Catholic childhood, and I tried to keep the other thoughts out. Soon enough, the energy was piling up in my shoulders and pouring down the backs of my arms and streaming outward through my held-up hands.

At that moment, the monastery made sense to me. Vows, penance, austerity, prayers, all of it: it was all a stunt, all the monks' grand method to get free of the ordinary distractions of life so that they could concentrate their minds and rev up their energies. They did it all day; they spent their lives at it. They probably have so much energy going, I thought, that they broadcast it; that's what I'd picked up when they'd filed out the chapel after the mass. Some of them must radiate it from every pore, all day long. Maybe they walked in the golden light I'd seen in Jackson Street. To them, the ordinary sunlight was probably nothing more than a memory. The idea dazzled me.

I began remembering those phrases the nuns had drilled into me in parochial school when I was a boy: "Jesus is the light of the world"; "God's radiance"; "Saint So-and-so was burning with the fire of the Holy Spirit." Of course I'd naturally assumed that it was just a way of speaking. But it wasn't. It was a real light they were talking about; it was a real burning. They told you that plainly enough, but for some reason they never let on that it was something everyone could feel if they practiced concentrating their minds. Instead, they harped on God and heaven and hell and all the rest of the rigamarole.

Before I'd even talked to Father Jeremy, I thought I'd found the confirmation I'd been looking for. Other people did know about the energy, and they not only knew about it; they devoted their lives to cultivating it. Then wait till I tell Margherita that my so-called crazy ideas are the secret rites of the one holy catholic and apostolic church! My head was spinning with it. I barreled out of the chapel to look for Father Jeremy. The old brother who kept the door to the main building said that the father sent his welcome and would see me in an hour.

I waited on the footbridge over the stream, watching the ducks upend themselves to feed in the pond. Their black and white tails twitched and pointed to the sky. Everything was bright; the mist was gone; the sun shone. For the first time, I could see that the monastery lay in a narrow valley between the hills, which burned with the yellow and orange flames of autumn. A fire tower stood on a summit in the distance.

I was right about moving to the country, I thought; you could concentrate your mind in such a peaceful place as this. Why else did you suppose the monastic fathers lived here in their valley? I could learn a lot just by noticing what choices the monks had made for themselves. If they kept to a tight schedule, for example, maybe it was because it helped them keep their minds focused. It was probably a mistake to think of their discipline as some kind of difficult penance. They followed the discipline because it helped them. You had to take a very firm control of your mind if you wanted to work on it; I knew that well enough now myself. Maybe Father Jeremy or one of the other fathers would teach me some of their methods; maybe it won't matter that I don't believe in their God. I can still learn what the energy is and how to control it, can't I, and how to keep away from the wrong turn into the dark emptiness? They probably have special techniques for concentration, special diets, even. It doesn't have to be connected with the saints and Jesus.

Plans to move my family up to the Berkshires, not far from

Father Jeremy, crowded into my mind. There was a small city nearby called Pittsfield—Brother Stephen had driven through it the night before; I could look for a job there. We'd rent out our house in West New York for six months, so that Margherita wouldn't feel afraid of a permanent break, and after six months of living in the country she'd be hooked. She wouldn't need to have a job, and she could stay with Vin again. We'd make new friends. She wouldn't want to go back to Jersey. For the first time, we would actually be happy.

Father Jeremy was standing next to me, resting his arms on the railing of the bridge. He startled me: his soft, handsome looks were gone. He'd lost weight, and the skin was tight around the tendons of his neck. I wondered if he had been fasting. Instead of contact lenses, he wore large octagonal gold-rimmed glasses that half-hid his thick eyebrows and made him look studious. In place of his trim clerical suit were the robes. His eyes were quiet with some inward thought as he asked me, with a smile, "How's West New York faring?"

"Faring? Oh, it's okay. Listen, Father, I wanted to ask you—well, first of all, thank you for letting me come up here."

"How could I resist after such a tantalizing letter?" he said. "I'm glad you came."

"Yeah, well thanks." I couldn't wait for any more of the formalities. "Listen, Father——"

"I'm all ears."

"Okay, now this isn't exactly what I came up here to ask you, but——" In all my planning about how I would learn from him, I hadn't thought about how to begin. "Look, you know when they talk about the light of Christ and the radiance of God and so on? What do they mean by that? I always thought it was just a way of talking, a kind of comparison, but now I think it actually has to be a real light, am I right?"

"I never would have guessed that was it," Father Jeremy said, looking at me with an amused expression in his eyes. He thought a minute, repeating my question to himself: "Is God's radiance real. Do you mean is God real?"

"No, well maybe, but I just mean is this light something you can see? Can you feel this radiance radiating? When they talk about it, what are they talking about, see what I mean?"

"These are things I don't know much about," Father Jeremy said. "It is God's nature to be radiant, and it is said that when a soul ascends to heaven it is dazzled by that radiance. But I can see this isn't what you're after."

I'd been shaking my head. "This is the way the Church talks about it, sure; I know that. But what I'm trying to say is——" I supposed they had to keep pretty guarded about the truth of the thing. You couldn't just spring it on people, as I already knew well enough. I'd have to come out and tell him. "See, I stumbled onto it myself, Father—the energy and the radiance. It wasn't through praying, though, it was by doing the stunts, like the one we did on you. I just concentrated on the stunts the way the little lady with arthritis in your congregation here concentrates on her Hail Marys, the way the monks concentrate on their chants, and watch out, there it was."

He was looking at me, very puzzled but smiling. "I've lost you now, Joey. Let's back up a bit. You were talking about. . .?"

What was this, I thought, their initiation test? Who knows? Maybe they have to do it this way. "All right," I told him. "I was talking about what goes on in this monastery—at least what certainly seems to me to be going on. Everybody here prays; they concentrate their minds, and their energy starts to pile up, because that's what happens when you concentrate your mind. The lady with arthritis does it with her Hail Marys; you and the other fathers, you do it with your chanting and whatever other methods you have, which I bet are very interesting; and I did it with my stunts. If you concentrate hard enough and you pile up enough energy, then the energy radiates from your skin. Isn't this what the Church calls God's radiance? If you radiate enough of it, it becomes visible, although I've only seen it once myself; maybe this is what the Church calls God's light, except that it's actually a light within yourself? Isn't that what all you fathers are doing up here—

building up your own lights and getting free of all the trouble of ordinary feelings?"

Father Jeremy was blinking his eyes and leaning over the railing of the bridge, staring at the reflections of the sun that glittered in the water.

"I hope you won't decide you can't tell me about this," I said, "because I'm not just talking when I say I know about it; except I don't know what it really is, and I don't know how to use it. Look, I can convince you, maybe, because you saw me yourself, the first time I caught on. It was the day we stole your limousine. The cops had finally stopped us, and you came walking up. Just then, the light was all around, and I didn't know what was happening. I always thought you saw and understood."

He murmured, "I thought I did, too. I thought you were on drugs, Joey." He looked at me sharply. "I'm sorry. Perhaps that wasn't it at all?"

I laughed at him. "Come on, Father, quit playing around, will you?" But he shook his head, smiling slightly, and said nothing. The thought suddenly struck me that he didn't know about the energy. But I didn't believe it. He was deciding how to deal with my unorthodox approach to the energy and with my using a nonreligious kind of concentration; that must be it.

After a minute he said, "I'm trying to place what you've told me, Joey. It's definitely true that people can have unusual sensations when they pray. I myself can feel very clean afterwards inside, as if I'd been swept out—unquestionably a physiological feeling, a real feeling in the body. One hears or reads also of the devout experiencing light, or radiance, or the presence of God. I take it you're speaking along these lines?"

"Okay," I said, "maybe I am. Except I'm not devout; excuse me, Father, but I don't even go to church, and I don't actually see what this whole thing has to do with God at all. Why does it have to be God's radiance? What about your own radiance? Can't you just develop the radiance in yourself? Isn't that what you do, Father?"

"No." He tapped his palm rapidly for emphasis. "Prayer

may be pleasant and bring pleasant sensations, but that is not a reason to pray. To make prayer into a kind of pleasure is a bad mistake that devout people can make, and it's a mistake for just the reason you admit to: this pleasure shuts out God. True prayer seeks to reach God. True prayer asks forgiveness, and it purifies the soul."

I was getting pretty impatient with him. "That all sounds real nice, Father, and I don't mean to be disrespectful, but everything you say assumes there is a God, it just assumes it, see? Because what if there isn't one? If the praying and the chanting and all the rest are meant to purify the soul like you say, then why do you want to put God in there to muddle up the purity? When you concentrate your mind and the energy builds up, then soon everything is filled with it, so there isn't any room for any disturbances, and everything is peaceful and pure and still; but the energy itself is empty. This is just what makes it pure. It doesn't have anything inside it. So how can there be a God in there? And a Christ and saints and angels playing harps? How can there even be a soul in there? That crowd of ideas you fathers pray to, it just seems like a lot of confusion to me, not any peacefulness and purity."

He'd been waiting to get a word in, and I was afraid I'd completely offended him. But in fact I'd finally got him interested. The inward look had left his eyes. "I agree that prayer can be misused, so that it clutters the mind instead of purifying it," he said. " 'God, please give me this, God, give me that'—you can litter it with begging, and you can also litter it with your grasping thoughts about the pleasure it's bringing you, can't you?" He turned toward me, raising his eyebrows. " 'Praying is such fun, and I'm really quite an excellent person to be so good at it'—That's not prayer, however; it's the opposite of prayer. As I see it, the point of prayer, the point of penance—one might even say the point of religion—is to forget oneself, is for you and me to abandon ourselves so that God may live inside us in our place——"

I'd been impatient to interrupt him. "Sure, okay, change

yourself, just completely lose yourself in the energy. I've sometimes thought about this, but what I don't see is why you keep
talking about God."

"Then let me make my point," he said, tapping his palm
again. "Say that you have emptied yourself of yourself, of your
desires and of your fears, and you have accepted God within
you as Jesus Christ our savior instructs us, only to discover that
God is empty, or worse, that there is no God after all, but only
the void—this seems to me a deeply frightening idea. Isn't it?
Don't you find it so? I mean, what would one have, then?"

I had gone up there to ask him, but he was asking me; and
what did I know? I was crestfallen. "The emptiness is full,
though, Father; it's full of energy and stillness. Your mind fills
with it and fills with it. It's not the void. It's empty the way
sunlight is empty. It's enough by itself; you don't need any God
in there. Because I know what you're talking about: you're talking about something else, when your thoughts empty out and
there isn't any energy there to take their place, there's just
empty darkness. You just become less and less, and that is
frightening, believe me. I thought I was going to die when it
happened to me. This is what I originally came up to ask you, if
you knew about all this, and if you had a method people can
use as a guide so that they can build up their energy while
keeping clear of any bad mistakes."

But I could see that he didn't know. He didn't know anything from experience about the energy and the stillness, or
about the darkness, either; he didn't know what I'd wanted him
to know.

"The bright, full emptiness and the dark, empty emptiness." He was nodding quickly. It intrigued him. I had the
feeling that once he put something into the category of an
intellectual idea, he could toss it up and down and around no
matter what it referred to. But I think he saw how disappointed I
was, and he let it drop. "I can tell you one thing, Joey. God is
there to struggle with us against the darkness to bring forth the
light, but we have to accept him in our hearts in faith in order

for him to help us. I believe that if you had faith and if you held to it, no emptiness could harm you. I think God has been seeking you, for he seeks all of us, and I believe you have been turning away from him."

"I'm not turning toward him or away from him, Father. I just don't feel him in there." At my raised voice, the ducks burst up from under the bridge and flew down the pond, trailing their hanging feet on the water, until they settled again among weeds that grew along the shore. "I just want to understand what I feel, Father. I want to know who I am and what I'm supposed to do. I don't want to argue about God or any of that; I'm real sorry I brought it up with you. I came up to see you so that I could get some instruction. It doesn't have to matter if we don't agree on what to call things."

He watched me intently for a while and then said slowly, "You can get some instruction here, of course. Celebrations of the Mass are open to the public, and instructional retreats are held for the faithful several times a year. I myself am a new-comer, though, and I have no skill and little knowledge. There are indeed some very remarkable people in this monastery who might well be able to enlighten you about the experiences you've had—though not all of them do very much talking. But I'm sure of this, Joey: no one here will teach you spiritual exercises so that you may employ them for personal pleasure or power——" I was going to interrupt him, but he waved his hand back and forth and added, "Or even for understanding, if by 'understanding' you mean knowledge separate from faith. Knowledge, pleasure, power—any augmentation of the personal self is not the path of the spirit. To use the spirit in the service of the personal self is the work of darkness and not the work of light."

"I don't believe in my personal self, either, Father. Good old Joey isn't very interesting to me, and he's a lot of trouble. I want to replace him. I told you this."

"What with, though?" he said. "What will you replace him with? You can't just replace him with nothing."

"The energy isn't nothing."

"What is it, then?"

"I don't know. I was hoping you would know, Father."

He shook his head. "I don't know, precisely. We each have our various experiences in prayer, and this is not one I've had. But even if I had had it, I still would tell you that you cannot do without faith. You are right to think that you need a tradition and a discipline to guide your steps and to clarify your goal. No contemplative father would tell you any different."

"But if you admit God is just a method, then why do I have to believe in him?"

He was silent, and for a minute he breathed heavily, as if he had been running. I wondered if I had upset him. But then he said calmly, "God is not a method, but faith is. You cannot make progress and avoid mistakes without it. You say you wish to renew yourself, and that is good; I doubt anyone would undertake a religious life without that wish. But good old Joey, as you call him, is going to be very stubborn; he isn't going to want to be renewed. That I can tell you from my own experience. Without the good God to go toward whom you believe in with all your soul, and without the discipline of Christ to slowly chip away at your old habits, you will never be able to let that old Joey go. He will be too strong. He will defeat you."

He was holding onto the railing with both hands, and the muscles were clenched in his jaw; it suddenly struck me that he certainly was fasting and that our conversation was exhausting him. I waited a minute before asking him, "Is that what you're doing here, then, Father? Replacing yourself with God?"

"Trying," he said, nodding and smiling. "Trying to try. Life is arranged here so that one does not need one's self, but one's self is not always eager to be unneeded. Sometimes one has to starve him."

"And you're glad you chose this—living this life?"

He was breathing heavily again; he swallowed and stared for a moment at the glittering water. He said then, "Glad, Joey. Even in the midst of this; I couldn't tell you how very glad."

"I'm afraid I've been giving you trouble a second time," I said.

"Oh, no, do not think of it. In fact, I wouldn't normally have seen anyone now, but I asked special permission to see you, and it was granted readily. You didn't know that you helped me with your escapades, did you? I was doing a job that I wasn't qualified to do. I have too many faults to make a good priest, too much vain love of fame and adulation and words. I was reinforcing my bad habits instead of trying to break them. You got me fired before I entrenched myself in a mistake."

He was watching me, still smiling, but I could see in his eyes a longing to go back to the inward place where his strength was awaiting him. We stood together for a while without speaking. "Lunch will be served soon," he said finally. "You'd be welcome."

"Thanks, Father. I'll go on, I think."

"I'll send you the schedule of retreats. Also, we do not restrict correspondence."

"Okay, Father. I appreciate it. Thanks for telling me these things."

In a minute he walked slowly off the footbridge, holding the railing. I tramped after him. Out from the weeds, like guardians of this quiet, the ducks swam back into the middle of the pond.

# 4

# MILLINOCKET

I walked out of the valley of the monastery, up a winding gravel driveway to the state highway on the ridge. From the stone pillars of the gate, a low stone wall ran north and south along the road. I sat down among the dry leaves of ivy that grew over the wall. Eastward, on the slope of the next ridge, a tractor moved in a long oval, plowing up the stubble of yellow hay. The tractor's sound was lost in the valley hidden between us; it seemed to glide in a golden silence. Trees crimson with autumn crowded above it along the bright horizon.

Below and behind me, the red walls and black roofs of the monastery buildings slept among green lawns. More than before, I felt that I understood the men who lived there, and I envied them. They had been called and had discovered what it was that called them, and they had found a place where they could give up their lives in answer. If I had been asked, not many months before, what I thought of a monk starving himself into submission, I would have laughed at him for being a lunatic, just as Margherita and every one of our friends would have done. But Father Jeremy's fasting seemed sane to me now, and the idea of letting myself be ruled by a strict discipline even attracted me. Look what the monastic discipline had done for

Brother Stephen, I thought; if it had subdued his madness, it certainly could control the bad tendencies I seemed to have. And that was only the negative side of it. They may have fasted and hauled themselves out of bed every midnight of the year to sing the Mass, but both of them had struck me as happy men. If their discipline required hard things that made ordinary people laugh, what did these monks care, if only it opened a way for them and set them free?

For a while I sat turning a curling leaf of ivy over in my hands and wishing I could walk back down the driveway to the monastery and never come out again. But I knew it was impossible. I hadn't the slightest intention of abandoning my family, and even if I had wanted to, I couldn't pretend to the monks or to myself that the Church could be my guide. Father Jeremy had said that his method was faith, but I did not believe. I tried to think of what there was in the energy that might make someone find God there, but I could think of nothing. The energy wasn't a person, human or divine. It was a force within myself—not Joey, certainly, not Celebrisi; something beyond name and thought and form, and present not only in me but in everyone. But the idea of praying to it seemed odd to me, even absurd. In one sense, that was a loss. From watching the fathers and the lady with arthritis I could guess what power their faith must be giving to their concentration method of prayer. I had no method, and my concentration had no power. Any emotion or distraction ended it. I wanted to learn to concentrate my mind till I could forget myself, just as Father Jeremy and Brother Stephen wanted to forget themselves; the destinations we looked toward were the same. But I couldn't take their road.

Without intending it, I myself had fasted since the afternoon of the day before. Slightly light-headed, I walked three miles along the ridge to the village of Sussex Center and ordered a large breakfast with a milk shake at the Town Luncheonette. As I ate, I looked across the street at the people coming and going among the stores beneath the trees: Keeler's Hardware, the Sussex Market, Wilson's Real Estate and Insurance. There were a post office, a single gas station, and a white wooden Protestant church in the middle of a triangular lawn where the state highway forked; that was all.

I wished that Margherita had been there to see the village; the peacefulness of it was exactly what I'd been wanting to find for ourselves. Especially because my concentration had no method and no power, I was convinced that I was never going to make much progress in it if we didn't have a quiet place to live. Even the monks, with all their training—I noticed they weren't living on Forty-Second Street. Their valley was an un-guarded fortress of stillness against the agitations of the world. Brother Stephen had said that just going home to Hackensack for a visit had brought back a little of his madness; I didn't think the dark emptiness was precisely a madness, but it was very dangerous, and West New York was undoubtedly where I was most vulnerable to it, because it was there I was most likely to get angry. It was true I'd resolved to keep my temper. But I didn't know how I'd have the patience to keep it in the face of the doubts of my friends and my family and Margherita's family, especially when they were all doing their best to console Margherita by telling her I would soon get over the very thing I wanted her to accept.

When I was home alone doing housework or taking care of Vin, there'd been enough quiet to concentrate my mind and hold to my own calm. Now my leg was virtually healed, and I wouldn't qualify for disability pay much longer. I would have to find a new job. That in itself would have been all right, if I didn't have to also go and talk to everyone and measure up again, join the group and play canasta and make people laugh again; the idea of all that playacting made me feel weak, half with anger and half with dread. Where would I find my calm then? I wanted to give myself a chance; I didn't want to bolt myself down to a future where there was no hope. I wanted to find a place where Margherita and Vin and I could be at peace, where we both would have the freedom to open our minds to the energy.

On an impulse, I pulled out the map of New England I had brought for the trip and spread it out on the table in front of me. I'd told Margherita I would probably be away three or four days and that I might not be able to call her; but so far I'd been away barely twenty-four hours. What if I could find a job in one of these New England mill towns in the next two or three days? Then I'd have something real to show Margherita, a real possibility for us. We could find a house in the countryside nearby, rent out our part of the house in West New York, and give a different life a chance for just a few months, to see how we liked being away. Right there on the road map were the states Brother Stephen had mentioned in the car the night before. Vermont began only fifteen miles to the north up the road, and New Hampshire another forty miles to the east; east across New Hampshire was Maine. Here and there were small cities, undoubtedly with mills in them: Manchester, Concord, Portland, Bangor. Without thinking further, I folded up my map, went outside, and stuck out my thumb at the northbound cars.

Dairy farmers stopped for me in their pickup trucks. I stared out the windows as they drove. In Vermont, the hills grew steeper, and the farmhouses changed: large and square and plain, white with green roofs, each one connected by a covered passageway to a barn just as plain. A farmer about sixty who took me east into New Hampshire said the covered passageways let you get to the barn when the snow was in. Near the towns, the highways were cluttered with motels, and along the main streets, large white houses with green shutters stood back behind clean lawns. Farmhand, motel maid, clerk in the hardware store: not the kinds of jobs they'd be offering an Italian guy from someplace in Jersey.

The city of Manchester was what I wanted. Through the center of the town ran a river lined with red brick mills. Each wore a little white steeple for a hat, and the name of the company was painted in fading letters across its face. The farmer who was driving me dropped me downtown in Manchester at the state employment office just before it closed. But there was nothing on the boards for me: just short-order cooks and clerk-typists. "Business is slow," the crewcut behind the desk said.

I stayed the night in the YMCA in Concord, fifteen miles north, and tried for jobs there in the morning. There was nothing. I tried Portsmouth, New Hampshire; in the afternoon I hitched to Portland, Maine, and looked there. "You could try the paper mills," the young woman in the state employment office in Portland said. She had a bleached white streak in her hair. "The paper mills start having some turnover about now, with the winter coming," she said. I asked her where the paper mills were. She looked at me as if she thought that I should be pitied, but that she herself didn't have time for pity. "Up north," she said. "Try our Bangor office. Will you tell them we directed you? We need that for our files."

It was my third night out; I had to call Margherita. I didn't want to talk to her, though, while there was still a chance of finding something quickly that might possibly look right. I was afraid that if I didn't have an offer of a good job, she wouldn't even consider the idea of leaving West New York. Riding through the towns, I had debated a hundred times with her in my mind, trying out ways to persuade her not to be too stubborn and to give what I wanted a chance. But the debate always ended with my feeling that I would lose when the time came. I knew that she felt her family and the neighborhood and our friends were the fixed center of her life, and that she would see living in New England as a kind of exile. My only hope was to offer her a situation that she could believe would make me more stable. After a few months there, maybe we'd know better what to do.

To postpone the argument but keep her from worrying too much, I sent her a telegram, which made me feel that what I was doing was very important, since I'd never sent a telegram before. "Up here looking around a bit," it said. "Will call in a couple days. Squeeze Vin for me. And you." The plump woman in the Western Union office embarrassed me by counting the words and reading them back to me with a smile.

In a '51 Studebaker, a teenage boy with a forest of black hair and a ready lecture on the Bible drove me into Bangor that night. The city was the next thing to still. Nothing was open on the main street but three bars. In front of them, pickup trucks smelling of cows were parked on the diagonal. It was cold; half an inch of snow lay beside the railroad tracks that ran through the town. I stayed in a brick hotel above one of the bars and lay awake with the noise of voices below. There was a telephone book on the night table. I didn't see any paper mills listed in it. It had begun to look like I'd have to trudge back home and tell Margherita that I still didn't have an answer for her. Maybe I'd have to settle for West Jersey, though that seemed too close to West New York now, far too vulnerable to the influences of our old life. I almost called Margherita, but I decided I would give myself one more day.

"Loader? Can you work a loader? Don't mind working outside, do you?" the old man in the employment office asked me in the morning. I said I could work a loader inside or outside. "Gets mighty cold up there, though," he said, nodding with a grin, seeming to enjoy the idea of me freezing to death while he spent the winter in the tropics of Bangor. "Up there" was Millinocket, seventy miles farther north. There were two big paper mills there. I walked back out to the highway, trying to feel confident about what I was doing.

A very fat greeting-card salesman in a grey suit stopped for me in his Plymouth Barracuda. As we drove north, the country changed again. On the ridges the red leaves were gone, and with the bare purple branches were mixed the green arms of spruce and pine. The farms were fewer and smaller and more weather-beaten; junk cars and old refrigerators without their doors lay unburied in the front yards. Later the farms dropped behind altogether, and the trees moved down close against the road. From one high point, I looked west and north across the ridges for what must have been fifty miles, and the trees grew over it all, without a house, without a road to be seen, though the sunlight glinted here and there in the distance on a lost pond. The Maine Woods had begun. The salesman who was driving me—he spent most of the trip describing a scheme of his to corner the pencil-sharpener market—said the woods kept right on going into Canada with hardly a break, and then better than seven hundred miles farther, through to the Arctic. Since I couldn't believe a man of his size would go anywhere near such a strenuous place as the Arctic, I assumed he didn't actually know about the woods and had exaggerated them a good deal for effect. Afterwards I found out that he hadn't.

As the road cut through the forest, with the edge of the trees close in one either side, I could see far in among the crisscross maze of dead lower branches, till they matted together in a black dark. I asked the salesman if people ever went in there.

"Loggers, hunters, oh, sure," he said. "Have a breakdown, freeze, get lost, go nuts—happens every winter. They go in, they don't come out." He chuckled with satisfaction.

After more than an hour, the trees suddenly halted, and we were driving down a green open slope patched with snow. Ahead at the bottom of the clearing, a black river, the Penobscot, crossed beneath the highway, and beside it stood another long old red-brick factory: the East Millinocket mill. Beyond it, two miles up the slope, the woods began again. We turned west along the river. The salesman told me that until a few years before, they used to float the logs down the river out of the forest to the mill. "They use trucks now," he said. "Less labor." Soon, above us on the slope, the green steel of the new Millinocket mill stood gleaming with a thousand windows.

"I'll show you where I stay when I'm here," the salesman said. "The widow likes an introduction." And he drove me down the main street of Millinocket, past brick commercial buildings and the white Protestant church in its green square and onto a side street of small wooden houses. "Rooms," a sign said in the window.

"Mrs. Rose," the salesman announced, "this young fellow may want bed and board on a weekly basis, if the mill takes him." Mrs. Rose was a tall thin old lady with white hair in a hairnet and a flower-print dress and a grey shawl on her shoulders. We stood in the hall, and she looked me over suspiciously. "He pays in advance," she said.

Mrs. Rose's house was as close with itself as she was with her money, and a good deal older, with low ceilings and low doorways and small windows that had tiny panes with circular flaws in them. On the doors were black iron latches you had to lift to open, and the living room was cluttered with high-backed furniture, with claws at the ends of the wooden arms, and with lace towels draped over the backs of the chairs where your head went.

"I'll drive you to the mill," the salesman said. He held up a fat finger: "Opportunities! Opportunities!" probably thinking of his pencil sharpeners. As he drove me up the ridge toward the mill, I looked behind at the white houses of Millinocket packed together along the river in the middle of the clearing. The woods climbed down the ridges from every direction and closed close around, not two miles out from the steeple of the church at the center of the village. The town was shut away even more than the monastery. I remembered the salesman's cheerful satisfaction with the menace of the woods, and they seemed in fact to be ready to flow down like a surf over the town. Yet if the town and the clearing held off the trees, I thought, still the trees held off the menace of the world.

They hired me at the mill. The job was to unload logs from the backs of the logging trucks, using a big pair of machine tongs mounted on a loader that wasn't much different from my hi-lo back home. The logs were swung four at a time end-on into the stripping saw, which ripped off the bark and sent the logs naked into the mill. I watched the supervisor run the loader for a while—the man I was replacing had quit—and then I walked back down into town, feeling scared. I knew I couldn't be positive that I was choosing something right. There was no one to consult with. Certainly nothing about Millinocket made me think I was likely to find someone there to explain the energy to me. The people I'd met on the road, at least, were just as ordinary as anyone else I'd ever met. How could I bring up the subject of concentrating the mind with a salesman obsessed with pencil sharpeners or with a kid who thought he was so saved that God was going to do everything for him?

Millinocket was quiet, though; that I could be sure of. I spent the day walking all the streets of the town while I looked at houses for rent and rehearsed what I was going to say to Margherita on the telephone that evening. There was hardly any traffic in the place; the town wasn't on the way to anywhere but the woods. At every turn of the streets, the dark ridges of the trees lay like shields on the horizon. I could only hope that if we lived in a quiet place where the energy could grow in peace, it would at last through its own strength reveal what it was and what I had to do.

I'd decided to call home after dinner, when Margherita would be rested and Vin would be asleep. There was a phone booth on the main street in a drugstore that was open late. I started calling at eight, but it wasn't till nine-thirty that she answered.

"Hey, Margherita? Hey, where you been all evening? I've been trying to get you."

She didn't say anything for a moment. Then, "Joey? Joey, is that you? Are you at the bus station? Joey?"

"I'm up in Maine, like I told you in the telegram, didn't you get it?" She didn't answer. "Hey, didn't you get it? Where were you tonight, anyway? Is someone else there?"

"No, I was at my course, I——"

"Your course? What's this, a course of what?"

"It's a refresher, for my cosmetology license——"

She stopped talking again, so I asked her if this was for her job or what?

"Joey, why didn't you call? Why aren't you home?" I could hear that she was upset, and I was afraid that if she didn't calm down she wouldn't listen to my plan.

"You knew I was going to be away for a few days, Margherita," I told her. "There's no reason to get upset. I thought you'd be glad to hear from me."

"I am—I am."

"I've had some good luck," I said. "Father Jeremy, the monsignor, he helped me quite a bit and explained some things, and I've seen some really beautiful country, really restful places. I know you'd like to see them, Margherita."

Again she didn't answer for a moment; then she said, in a cautious and nervous voice, "Are you all right, Joey?"

"All right? Yes, I'm all right. It's very easy to stay calm and keep your temper in a peaceful place like this; that's what I want to talk to you about. Everything I've been trying to tell you about living in the country, you remember? Well, I've been checking it out the past few days, and it's true. Houses are really cheap up here, and the pay is good, and everything is quiet and peaceful."

She said cautiously, as if to humor me, "That's real nice, Joey. Are you coming home, then? Vin's been asking for his daddy."

"Yeah, I've missed him a lot. So what's he been doing?"

"Carmella said the kids fought today. He's been a little fussy. He's used to having you around."

"We're going to get him out of that situation. Listen, Margherita. I want you to come up and see this place I've found."

"What do you mean 'see it,' Joey?"

"I mean come see it, come take a look—you don't have to be so nervous, Margherita. I want you to give me a chance and try what I've been suggesting, just come and give it a chance, that's all I'm asking."

"You mean come up there?"

"Yeah, I mean come up here." Annoyance was in my voice; I tried to clear my thoughts of it. I told myself to go slowly with her, since it was obvious that she didn't completely trust me any more. "Just for a few days, to visit and see for yourself, and we can discuss things."

"I've got a job, though, Joey. I can't just take off like this."

"Sure, maybe not usually, but this is for something important. That guy Rosen's been real nice to you."

"That's just it, and now he's gotten me into this refresher course so I can be a hairdresser, and what am I going to tell him? That I have to go see some stupid place my husband's——"

I interrupted her: "That's just the point, Margherita, that's just the reason. You think it's some stupid place because you haven't seen it and you don't know what it's like, and you just write it off without giving me a chance."

"Okay, Joey, all right, but we can discuss it at home. We can discuss this at home, because you don't have a job to take time off from."

"I do, though, Margherita. I got one this morning, right here in Millinocket. That's the good news I've been wanting to tell you."

That silenced her for a moment. She said then nervously again, "What'd you get a job *there* for, Joey?"

"Because I wanted to prove to you that my ideas about moving are possible, see what I mean? It's running a loader at a big paper mill, and the pay is almost as good as what I had at the terminal, just to start, and the houses are a whole lot cheaper than in Jersey, and they're all one-family and they all have yards with little fences and flower beds, and there are a hundred different lakes all around here for swimming in, which is just what you like. You can skate on them in winter, too, which I also know you like."

She said after a minute, "Can you come home Friday, and we'll talk about it?"

"I want you to come up here, Margherita. I want you to come up here and see it."

"I don't know how soon I can get time off, though. I don't know what he'd say."

"Ask him, Margherita. Just ask him."

"Ask him, but what am I going to tell him?"

"Just tell him your husband wants to try something different, and you guess you owe it to him to check it out."

"Okay, all right, Joey." Her voice sounded weary, and I could tell that she had decided she'd have to humor me.

"Don't worry, Margherita. Everything's fine. This is a very good idea, and it isn't for sure you're going to lose anything by it. Maybe you'll look back and think of this as the best thing that ever happened to us—try to think of it that way."

"Okay, Joey. I'll try."

"I'll call you tomorrow night, okay?"

"Okay."

"Hug Vin for me."

"I will. Take care, please, Joey."

"Don't worry, will you? I'll call you tomorrow."

"Okay then."

"Okay."

Walking back to Mrs. Rose's boardinghouse, I felt sorry that the call had ended the way it had. I wanted a chance to have things my way, but not at the expense of forcing her. I didn't want to steal her hopes from her; I wanted her to be happy with what I had for her, and I wanted us to help each other. I also knew how stubborn we both were, and for the first time the thought entered my mind that I might lose her.

The electric sign on the Great Northern Federal Savings building said nine degrees above zero when I walked up the slope to the paper mill in the morning. All I had was a jacket and scarf, and my fingers were red and numb by the time I punched in. The supervisor on the loading dock, whose name was Gordon Higby, thought I was joking when I told him it was the coldest weather I'd ever been in. He said maybe I ought to get a bit used to it, since it got down to twenty-five, thirty below there in January and February. At first I thought it was him who was joking; then I thought Millinocket was obviously out of the question as a place to live, since Margherita wouldn't be able to stand it, and even if she could, I couldn't. I decided not to mention my doubts to Margherita, though, when I called her back that evening. She told me that her boss had agreed to let her go the day after Thanksgiving, which would give her four days off, so that she could travel during the daytime and still spend two days in Millinocket.

"That's not so bad, except that it's more than three weeks till then, Margherita."

"You can come home next weekend, then," she said.

"Yeah, I don't know."

She put Vin on the line, and his little voice almost made me decide to go home as she asked; but I knew that unless I stayed away, she would never consent to leave West New York, even for a four-day visit. Vin asked me if I was coming home tomorrow, and I bit my tongue against saying yes and told him no.

I changed my opinion about the cold. As I learned the new job during the next few days, the freezing air helped calm my mind. Like a blowtorch, but smelling of the sawdust of clean pines, the air stabbed into my head with every breath and cut out my worrying thoughts. I tried to concentrate my mind on moving the logs, and the energy stoked up inside me, burning on my skin and keeping my hands and feet warm. Far off into the bright air, in the woods beyond the river and the clearing, dark lakes sparkled in the sun. I wanted to make my mind as clear and still as that distant water. The whine of the stripping saw and the endless growl of the logging trucks as they backed and filed blended together in my ears into a roaring silence.

Gordon, the dock supervisor, became friendly when I told him that I knew about cars. He himself was a fanatic about Volkswagens. He invited me over to see his junkyard. "I just got another '57," he told me. "Good year." He never said more than ten or fifteen words at one time. His backyard and barn were a horticultural nursery of Volkswagens in various stages of budding and grafting and flowering. He had all the parts perfectly organized down to the last machine screw, and there wasn't a spot of grease out of place anywhere.

Gordon was a little grey-haired guy of about forty who kept his lips pursed all the time, and indoors and out he wore a grey fisherman's hat with little round holes in it. He kept taking it off and scratching his head and putting it back on again. His wife, Joyce, who was blond and slow and bigger than him, didn't like to talk much more than he did, and when they did say something, at first I had to ask them, "What?" half the time, because their Maine accents were so strange to me. They never raised their voices. It seemed like the years of cold had frozen their lives to the essentials, as if they'd stashed their feelings a long time back in some deep, icebound cellar and had mostly forgotten them. Probably for that reason, they didn't seem to have any interest in gossip. I worked the entire next weekend on Gordon's '57 Volkswagen—later, after we'd rebuilt it, he gave it to me for seventy-five dollars—and not once did he or his wife ever ask me why I'd left Jersey, and did the ring I wore mean I had a wife and maybe kids, and did I go to church or play cards or watch football, and what did I think about politics? I thought we probably could live in Millinocket ten years without anybody asking us for an explanation of why we were there.

Each morning when the logging trucks woke up the town by roaring into the woods, I felt surer that I had found the kind of place I had planned on. The people were decent and not nosy and wouldn't bother us; the pay was good and the housing cheap; Margherita could swim in the summer, and Vin could go sledding in the winter; what more could we ask? Next to this peaceful Yankee clearing, West New York seemed like a jungle. Far more than at home, the energy stayed with me; it was there in the morning when I woke, transforming the hurry of Mrs. Rose's house, heavy with loggers' boots on the stairs, into a natural ease; all day it warmed me and kept me alert on the loading dock; after dinner, as I looked out at the night sky crowded with a thousand stars that I had never seen from the city, it lightened with hope my fearful thoughts about my life.

On some days, especially on days after I'd talked on the phone with Margherita, nervousness would take hold of me. Hour upon hour my mind was a courtroom of debate. I couldn't persuade her. Yet the thought of trudging home to the dead end of West New York, to live out my life without any hope of finding out who I could be, filled me with a kind of fright. My fears and debates wouldn't let me concentrate, and the energy would fade. I'd be cold on the loader. One nervous afternoon, after I'd been in Millinocket about ten days, I pulled the wrong lever and dropped some logs on the dock not five feet from where Gordon was standing. He didn't say a word; he turned his back on me when I apologized.

That night I went down to Bangor with a couple of the logging-truck drivers to see a Western movie. I didn't think I'd be able to stay very calm in my room. After the movie, on the way back to Millinocket, as I slept sitting up in the back of the car, I dreamed I was sitting in the lobby of a big old wooden hotel, the kind there'd been in the movie. I seemed to know it was in California, in the eighteen-eighties or nineties. It wasn't exactly myself sitting there, but somebody else who was myself, the way it can happen in dreams. Couples kept going past me and upstairs—that was the kind of place it was, but with a very respectable air about it; it was something acceptable on the frontier.

I was waiting, but I couldn't remember for what or for whom. Finally a woman I'd seen walking around in a fancy long red low-cut spangled dress, the kind the bar hostesses had worn in the Western, came over to where I was sitting and said I should go on upstairs. She mentioned the name of a woman, but I didn't hear it very well. I walked up a big curving staircase with a banister painted gold and down a long corridor with red plush walls. I could hear laughter in the rooms behind the doors. Then on one door I saw the number 516, and there was a rush of feeling in my throat and eyes, half of pain and half of delight. Without opening the door, I was in the room. A woman was standing with her back to me at the edge of a modern shower stall, rinsing out a pair of khaki pants in the shower. She'd been in the water herself, and her hair was up in a towel. Her bare skin dripped and shone. She turned around, and we embraced with an emotion that burst up from under my stomach and flooded my mind so that I forgot what I was seeing; it was a more powerful desire than I'd ever let myself feel when I was awake. As she unwound the towel from her hair, which was black and straight, I noticed she was an oriental woman. Then I remembered that this was what kept us from being together.

Just then the dream changed. I was standing in a pavilion, a sort of porch without a house, a little like the kiosk in the Millinocket Common where the town band sometimes played on Saturday afternoons. In the dream it was built into the side of a hill, and across a small canyon, a hundred feet from where I stood, a waterfall shot down a wall of rock and churned up a circle of white water in a dark pool below. Beside the waterfall, vines with enormous green leaves hung down the rock wall. A woman stood facing the fall, rinsing her clothes in the pool. I saw myself then: dressed in heavy embroidered robes, I was watching the woman from above, half-hidden in shadow in the pavilion. Her bare back was turned to me; below her waist she was hidden in the white water. Suddenly she stopped her washing and walked under the waterfall so the stream of it blasted down on her upturned forehead, and she shook herself and whirled her arms so the clothes in her hands whipped around like flags. My throat tightened with a longing to call out her name, but I knew that if she saw me there she would be very angry. I thought I would give up my life to see her full form without her knowing. Suddenly there was a splash below me, and, naked himself, a man was bounding out into the water. I recognized him; I was amazed that he was her lover; I was stunned that she would have a lover. He paddled toward her, yelling happily a nickname that I didn't know she used. I was sure that in a moment she would turn around to him and that I would see her form at last. I knew she would also see me spying on them. But I couldn't force myself to turn away.

Again the dream changed. It was a single picture. I was standing in a dusty street, knocking on a rough wooden door in a long wall made of mud and straw. I was young; fifteen, maybe. I knocked, and from behind the wall came the sound of splashing water and a girl's laughter. I banged on the door with both fists. There was no answer except more laughter. I wanted to scream at her for mocking me. I woke up. We were in Millinocket. The other men were riding me for talking in my sleep.

The longing I'd felt in the dream was still tight in my throat in the morning, and it remained for days afterward. Suddenly I was looking at women again. The glimpse of a girl's walk or the angle of a face would remind me of the women in the dream, and desire would rush through me like a hot breath. Thoughts of sex had a strange effect on the energy: it seemed that they exhausted it. When I watched the secretaries at lunch hour, energy flowed out toward them, instead of circulating through my body as it did when I concentrated my mind. Instead of feeling invigorated I felt drained.

When I lay in bed thinking of Margherita with desire, sometimes I would give in to panic that I had closed myself into a trap: she would never agree to a change to what I wanted, and I would never be able to return to what I was. Then I blamed the energy for taking me away from my old life. Hadn't I been happy enough before it came, or at least more or less content because I hadn't known anything else? And yet what was this something else? I still didn't know. If they'd only given me some space at home, it would have come clear by itself in time. If only Margherita hadn't been so stubborn and had been willing to compromise, I wouldn't have gotten myself stuck up here, halfway to the Arctic.

Three days after the night of the dream, I spent the afternoon in Gordon's yard, putting the finishing touches on the '57 Volkswagen. I brushed solvent on some tar spots on the fenders. As I picked up the hose to wash the fenders down, two high-school girls out on the sidewalk let out a glad shriek, the way they do when boys come up behind them. Just then, a moment I'd completely forgotten, from the time when I'd first begun going out with Margherita, splashed up in my mind. After I'd taken her out to see a couple of baseball games, without its drumming up much interest on either side, I'd decided one Sunday on impulse to walk over to her house, having nothing else in particular to do that day. No one answered the door, but just in case she might be out back, I went up the side alley to the yard behind the house. There was Margherita, dressed in shorts and a man's shirt too big for her, watering her father's flower beds with the garden hose. That was why she hadn't heard me at the door. She caught sight of me: zip! She trained the hose on me. Of course I closed in and wrestled with her for the nozzle, and soon enough we were both soaked.

Shriek! went Margherita, when she noticed how wet she was—it was the high-school girls' shriek in Millinocket that had called up the memory—and she ran up the back steps of her house to go inside to change her clothes. But in order to open the back door, she was forced to turn toward me a second. Her soaked shirt clung to her skin, and I could see through the cloth to her shape as she turned, as well as any young man could ask. It was this that I had forgotten. She was slim then, and her hair was short and straight to her shoulders, instead of the bubble cut she'd had done soon afterward. I'd forgotten that; I'd forgotten her as I'd first desired her, just as I'd forgotten everything else that was now clear in that memory: the red wooden steps that had long since been ripped out for concrete, an out-of-date radio aerial like a helicopter rotor strapped to the drainpipe, a potted gardenia in the kitchen window, and the day's scattered clouds in a blue sky. That other afternoon in Gordon's backyard in Millinocket, as I remembered her standing for that moment six years earlier with the sun on her wet skin, the longing of the dream pressured up into my eyes and flushed out with a feeling of happiness. I recognized the women of the dream: they were all Margherita. The slim form, the straight hair dripping at her neck, the black eyes, the same playful nature—they were the same.

Suddenly I thought I knew just how to persuade her to stay in Millinocket. There was no need to argue about whether the energy had any sense to it. I'd just ask her to stay so we could be in love again. I remembered how after we were married, and especially after Vin was born, she had lost her playfulness; the respectable laws of West New York had bottled up her youth. I remembered how in the beginning she'd loved me because I didn't completely believe in the laws and even disobeyed them; but then she had forgotten. I was sure she could remember now in Millinocket because there was no one to confine us, as long as we kept to ourselves. In my mind I won our argument at last.

Thanksgiving drew near. Margherita told me on the phone that she wouldn't be bringing Vin because the trip on the bus would be too long. I let her have her way without protest. I told myself there was no need to be depressed; she was going to be won over, and Vin would be there every day soon enough.

I did my best to prepare for her. In another widow's house I found a sunny double room looking out on the street. I bought her some warm gloves and a warm sweater and scarf. I found the best eating places and the two best houses for rent to show her. I bought the Volkswagen from Gordon with part of my first paycheck, and I got a Maine license plate, which I thought would make me look settled. I drove down to Bangor to get the schedule for the cosmetology classes at the junior college there. I sent Margherita money for her bus fare. All I could think of was the memory of her standing in her soaked shirt on her father's doorstep. I stared at couples walking on the sidewalk or driving by in cars and imagined the happiness of soon being like them. I spent the last week of waiting in a frenzied agitation of hope and desire.

Margherita was already waiting in the bus station. Right away as she stood up, I could see that she was thinner, the way she'd been when I first knew her. She came across to meet me. "Hey, Joey." We both felt embarrassed; we didn't know how to greet each other. She stood there holding her suitcase. I asked her; "Listen, would you take off your hat a second? I want to see how you look." She had one of those fur hats that are folded over the ears and tied under the chin by a string.

"Oh, I'm growing my hair out," she said. "I didn't even want you to notice, and here you——" She had her hair straight now and shaggy, with the ends close on the back of her neck. She looked younger. I wondered if she, too, had been trying to remember how we had first been together. "What do you think of it?" she was saying. "It's got to grow out first, but it's two nine-dollar haircuts, and Mr. Rosen's doing it for free, isn't that great of him?"

"It looks great, it's just the way you used to have it, did you remember?" I took her suitcase. "What do you have in here, bricks?"

"Magazines. It's eleven hours up to here."

The desire that had made me sweat during the drive down to Bangor to meet her seemed to have frozen in the embarrassment and the cold night. We went to a pizza parlor and talked a blue streak about everything we'd been doing since we'd seen each other; it was as if we were old friends trying to catch up on news. We talked about Vin.

"He asks for you, Joey. He wants to know when his daddy's coming home."

"Yeah, well, we're going to fix that." I told her about my visit with Father Jeremy. "He didn't think I was crazy at all, Margherita. He just thought I should be a Catholic. Don't worry, I'm not planning on it. The way religious people pray, though, and the way these monks chant—you should hear them, it's something very out of the ordinary. It's a concentration method, see, more or less the same kind of thing I do. He agreed with a whole lot of what I've been saying, except he thinks you have to do it with the Church." I didn't tell her that he warned me against practicing concentration without faith. I was afraid that if we discussed it too deeply and I told her how unsure I still was, she'd turn against Millinocket before she'd even seen it. "Anyway, there's nothing to make me nervous or angry up here, except your not being here. Wait till you see the place."

"Aren't I seeing it? It looks like any other city, Joey, if you ask me, though."

"No, didn't you listen? This is Bangor. Millinocket is seventy miles north of here."

"Seventy miles? Seventy? Do we have to cross the border into Siberia to get to it?"

"You used to make a whole lot of jokes like that, Margherita."

She smiled at that. "It's cold here, though."

"So you shouldn't have worn such a short skirt."

"I wore it for you, didn't you know?"

"Sure, no problem, we'll buy you some ski pants. You get used to it; you get to like it. It's probably why these people up here are so quiet—it's too cold to have fights and problems. They'd all think Jersey was a nuthouse."

"There are a lot of nice people in Jersey, and you know it."

We changed the subject; we didn't want to talk about any disagreement. On the way to Millinocket, she joked about whether we were going to pass any dog teams on the highway, and did I get us a room in a motel or an igloo? "Come on, Joey, mush! Mush!" she shouted when I had to shift down on a hill. Our talk got more and more playful, but when we got to our room the perfection and the happiness that had been in my mind before she came was not there. It was cold, and a television was very loud in the next room. I told her I'd go ask them to turn it down.

"That's all right. I could sleep with a subway next door, after that bus ride."

"Are you glad you came up, though?"

"Well, you didn't give me any choice."

"Are you, though?"

"I don't know, Joey. We'll talk in the morning, okay?" She went to sleep, and I lay awake telling myself to be patient and to hold onto my hope.

We didn't talk in the morning, though, since it was Friday and I had to work. We met for lunch, and in the evening we went to Gordon's for dinner. Everything was friendly. Margherita and I had always gotten along well in the day-to-day aspect of things.

Now and then, I hinted at what I wanted: "You have to admit this is a real pretty town, Margherita."

But she wouldn't give any ground. "I guess it is nice for these people, if they like being out in the sticks like this."

I'd given her some money to buy more warm clothes, and the next day, Saturday, I drove her to one of the lakes a few miles outside of the town. We walked through the fields toward the edge of the woods. Nine inches of new snow had fallen in the night, and as we walked, the snow began again, one of those perfectly quiet falls that you notice only when it lands there on your hand. The sky had dropped a white ceiling that seemed to be only a few feet above our heads, and the flakes that twisted down out of it were larger than either of us had ever seen before, half an inch across.

We watched their starry shapes melt and vanish on Margherita's sleeve. "You ought to be able to keep them," she said. She lay down and patted out angel's wings with her arms stretched out in the snow. As I watched her, the longing of desire that I had felt in the dream grew in me again. She was absorbed in her own thoughts, and she seemed distant, someone never to be reached, as foreign as the women of the dream. As she stood up from the snow, then looked at the angel's form disappearing under the falling snowflakes, then lay down again to pat out another pair of wings, she seemed reachable only if she would let the circle of her own longing expand outward from herself until it touched and overlapped my own. We had stepped into each other's circles almost by chance that day in her father's backyard, by lucky chance; watching her there in the snow, I was sure that we could bring our circles together again, if she would only stay in Millinocket and allow it to begin. I thought I would be happy to let all my energy flow out to her, if she would accept it. I lay down beside her. The snow seemed warm; desire kept us warm. She seemed just at the edge of the circle. Afterwards I thought that if we had only forgotten our bodies and made our love just then, just there, despite the wet and cold, we would have lain in our circles together. But we went back to the car, and as we drove back to town the longing drained out moment by moment till the circles dissolved, and we were just two people on a bed in a room, as it always had been.

She went down the hall to take a bath, and she spent a good while there. When she came back she turned her back to me and got into her clothes quickly. She was shivering. "I can see why you like the snow, but the cold I can't see," she said.

"Sure, but this is a widow who is chintzy with her boarders, Margherita. Most people up here keep their houses like a hothouse in winter. You dress right, that's all. I told you this."

"Okay, you told me." She came over and sat next to me on the bed with a determined look about her mouth and eyes. "Now you tell me what we're doing in this place."

"We're seeing it, Margherita. We're looking it over, since how else are we going to understand what kind of places there are besides Jersey?"

"And what's wrong with Jersey?"

"That's just what I've been trying to tell you by showing you this place."

"How come you don't want to come home, Joey?" Her voice seemed very loud in the room.

"Okay, now take it easy. We're going to talk about this, so you think a minute. What do I have to go back home to, except an unemployment check and a lot of one-time nosy friends and a bunch of nervous in-laws who worry all day about whether I'm going to cause trouble and embarrass them?"

She was already telling me, "You just keep quiet about my family, Joey Celebrisi, since I don't see how I ever could have gotten through this time without them——"

"You rely on them so much, no wonder you don't understand what's been happening with me. You never used to listen to them like this, Margherita."

She was shaking her head and plucking at the bedspread fitfully. "You write off everybody you know, then who are going to be our friends now? The only reason you think these people up here won't bother you is because they don't know you and they aren't your kind of people. If we lived up here, we wouldn't have anybody to really talk to, and we'd be climbing the walls."

"We would know people, though. We would, Margherita. We'd get to know them. You start again, that's the whole reason for this, see what I'm trying to tell you?" I was speaking quietly and stroking her shoulder. I could see she'd never understand if she couldn't see it calmly. "We can start again; I know this. That's what the whole upset back home was all for: just so we could change and bust the routine and remember and start loving each other like we were supposed to do. Do you remember that day when we had the water fight at your father's place, when we first knew each other?" She nodded after a minute, frowning. "Well, the other day I suddenly remembered it like it had happened yesterday, like it was happening over again. I want it to be like that again now, Margherita. It can be, if we start again and just have each other and Vin."

She said bitterly in a low voice, "And what if you have trouble again, Joey. Then what happens. Then where are we."

"We'll be perfectly okay because there isn't going to be any trouble. The energy and everything else that happened was just to bust things up so we could remember and begin again; I know this. If you and Vin come up here, it's just going to be clear sailing." I knew that wasn't true; the energy came for reasons that I didn't understand, and there was no guarantee at all of clear sailing. But I wanted to persuade her, and I wanted it to be true.

She shook her head and blinked, with her hands tight in fists in her lap. "What if you get it in your head to run off again, and leave me with Vin in this godforsaken place, Joey? Can't you see this?"

"I could see it if there was a chance of it, but there isn't, Margherita. After all we've been through to get here? There isn't a chance. Believe me."

She turned away from my hand. "I don't believe you."

"You've got to, though. You've got to understand."

"I don't understand. How can I know what you're going to do? I don't understand you." She got up and walked over to the dressing table and held onto the chair with her back to me. "There's no way I can know what you'll do."

I didn't know whether I should go over to her to try to comfort her. I felt angry at her and afraid of her. "You would know what I'd do, Margherita, if you tried to listen to what I've told you all these times, like if you ever really listened about the energy and gave it a try, instead of just assuming I was doing something wrong and crazy, the way everybody just assumes it."

She was shaking her head. "The things you say don't make sense, Joey. They just aren't good for anything. They aren't what people have to do."

"You don't know this," I said to her, my voice rising. "You just figure you know the right way for everything, and you don't care what anybody else might want——"

"Oh, is that what you think?" she said, turning around to me quickly. "Is that the way I am, while you——"

"It is the way you are, about this."

"And what about you? You're always trying to do for the other guy, is that it, Joey? Except who is it who gets himself in jail and throws his job away on some stupid race and shames his wife in front of everybody over and over and makes everybody go wild with not knowing what's happening to you——" She was holding onto the back of the chair and leaning forward and almost hissing at me. "You say I should listen to you and understand you, but you don't even bother to ask about me, because what do you care about what's happening in my life? You don't care if I better myself or if I end up on the dole. I had to borrow the money for this course I'm taking, and you don't care if I pass and get my license or not. You haven't asked about it once, because you don't think about me."

"I do so. I think about you all the time. You can take the same course down in Bangor, I called up and checked it out for you."

"Did you? Did you find a job for me too, Joey?"

"No, but——"

"Since what makes you think I could get one in a place like this?"

"You could start your own business; I had this idea, Margherita."

"With what kind of money? Where would we get the money? You have all these crazy ideas, and maybe you try to work me into them, but that's not thinking about me, Joey. I want a decent life so I can be upright in front of people and have Vin grow up to be something, and I don't want him or me mixed up in your ideas, because your ideas aren't of any use. They're worth nothing."

I was stunned by this. I had no idea she had all that anger in her. She was standing over me and shaking. She said after a minute, "I'm going home and staying home whether you come home or not, and sometimes I think I wouldn't care if you just didn't come back at all."

"I'm afraid to go home, Margherita." I plucked at her skirt as she stood in front of me. I felt deadened. "I don't know if I can."

"Then stay here." She walked away and sat down at the dresser.

"If you and Vin aren't here, then I don't want to stay here either, can't you see this?"

"Then you can come home," she said in a flat voice.

She sat looking at the floor and working her hands, and for a moment I thought she might agree to stay. But she shook her head and said quietly, "You come home and be my husband like before, and I'll be your wife like before. That's all I can give, Joey, even if it isn't enough for you."

I didn't know what to answer. I couldn't face carrying what she said any further.

Minutes went by. After a while she asked, "Is there a movie theater here?"

We sat through a double feature, so that we wouldn't have to talk. Back in the room, we both lay awake for a long time.

In the morning we were carefully friendly again. We wanted to protect ourselves from any strong feeling. I didn't know what I should do about her leaving. I felt fearful and numbed, and I didn't want to think about it. We chatted our way through breakfast and the ride down to Bangor, mostly about Vin and the appealing childish things he'd said and done since I saw him last. We checked Margherita's suitcase and stood in line for her to get on the bus almost as if we didn't know what we were doing, as if we were home and I was putting her on a bus to see her aunt in Staten Island. The driver started taking people's tickets. The line moved up. She gave me a hug, the kind she'd give a cousin or her brother-in-law. "Take care, Joey."

"Maybe I can come home soon, Margherita; maybe a little longer, I can't tell."

"Sure, Joey. You see." She gave the driver her ticket.

"Tell Vin I'll see him soon," I said. "Tell him I think of him."

She got up on the first step and turned sideways to answer, and I saw her as she was on her father's back steps in the memory and as she was in the dream. The resemblance leaped into her face and shone there. The longing of the dream burst up through me and seemed to spread out in a circle to touch her as her lips moved. The sound of another bus revving up nearby covered her words.

As she turned and stepped into the bus and moved down the aisle, I felt as if she was taking something from inside me along with her. It seemed to stretch between us, stretching thinner and thinner. I wanted to push in after her to stop her, but the entrance to the bus was jammed with people. I rushed along the side of the bus to look for her in the windows. I shouted her name. I couldn't find her. It wasn't till the driver was backing the bus out of its dock that I saw her in a window on the upper deck, talking to the person next to her, leaving the circle of my longing behind her, gliding backwards out of my life.

# 5

# SNOW

Driving back to Millinocket, I stopped half a dozen times and tried to work up the courage to turn around, drive south, and catch up with Margherita's bus on the highway. I'd beep my horn, and we'd shout at each other at sixty miles an hour, and she'd rush off the bus at the next station—then I'd see the anger that had been in her face, and the daydream would fall apart. All the rest of the day, the memory of her standing there shaking and telling me she was finished with me kept stabbing into my mind. There was no way to answer her. It was obvious that any wife would have done just what she had done.

I sat in my room, staring out the window at the woods till my eyes burned from not blinking. I tried to figure out how I ever thought she would want to move up to Millinocket and get involved in my ideas. She'd always despised them, and she was right to despise them. That seemed as clear and cold to me now as the winter air. I didn't know why I had made such a ridiculous fuss about the energy in the first place, throwing up my job and my family and my home for it—just for an odd feeling that as far as I could tell nobody but a few monks in retreat had ever heard of. I didn't know what I had cared about it for. I'd never even known what it was. I'd thought it would lead me to the meaning of life, and for that I had given up living my life. How could my ideas be anything but wrong? How could Margherita feel anything but scorn? She seemed gigantic and terrifying to me; I wept, thinking of her.

At length my mind quieted, and I went downstairs to watch football on television with the loggers for the rest of the day so that I wouldn't have to think. In the morning, and all through the next week as I worked the loader at the mill, I searched through my memory of the argument with Margherita, trying to find a place where I could have said something different to persuade her. A hundred times I rehearsed a new argument that we could have if I went home the next weekend. Yet when Friday came and it was time to go down to the bus station, I knew there was no hope in going home. She would never give up her Jersey view of life. She would never compromise.

Then I blamed her instead of myself. In the mornings, when I woke up and Vin's voice wasn't there babbling over his toys from the room next to ours, I asked her in my mind what kind of wife this was, not to give her husband even a few months' chance to make a change? Her idea that you had to do forever what you started out doing, whether it made sense any more or not—this was just too stubborn, just too stupid. I thought I'd married a woman, not a piece of wood nailed across the door. She thought she had to bring up Vin to be upright in front of people, but upright like a fence post, so he could never move? Was it all right for him to breathe, Margherita? If some people down the block don't approve of him a few years down the line, that isn't going to kill him. If he finds some friends who don't look perfect in the slits you have for eyes, are you going to shut him up in the garage? You're so nervous to have him upright that you've stolen him from his father, and you're going to bring him up without me. That's certainly upright, Margherita, and everybody's going to cheer for you. Hurray for Margherita! Hurray for you!

During the weekend I took overtime at the mill—they were doing year-end inventory—because I didn't want to spend two days in my room alone with my bitter thoughts. As I walked around the lumberyard counting logs, I tried to tell myself to remember my rule not to be angry, but that only made me angry at myself. What good had my rule done me, except to let Margherita walk all over me? Staying calm was supposed to keep me from the dark emptiness, but maybe the dark emptiness wouldn't be such a bad thing now if it came and took my thoughts away from me. I never would have felt it anyway if I hadn't started experimenting with my mind, and what good had that done me? What good had any of my thoughts done me, what good had the energy ever done me, except to rob me of my wife and my boy?

Since the dream of the women I hadn't felt much energy anyway—first I'd been agitating about Margherita coming and now about her leaving—but as far as I was concerned, the energy could fly off and never come back again. I didn't care if I ever felt it again. What use could it be now? If it wasn't there to keep me warm, I could just wear the extra sweater and the ski parka I'd bought for Margherita, since she hadn't taken it back with her—she probably felt they were contaminated. But I didn't wear them. I wanted to be uncomfortable and miserable.

At the end of the second week after Margherita had gone, a letter came from my mother asking me when I would be coming home. "Vin's asking for you, Joey," she wrote, "and I know Margherita wants you back again." I was ready to call my mother and tell her to go get Vin and send him up here on the bus if he wanted to see his daddy, and send Margherita, too, if she really wanted to live with her husband again. In the next thought I was ready to get on the bus myself and go back home and take over. But I didn't call, and I didn't go down to the bus station. I knew that no matter what I tried, I would never win. Jersey was Margherita's fortress, and I was already outside the walls. I wrote my mother that it was up to Margherita if she wanted to patch the thing up, since she was the one who had decided it should be broken. I told her I didn't know when or if I was ever coming home.

At night, I sat in my room and stared out the window at the cold stars. It wasn't a method of concentration now. What was there to concentrate on, except my own hateful thoughts? I sat there because I had nowhere else to go. I became more and more frightened that I had trapped myself in Millinocket. I thought I was doomed to circle around in that winter clearing, lugging the burden of myself for years and more years.

Sometimes I thought of going back to Father Jeremy's monastery and trying out the life of a lay brother. But the monks' fortress, too, was open only to the people who belonged. I felt angry at the monks for being so inaccessible, so selfish with their teaching that they wouldn't share it with unbelievers. But at the same time I knew that they were right and that their caution was the opposite of selfishness. Spiritual exercises, as Father Jeremy had called them, were dangerous without a right way of life to contain them. Hadn't my own attempts at them shattered my life? How was I to find a way of life for myself, though? I despised myself for not knowing what to do, for not going on to look for what was right. But despising myself didn't help, because I had nowhere to look. As the days passed, it slowly dawned on me that I was alone.

More and more often, fits of nervous jumpiness attacked me. Sometimes at night I couldn't lie still for more than a few seconds. I'd get exhausted from shifting and clutching myself and turning. I bought some tranquilizers, but they made it worse; my body disappeared into a stupor, and my thoughts hurtled around in my mind like insects in a hot closed room. I took to sitting up most of the night and staring out the window across the dark fields to the woods, till at last a heavy sleep would seem to glide down off the black shapes of the ridges and over the fields, then up through the window and into my mind.

Each morning when I awoke, I was still more frightened, and I would quickly throw myself out of the room without changing my clothes and walk around the waking village until it was time to climb the slope to the mill. There, from the loading dock, I'd look out over the distant trees that stretched back on their dark ridges for endless miles under the grey sky. They slept in the long emptiness of winter. I, too, wanted to sleep, to let my mind rest in emptiness for a long time.

I had never gone into the woods before. People said it was dangerous to go in alone in winter, and even with a companion it was better to carry a two-way radio. If your car broke down in the cold or if you were caught in a blizzard, you could freeze before someone found you. But I wondered whether the silence of the woods, which seemed to move down off the ridges and bring me sleep in the night, might lay its weight on my mind during the day and take my painful thoughts from me if I let it surround me. Even if I forgot myself for only a moment, it would be worth some danger, and I didn't believe there was much to be afraid of, anyway, with a dependable car like the Volkswagen, if I listened to the weather report before going in.

The next Saturday morning, the third after Margherita had left, I turned down the offer of overtime and drove the Volkswagen into the woods. At first, as I followed the main logging road, summer house trailers and directional signs held off the presence of the trees. But after about ten miles, the pavement narrowed onto gravel, with long fingers of ice in the ruts. Snowbanks three and four feet high closed in on either side, so that the road was a trench between white walls. Pine trees and firs and bare birches crowded down to the banks. I stopped the car and began slowly walking in among the trees. The trunks stood very close together, and all the branches were dead for twenty feet up, sticking out in sharp stumps that met and crossed like the arms of turnstiles. I couldn't take a step without my clothes becoming snagged and my face being whipped. Ahead the trees seemed to close together in a grey black wall. I cried out a moment when a branch stuck me beside the eye, and after my voice died out, I noticed that the woods were completely still.

I knew then why the people of Millinocket huddled together in their clearing. It wasn't the cold of the woods or the snow. It was the emptiness. There was nothing there but the grey black branches and the white snow. It could almost have been night, lit by a very bright moon. My feet crunching and the branches cracking in my path and even my breathing sounded loud and hectic and conspicuous. Whose mind could hold itself together after an hour, two hours, after a day in this silence? Whose thoughts wouldn't scatter and be lost among the endless trees? Sometimes a crash would come faintly from away in there, and then the stillness would flood back in again and wash over my mind like a surf. Then the surf would recede, and the hot hurting thoughts would be there again, telling me of Margherita and Vin and the emptiness of my own life.

I stood there for half an hour, trying to let the still moments in my mind stretch longer and longer, until I noticed that the cold had seeped through my clothes to my skin. I worked my way back to the car to get warm while I drove on. Ten miles farther, I stopped and walked out again among the trees. I went back to town to eat lunch and then drove out into the woods again.

The next day I took my lunch with me and drove a hundred miles before turning around. I had a map, but I didn't use it. It was just that kind of thinking and planning that I wanted to escape. If I stood long enough among the silent trees, blankness would settle on my mind, and when thoughts came they seemed to be spoken somewhere slightly distant, somewhere above and behind me. I could pretend to myself that they belonged to somebody else.

All week on the loading dock I looked with a kind of longing across the roofs of the town to the ridges of the woods. I saw now that I was trying to bring back the blank emptiness that had attacked me in the kitchen back at home. It had frightened me then; I had been afraid of dying in it. Now I thought that what it would take was not my life, but my mind for the time that it lasted; it was a kind of sleep. My mind would return, just as it did every morning, just as it had that day in the kitchen. I warned myself that I was playing with something far too dangerous, but then I argued back angrily that I was tired of being cautious. I was tired of caring. I wanted to sleep and let my mind go. I could worry again when it came back. When it did come back, maybe some of the pain would have lost its way in the woods and not returned.

I drove back into the woods the next Saturday morning. A warm comfort settled over my mind, as if I was a child drawing up his knees under the bedcovers while snow fell outside in the night. I wanted to drive to the center of the woods and forget myself there and dissolve into sleep. I wanted to drive till the woods and the widening circle of my longing for them were one. I drove for what must have been hours, up the ridges and down again, jouncing over the icy track beside the unchanging trees. I listened less and less to my frightened thoughts. After a while they were nothing but blurred and scratching sounds that mixed with the rattling of the speeding car. Closer and closer the silence of the woods surrounded me, seeping first into the back seat, then next to me, then around my shoulders and head and neck, then into my emptying mind, till I could no longer tell the presence of the trees from the presence of my longing to be lost among them.

Heavy clouds had been moving over the trees. That morning the weather report hadn't said anything about a storm, and the air hadn't smelled of thaw or snow, so I hadn't paid much attention to the clouds. But now snow began to fall in large, wet flakes that clogged the windshield. The car began to slip and whine. Above the sound of the engine, I could hear the wind rising and sighing. I turned the car around and shifted into low gear and tried to keep up my speed. I wanted to call my mind back to concentrate on the driving, but most of my thoughts had already scattered out into the trees. I couldn't find my own mind's voice among the voices of the wind. Slowly the grey curtain of trees along the side of the road faded from sight; then all I could see through the windshield were white flakes driving out at me from a white cloud. I kept forgetting whether I was driving now or whether it was a memory from another year. I suddenly noticed that the car was spinning around; it quietly floated broadside into a drift.

The wind shoved at the car and howled around me, climbing and falling in a thousand voices. I thought the trees had been driven mad with longing. Other thoughts came: I should stay in the car and leave the motor running, and maybe I'd be safe, someone might be coming through with a plow—the thoughts shouted urgently across the empty spaces in my mind, and for a moment I wondered curiously who was being talked about. But I was already pushing the door of the car open against the drifts. I had decided what I wanted was to go outside and find the thoughts that had been taken by the wind. As I opened the door, the storm burst in howling and filled the car. I thought it would shatter outward. Then the next minute I couldn't remember if it was the car that might shatter or my mind. I noticed that I was stumbling around in the road. Thick flakes whirled around in the wind, so that I couldn't see farther than the length of my arm; when I shot out my arm to keep my balance, my hand disappeared into a white darkness. I wanted my hand to disappear; I wanted to forget and to sleep. Why should I know anything but the whiteness or hear anything but the wind? The wind and the whiteness were welcoming me. They pressed and pressed lovingly against my senses till it seemed my mind and my body were slowly parting like a fabric that had been stretched too far. Soon it would be my own voice howling; it would be my darkness. My thoughts seemed to fly out into the storm. After a little while, I noticed someone slogging around in a blizzard; I didn't know who it was. It seemed to be a snapshot I was looking at. In the snapshot, someone was looking at another snapshot just like it, and in that other snapshot, a man was holding still another. As I looked, I seemed to fall down through endless shimmering photographs into a white silence.

# 6

# THE BIRLAK STUNT

When I lost consciousness, I fell down in a kind of shelter between the car and the snowbank. There two snowplow drivers found me. They hauled me into the cab of their truck, shoved brandy down my throat, jabbered into their radio, and yelled when I started to pull my gloves off my aching hands. I didn't understand one word they said. Afterwards I understood the reason: they'd been speaking French. I had driven across the border into Quebec on the logging roads. But at the time I had no idea where I was or what was happening to me. Large patches of my body had disappeared from my feeling, and as the truck barreled through the woods, there were long silences in my mind. The drivers kept shaking me out of a daze.

Later I remember being helped into an ambulance. The sky in the window was streaked with the colors of evening. Up ahead, across a river, a city stood at the summit of high cliffs, with a castle looking out from the edge. I remember I wasn't sure if I was seeing an actual place or a television advertisement, and I thought there would be girls striding across the bridge at me and swinging their hair in the silence.

It was the city of Quebec. For a week I lay in a hospital, waking with a start every few hours, and looking around the room, wondering who I was. Strange things were there in my mind: shouts and monsterish faces and crowds of people in bright-colored clothes. The doctors gave me drugs against the shock, and they cleared up the frostbite on my nose and feet and cut off the last two fingers of my right hand. Then brick by brick, the house of my mind gradually rebuilt itself as I slept, and at length I remembered myself and everything that had happened to me much more vividly than I wanted to.

I had my life back and my mind, and despite what I had lost I was very grateful. I walked around that wet chill grey city, full of childish joy at the foreign people and things I'd come alive again in the midst of—the dumpy ladies serving coffee from their large bright steel steam espresso machines, the red-and-white oilskin tablecloths in the cafés, the prim spiffy secretaries hurrying through the snow flurries, the construction workers, all small dark men like myself, in their blue berets. I was glad they were foreign; I felt foreign to myself. The man who had lost his family and who would have succeeded in killing himself if a certain blizzard had lasted longer and had kept the snowplows away longer—this man seemed to belong not just to another country, but to another lifetime. I could hardly feel him. The hurt and the longing, and the excitement of the energy, were buried in a kind of dullness. As for something new, where was a hint of it? There was just one day and then the next and the next, each floating by in a foreign language. To survive was enough for me.

I found a job cleaning vats in a chemical factory. I dressed up in what was more or less a space suit, climbed down into the empty vats, sprayed solvent with a hose, and scrubbed with a long steel broom. In the evenings, I sat in the café on the first floor of the hotel where I lived and watched the strange, jabbering, confident life flow by. It was obvious the people there all thought they knew who they were. Dumpy Madame Surtis, now, she was the lady who ran the Hôtel du Clos and made *café au lait* all day with her steam machine and served shots of brandy to her husband Jean-Hébert, the foreman at the chemical factory, when he came home after work full of racial remarks about the West Indians. That's who she was, and Jean-Hébert was who he was. Maurice the red-haired postal clerk, who nipped in for his anisette every night at six ten exactly, and said "*Exactement, exactement,*" to Jean-Hébert's remarks, he was exactly who he was. It was fixed, it was all settled. What if they were fired, widowed, crippled, deported? What if something erupted from the bottom of their minds and exploded their lives apart? Would they survive? Probably, yes; but they would be different. Then who would it be who'd survived? Who was it who'd lived through that blizzard and was sitting there watching them?

Now I understood more clearly what I'd meant back home when I'd said to myself that people's lives were a play they thought was real. They thought who they were and what they did were fixed and necessary things, to be counted on and defended and believed in. But what they trusted as fixed became different without their planning it; what they took to be necessary was forgotten in the next year and unknown in the next town. Their lives were houses built on air. I saw that plainly not only because the house that had been Celebrisi was razed, and yet I was still there. It was also because I was living in a foreign country, where people's habits and clothes and gestures and even their words seemed to have been made up for no sensible reason. I smiled a moment thinking of the half-fearful, half-disgusted look Margherita would probably have given me if I'd said to her I'd found out the word for "dog" isn't "dog" at all, but *chien.* Of course everybody knows that there are different languages. But if each language names each thing differently, then all names are false, and no language is true. It was the same with people's habits, their thoughts, their emotions, their ambitions, and their ideas of who they were. There was nothing about their lives that couldn't just as easily have been something else.

I realized that in one sense these thoughts were obvious and that in fact everyone's opinion was the same as mine when it came to people who were different from them. Back at home, it was an article of faith, repeated in the catechism of every bit of gossip, that other people were strange and inexplicable and therefore not as good as ourselves, especially if they lived in New York City, or if they spoke Spanish or weren't white, or if they did or said outlandish things. Why did they insist on such unnecessary behavior when it was so easy to be like us? That was what was so distressing and so hard to fathom. But it was one thing to see that other people's lives were in the last analysis unreal; it was altogether another matter to see that your own life and your own personality were also a structure no less arbitrary than the rest, with its foundations built no less on the empty air. I'd thought Richard must have suspected it sometimes; perhaps that was what had made him a more tolerant person than the others. As for Margherita, when I'd suggested to her that her life was unfixed and could be changed, she'd only tightened her grip on what she believed and held on with both hands, even though it meant letting me go.

Father Jeremy knew, of course, and Brother Stephen. They hadn't wanted their false personalities and their old lives. Looking back on my meetings with them, I realized that this had been our kinship. Their ambition was a complete rebuilding, though not of the kind an ordinary person might want after the destruction of a sudden widowhood or a long illness. A new job, a new wife or husband, new friends—they wanted to sweep all of that aside and bring God into the empty space that was left.

I felt no temptation now to go back to their valley. I was still convinced that what was calling me called from within, and not from outside me, like Father Jeremy's God. I wanted to find the energy again and to know its secret at last. But having known Father Jeremy and Brother Stephen, I knew that there were people in the world, and undoubtedly always had been, who believed it was not only possible but essential to see the ordinary self as false, to do without it, to fight it off if necessary, to find peace and truth through letting it go.

The energy had not returned. I hadn't felt it since the dream of the women had aroused my longing. Then the agitation of preparing for Margherita's coming, her presence and her loss, and the idiocy in the woods had all exhausted me. I didn't try yet to call the energy back. I was content to rest and to wait. I knew I wasn't ready to decide what to do or where to go; I was too fragile and too drained. It was only important to stay away from any strong feeling and above all from anger, which I recognized well enough now as the gate to disaster. I never would have tried to throw myself away in the woods if I hadn't been angry at Margherita and at myself.

Back at home, I'd wanted to understand everything immediately, so that I could explain it to Margherita and win her over. Now there was no hurry. As each day went by, I saw more clearly how unlikely it was that I would ever go home. It slightly horrified me at first to realize that I was happy to be alone. But the truth was that I didn't really miss Margherita very much. It was a relief not to be living with someone who I always owed explanations to that I couldn't give.

That Margherita was more or less happy to be rid of me wasn't difficult to guess. My mother kept writing and asking when I'd be home, but Margherita never asked me; in fact, she wrote only once during the four months I spent in Quebec, and that to ask me where the keys were to the safe-deposit box. I sent half of my paycheck home every week, and I mailed Christmas and birthday presents home to Vin, but she never let me know if she received any of it. My mother finally admitted in a letter that she thought Margherita was very angry with me. I should come home soon, she said, if I ever wanted Margherita back again.

I myself was angry sometimes, because I felt that by refusing to move to Millinocket she had taken Vin from me. I tried to cut the anger off as soon as it arose, but I couldn't cut off the thoughts of missing Vin. Slowly I accepted them as painful thoughts that I would have to live with, like the phantom pains in the missing fingers of my right hand. Vin had to live with one of us, and that had to be Margherita, since I had nothing to give him now.

With the help of a book from the public library, I learned to get along in French, which didn't seem so far at all from my grandparents' *Napolitan,* once I saw the pattern of it. The people who worked at the hotel befriended me. I went to my job, and I held onto my thoughts quietly, without panic. I let the cold months pass.

Then one afternoon at the beginning of April, a government inspector in white coveralls came around to the chemical factory, tapping his pencil on his clipboard. He was very insulted when he found out that the fellow in the space suit down there cleaning vats was an American without the proper identity card and working papers. Jean-Hébert was furious. He hurled down his hardhat for emphasis. Would the American do better work if he had the papers? He challenged the inspector to explain the use of an inspector's existence. The inspector didn't say. He tapped on his clipboard and wrote out what he called a notification. To Jean-Hébert's annoyance, I thought the whole thing was extremely funny. Since the inspector was collecting identities, would he mind letting me look through his files, because I'd been needing one? I'd thought you had to have an entire structure of a life for an identity, but maybe the government up here had figured out a way to put the thing into a computer? Had they been offering this information on exchange to the American government? I bet the people down there in Washington would be anxious to get hold of it. I was sputtering with laughter, swinging my space helmet in my hand and trying to get my meaning out in French.

Afterward, Jean-Hébert offered to help me go after the proper papers. But I decided the time had come to move on. In my hotel now and then in the mornings, a sweetness in the air had been slipping in through my window, and I had already been eyeing the Volkswagen as it rested in the parking lot behind the hotel. I'd been thinking of the dream of the fish that I'd had back at home; the hope they had given me had slowly returned. They had told me I would change, and I had begun to change; they had told me not to get angry, and it would have been better to have followed their advice. They had also said I would find a new place, and I still believed them. I would find a discipline, a method, an explanation—something to guide me would be there, somewhere farther away than I'd thought at first, but not forever beyond my grasp, somewhere south and west, toward the spring.

That weekend, I beat out the dents that I had made bumping into the snowbanks in the blizzard, and I tuned up the engine. I cashed my last paycheck and drove out of the city onto the farm roads. In the villages, each one named for a saint and each centered around its grey wooden church, old women dressed in black, like the Italian grandmas back home, stood in the doorways of grey wooden houses and called out to children in the street that a car was coming. I drove on, bypassing Montreal, into southern Ontario, where the farms and the people suddenly looked like they had looked in New England, except that instead of hills there were plains.

The flatness of the plains amazed me. It was the empty landscape inside myself. The black plowed furrows shot out across the fields to the horizon without a single hill to break their aim, not a rise, nothing in the way, so that when I stopped the car on a back road and stood up on the roof, I stood in the center of a vast circle, as bare as my own life. In a minute a pickup truck jumped up from behind the horizon and zipped along a dirt road, spitting mud behind. I watched it cross the circle and drop off the edge again. As clouds moved, sunlight revealed tiny upright slivers of a new crop that covered the field in front of me with a green down. I walked out into the furrows, where the black loam was cold and rich as cake in my hands; it smelled metallic from the melted snow. I stood there and daydreamed about traveling all spring, about crisscrossing the bare lands that hinted at new life, back across the border into Michigan, then Indiana, Illinois, Iowa, Minnesota, the Dakotas—the names resounded like promises in my mind.

I knew it was still impossible. Whatever my hopes, I would have to stop and find another job. I hadn't saved much money from what I'd earned in Quebec, and the Volkswagen needed some welding work and a couple of new parts in the engine. Two days later, back in the States, on the Indiana Turnpike not far from Chicago, the car suddenly lost power. The fuel pump had given out even sooner than I'd expected. I parked on the shoulder, and the car rocked with the wind of the trucks roaring by. I looked out over the flats between the turnpike and Lake Michigan, where shapes of immense factories stood darker than the night against the sky. Plumes of bright orange flame flew up from them. The idea of another marginal job in a place like them made me feel pretty weary. A state cop swerved up and told me I had to get my car towed. I didn't have much money left after that.

At the state employment office, they told me they had nothing for me in the steel mills—the fiery places I'd seen beside Lake Michigan. But they said there was always some turnover at the packinghouse in East Chicago. I didn't even ask what the packinghouse packed. I figured I'd be lucky if I kept off the dole. The East Chicago city bus wound through neighborhoods of two-story red-brick houses. Then it dropped me at the gates of a black fortress of smokestacks and piled-up cookers and block-long sheds with sooted-over high windows. A blackened sign rose from the highest of the roofs among the smoke. I could just make out the brand name of the breakfast sausage that Margherita would sometimes buy for Sunday mornings. What they packed was meat: it was a gigantic slaughterhouse.

The steely haired woman in personnel gave my application form a bored look. "Where were you last week if you wanted production mechanic?" she said. "You can sit on the line, or you can leave your name."

"Anything you might have, Ma'am."

She nodded wearily. "I have a place in Building Five." She put me on the assembly line to pick pituitary glands out of hogs' heads for the minimum wage.

It was actually a disassembly line. There were forty or fifty of us, women mostly, sitting on high steel stools around a bench that ran around the four black walls of a huge high-ceilinged room. Slow three-bladed fans drooped down from above, and iron walkways scattered this way and that over our heads. Various supervisors and occasional troops of tourists led by a little man in a white coat tramped above us on the walkways.

A conveyor belt was sunk into the bench in front of us. In rode the pigs' heads, looking waxy and solemn. Each person was assigned a certain bit of anatomy to rip out of each head as it passed by. The backs of the heads were gone when they got to me. Using a long pair of curved scissors with a blunt guard, I had to nudge aside the brains and snip-snip, pluck out the pituitary, a bright pink pea. Two peas a minute made one hundred twenty in an hour, nine hundred sixty in an eight-hour day, till I ached with the burning stink of the place and my head was a blur.

I'd wanted to start trying to concentrate my mind again in the evenings, to see if the energy would come back. But the assault of a day at the slaughterhouse was too exhausting. I'd rented a room in the red-brick neighborhoods, in the basement of a family's home—I hardly even noticed their names at the time—and I leased a television and flopped down in front of the comedy shows every night in a drugged daze. The job even ruined my habitual hamburger dinner. The animal juice bubbling around my teeth made me retch, and I had to switch to pizza and peanut-butter sandwiches. I remembered the German vegetarian I'd shared the hospital room with after the hi-lo accident. He'd said he couldn't stomach the idea of eating dead bodies. At the time I'd thought he was an interesting oddball, but now I understood exactly what he'd meant.

I told myself I'd quit the slaughterhouse as soon as I'd built up some cash and fixed my car. But long before I was near that point, I got used to the place. The stench of it no longer bothered me, and the pituitary snipping became so much of a routine that I'd get completely lost in my thoughts and forget where I was for ten or fifteen minutes at a stretch. Then suddenly I'd notice myself there, snipping away like an automatic machine. It was obvious that this was how the steady workers stood the job: they just naturally shut off their minds. Since they were hired to be machines, they lived up to the idea. At eight in the morning they came in as people and inside of ten minutes they were transformed into rows of automated arms with tools sprouted from them, jerking down at the pigs' heads in a perfect rhythm, while their unnecessary minds wandered off into anyplace.

I decided to try practicing concentration right there on the job. It was far better than letting my mind slip off into painful memories. I took to staring at the rhythm of my hands as they moved on the line. One afternoon, not many days later, the energy was there again, flowing silently in my shoulders and under my scalp. It felt no different than before, as if the months of turmoil since it had last appeared hadn't touched it at all. I opened myself to it with a feeling of welcome. As I concentrated on my hands, the cool burning on my skin grew, then died out, then returned. It came and went all that afternoon, and I left work feeling invigorated and relaxed. The television shows seemed stupid. I went upstairs from the basement and for the first time struck up a friendly coversation with the couple whose house it was.

During the next few days, as I watched my hands, the energy would gather slowly upward through me, seeming to draw with it all the energy in my body, first from my legs, then my stomach and chest and arms, till I could no longer feel them. They were lost in a burning glow. The energy would pile into my head and push hard against my scalp from underneath, at a spot an inch or so in diameter just behind the center of the top of my head. The flowing energy seemed to want to push open a barrier there and to escape up into the air. But not to escape from me; instead I felt it wanted to escape with me. It wanted to carry my mind along with it, away from my physical brain.

My thoughts had risen out of my body that first day, at the end of the monsignor stunt, but never since then, probably because the idea of it had frightened me a little. Now I was ready to follow wherever the energy would lead me. There was no one now to hide it from or justify it to, and there was nothing for me to lose anymore. If my mind was calm enough again for the energy to return, then I had proof enough that I was ready to work again. I was getting well.

One morning just before lunch hour, the sad-eyed lady who sat next to me on the line suddenly began nudging me with her elbow and talking to me. My sensations had all moved into my head with the energy, and for several moments I couldn't grasp hold of my attention and move it to listen to her words. Her face was puzzled and concerned. She was pointing to my hands. The blood on them was thicker than usual. Suddenly the thought spoke in my mind: She's probably telling me I've cut myself. Immediately the energy bolted back down from my head into my body. The second finger on my left hand suddenly ached and stung. The sad-eyed woman had already called the supervisor, who had stopped the line. He was behind me, saying, "You'd better get to the nurse with that. Over in Administration, you know where?"

He took my seat. As I walked out of the building into the courtyard, wrapping my finger in my handkerchief and squeezing it against the pain, the thought occurred to me: Why should I bother to feel this? I wasn't feeling it before, was I? I stopped walking and concentrated my stare on the smoke floating up from a nearby stack. The energy began flowing again, and I found that if I willed it, I could pull it up from my body faster than before. The pain in my hand was lost again in the invisible glow. The space of my mind filled more and more tightly with the energy till I thought the barrier at the top of my head would have to give way to the pressure.

Suddenly I felt that my body was lower down from my mind than before. Without my noticing it, the energy had expanded around the top and sides of my head. The pressure had gone. The energy was burning there in a sort of round shape, but elongated and a bit pointed at the top, with vague borders all around. I could feel it flowing quietly upward to the smokestacks and the blackened high windows and out to the workers hurrying on their lunch break into the courtyard. The place of my thinking moved upward with it, but only to an inch or so above my head. There my thoughts rattled on, noticing this, noticing that, while everything else was still. As I crossed the courtyard, I couldn't feel my feet on the cobblestones. My body seemed to weigh nothing at all. I thought I could have walked for days.

The cut on my finger turned out to be minor, but I took it as a warning to be careful. I decided to confine any experiments with the energy to my free time, when I was alone in my room. I allowed myself to concentrate on one thing only: a photograph of a lake that I found on an out-of-date calendar hanging on the stairs to the basement. I also resolved not to stare at women, because that always disturbed me by making me think of Margherita, and then resentment and self-pity would drag my thoughts down and make concentration impossible.

Avoiding being mired in anger and desire and attacks of missing Vin was not as completely impossible as it had seemed to me at first. Just as it could burn away the physical sensations, so that as long as I held to my concentration I would forget about eating or drinking or any other business of my body, the energy could also lift me out of my emotions. The stronger the feeling, the more stubborn the concentration I needed to free myself; that was all. Sometimes the painful emotions would return when I leaned back to rest my eyes; but other times they would be gone, and I would feel a happy relief that at last I was maybe beginning to learn to control my disobedient mind.

I returned to the thought I'd first had in West New York, that the energy was actually something very straightforward: it was the basic energy of my mind and body, the power source for all the functions of my life. When concentration quieted my feelings and set aside distractions, it wasn't that the energy rose from some secret corner of my mind to take their place. It was the very energy that supplied the fire of my anger, the heat of my desire, and the power of the sensations in my body. I found it easy to think of my concentration exercise as a circuit breaker. It routed my normal energy out of its usual channels. It freed me of my anger by pulling the plug on it. The firmer my concentration, the more my habitual channels of sensation and feeling surrendered their share of energy, and their power would flow free through my body, into my head or out through my skin, and into the air. That was why concentration rested me and exhilarated me at the same time—something that I had always thought was contradictory. The tiring emotions were disconnected, and their liberated energy leaped through me like a charge.

I stopped thinking of people's lives as structures, like the houses they lived in. It made more sense to think of people as building their selves out of electromagnetic systems, which they powered with their own basic energy. It was obvious why most people didn't feel their energy as a separate sensation: it was constantly being eaten up in their normal systems. They didn't notice it because it was all in use. You had to slow down the systems, or even stop them, for the energy to appear on its own. I remembered telling Margherita once that I thought people could probably radiate light: "I bet that's what the halos are on the saints in church, did you ever wonder what they were?" I'd thought this was a wonderful notion, but she looked at me like I'd lost my senses. But where did she find the power to stand there shaking and tell me she was finished with me? The power that made her shake was the same power that shone from the saints, except that one was imprisoned in the dark circuit of anger and one was focused through the bright lens of prayer.

Concentration became easier for me. I got up early, and for an hour in the mornings and two hours in the evenings—all morning long on Saturdays and Sundays—I stared at my picture of the lake in ten-minute bursts, with three-minute breaks in between to rest my eyes. I hardly left my room except for work, for the local market and the pizza parlor, and for walks down to

Lake Michigan on weekend afternoons. I couldn't have called myself happy, because I still missed my family, and the future was still too uncertain. But I had never in my life been as calm or as vigorous.

Only one thing baffled me: the rattle of my trivial thoughts. Trains of them would ride across the field of my mind and take my concentration off with them. When a series of thoughts had exhausted itself, I would suddenly realize that my concentration was lost. The energy would be dispersed, and I would have to begin over again. In the past I had never encountered trivial thoughts by themselves as an obstacle. The noise and distractions of life in West New York, all the emotions and the worry, had always been the louder disturbances. Now that I was living quietly and alone and practicing concentration according to a schedule, the emotions were usually distant, and the simple thoughts came far closer to my mind's ear than before. I noticed for the first time how useless most of them were. They told me I had to do my laundry tomorrow, they wondered if those two new guys on the line were really union organizers like people were saying, they nagged me that my mother's birthday was coming up in two weeks. I told them to be quiet, since I couldn't buy my mother a present there in my room, and I didn't care right now if they put too much garlic in the pizza in that place. Yet I did care. My thoughts demanded my energy and took it. Their circuits were woven too fine for me, and I couldn't grasp hold of them and pull the plug on them.

Some evenings, if my feelings had been quiet all day, the energy would flow free out into the room and through my open window into the spring air. I felt that if only my thoughts, too, would be silent, so that all the systems of Celebrisi could be completely still, my mind would fly with the energy over the city and hold the spring in its embrace. I thought again of my belief that the energy burned in everyone. I wished that all of us knew how to quiet our minds, so that we could leave the systems of our selves behind and fill the bright air together. What would hold us down if all our thoughts and feelings were still?

What could divide us from each other and bring us pain? We believed that we belonged to our bodies and our feelings; but we were prisoners there. Our pain came from our captivity. Our true mind, our fundamental energy, was made for freedom and delight.

Because I could see my own captivity, other people's seemed equally plain to me. Right upstairs was a family of people who were led around pitifully by their systems like bulls by the nose. It was easy to see that they believed in their systems and they hated them. Birlak, their name was, Ned and Lonny and June. I'd become friendly with them by then. Ned, the father, had thick black eyebrows and black hair that stood up straight like a bristle brush; his job was to push a pencil in the purchasing department at one of the steel mills. His wife, June, worked the cash register in a shoe store in a shopping center. She had a very round, blond face and was one of those women who are always looking around vaguely because they're too vain to wear their glasses. Ned and June had a thirteen-year-old son named Lonny, dark like his father and tall for his age, already taller than his parents. I never found out why there were no other children.

Lonny paid for being an only child. His mother was possessed by the nightmare of losing him to pneumonia or the traffic on 141st Street or the tough boys in the ninth grade. She was always fussing and hovering and fluttering over him and adjusting his clothes and warning and reminding and telling him. He thanked her by making the kind of sharp, sarcastic remarks that kids his age are sometimes very adept at. Ned didn't take sides in this. All he wanted was for them both to be quiet. He'd pace up and down the house getting blacker and blacker under his black eyebrows till I thought he would blow up the house with the force of his frustration. June knew she was infuriating her son and her husband, but she couldn't stop. I'd watch the pressure head of fussing steam burst out of her even as she tried to hold it in. I believe that she had once fussed over her husband but that it had somehow transferred itself to the boy; and now she was too afraid of her husband to transfer it back again. I think he wanted it back, too, but he was too confused and too proud to ask.

Ned and June still shared one thing in harmony: plants; flowers. The house was thick with green leaves hanging from the ceiling, on windows, on shelves; and the front yard, back yard, side yards were a crowded garden of flower beds and shrubs and ornamental trees. June took me around for the grand tour. I remember her pointing to some green blades that were fattening at the top with unborn blooms. "Iris," June said. "Now these will be the yellow-and-whites. Ned," she yelled, "What are the yellow-and-whites? By the water meter? I'm showing Joey."

"*Ad astra*; yellow hafts and standards, white falls and beards," came his voice from behind the house, where he was building a greenhouse off the family room.

"He knows all the names," she told me. "He's always wanted to own a nursery. I just wish he'd do it."

It was the beginning of May. I helped Ned pour concrete and lay the steam pipes for the greenhouse. As we worked, he poured out complaints about his year-in-and-year-out pencil pushing at the steel mill. He said he couldn't afford the pay cut of working for a nursery, and he couldn't take the risk of borrowing on his life insurance to go into business for himself. "There's all this," he said, nodding toward the house, and meaning his nervous wife and his smart-aleck kid and the mortgage and the payments on the car and the washing machine. It was plain to see that his wife would have moved into a four-room apartment and gone to the laundromat without a complaint, just to have him come home content at night. But he couldn't see it. His anger had closed his eyes.

I felt sorry for them. It wasn't like my own marriage. These people didn't have any basic disagreement about things. They were just caught in some bad routines. I was very tempted to try and persuade them to take up concentrating every night for half an hour on a Christmas cactus or something, so they could calm down and build up some energy and look at themselves for once. I thought if they could get out of their fussing and anger systems just once even for a minute, they might be so amazed at the feeling of freedom that they'd resolve to try to get out completely, over the long run. But I knew that if I spoke about it, they'd think I was crazy.

They almost never went out together in the evening. June wouldn't leave Lonny home by himself, and he made a terrible fuss if they tried to slap a sitter on him. He never went out with friends. I don't think he had any. He kept to himself, like a lot of kids his age. The three of them spent every evening in that house, saturating the air with negative force.

Lonny had a passion for fighter-bomber airplanes. He had models of them stacked on clear plastic shelves all around his room, as thick as his mother's house plants in the living room. He had books on the subject, full of photographs and diagrams, and he knew all the names, specifications, speeds, maneuverabilities, heroic pilots, and famous bombing runs of history, complete with casualty counts and degrees of destruction in terms of dollars. He'd reenact them in his room at night. I could hear him above me there, imitating dogfights and explosions. He'd lecture me on it, frowning with his dark eyebrows to make sure I didn't interrupt or doubt anything he said. A certain amount of the statistics I believe he made up. I liked him. He was a nut on his subject, as I was on mine.

I wanted to try to rearrange the energy in that house without letting on that I was doing it. I hit upon a plot. In a hobby shop in the Near North Side of Chicago, I bought the components of an electric motor, and I told Lonny I'd show him how to assemble them. He fell for it. The very next night we had the components laid out on the floor of my room in the basement. When it was assembled, we hooked it to a grindstone, to sharpen his father's garden tools. Naturally, the motor made a trip to Lonny's eighth-grade science class, and he came back with a note full of praise from the teacher. Before long he had out a fat book on electromagnetism from the high-school library and was lecturing me on the various principles.

"That's real fine, Lonny," I told him, "but you have to understand it in your hands, too. Your father knows all the gardening rules, but he'd be nothing without the instinct."

"I have the instinct," Lonny said, "I have lots of instinct."

"Sure, I think maybe you do. If we took the motor apart, for example, do you think you could reassemble it?"

"Sure I could. That's easy," he said.

It wasn't easy, especially since he didn't enjoy taking advice, and after the third evening of failure at it, he spent a couple of hours in his room doing bombing runs. But he was as basically stubborn as his teacher, and on the fourth try he put the motor together. "We're doing a shortwave radio next," he said.

"Okay, but first we fix this old hot plate I picked up, so I can cook without bothering your mother."

"Yeah, my mother," he said with poison in his voice. "Let me see this hot plate." He looked it over. "This is nothing."

His parents hardly saw him now. Lonny and I even ate dinner in the basement among the wires and components and tubes. One night Ned took his wife to the movies. Then it was the flower show on Sunday, then greenhouses at the University of Chicago. Some of the tension that went out the door with them didn't return. I was pleased with myself. I had to give up most of my evening concentration time, but what good was the energy if I used it just for myself? I had always wanted to share the happiness of it. Besides, it made me happy to be around a boy again. If I couldn't help Vin now, perhaps I could help Lonny. If I still didn't understand very much, at least I could make use of the little I did know. I called it my Birlak stunt, and I wished I'd had the sense to do stunts like this one when I'd been home.

Eventually I couldn't resist trying out a few of my ideas on Lonny. I thought that since he was young, his mind wouldn't be set against something that might sound unusual. I warned myself: Here you are listening to your wanting-to-explain-it system again, and it's always gotten you nothing but trouble. But the desire to pass on what I thought I knew was too strong.

"People operate according to electromagnetic principles of their own, did you ever think of that?" I asked Lonny one evening.

"Sure I did. What do you mean?"

"I mean people work by means of systems, and they power the systems with their own personal energy."

"Oh, yeah. This thing isn't working, Joey." He was trying to tune our shortwave radio.

"For example, like your mother," I said. "You get mad at her for fussing at you, am I right?"

"Naw, I'm not mad at her."

"Well, I'd say you sometimes get mad at her, but here's why you don't have to: this fussing habit of hers is just a system she's got herself caught in. It isn't actually her, see, any more than the tuning dial is the whole radio. If the tuning is busted, what do you do? Blame the whole radio?"

"It isn't the dial. We need an antenna."

"I told you we need an antenna. You're smart, Lonny; you already know the principle. Your mother fusses because her fussing system isn't tuned right: it goes on too often. You ought to get angry at it, not at her, because she isn't the same as it."

"Yeah, she makes me sick."

"The reason you get sick is your own anger system, which is tuned to go on every time she fusses at you. Every time it goes on, it makes you uncomfortable. You ought to do some work on it. Adjust the tuning a bit. I'll show you how, one of these days."

He was studying the radio intently. "You're screwy in the head, you know that?"

"Oh yeah?" I didn't like hearing that.

"Mm-hm, my father told me. He says that's why you don't have any family or friends or anything." Lonny gave me a satisfied look. "Think he'll buy us an antenna?"

"What's this 'buy'? We can make one."

It annoyed me to find out that the Birlaks had already de-cided I wasn't normal, when I hadn't even mentioned my ideas to them. Obviously they'd been speculating about me during those weeks when I'd sat alone in my room after work. I was sorry I'd even hinted to Lonny about the energy. I hoped he would forget about it. Instead he adapted it to his uses immediately. The next day after work, there were heavy feet on the stairs as I sat there staring at my picture of the lake and trying to clear the pig stench from my head. In his short-sleeved white shirt, Ned stood leaning forward in the stairwell, frowning at me.

"Would you mind telling me what you're teaching my kid?" he said.

"We're still on the shortwave radio. We're going to put up an antenna, if that's okay."

"Would you like to know what he said to his mother this morning?"

"Sure, what was it?"

"He said he didn't have to listen to her, because Joey said she was just an electromagnetic system."

"That isn't what I told him, Ned."

"Oh? Just what did you tell him, if you don't mind?"

"I tried to explain to him that June couldn't help fussing over him sometimes, so there was no reason for him to get mad at her." Ned was glaring at me. I went on: "I said habits get hold of people, like they're electrical systems working inside, and there's no point in getting mad at an electrical system. Sort of along those lines."

Ned studied me for a while. "Well, would you mind stick-ing to motors and radios and keep out of my family affairs?"

"Yeah, sure Ned, no offense, hey."

I expected some sharp parting remark, but instead he waited around for a bit, looking at his feet. "Listen," he said. "We've been planning to go up to the lakeshore over Memorial Day. A place up in Michigan. June and I. Would you look after Lonny while we're up there?"

"Sure, be glad to."

He nodded. "I appreciate this. You can forget the rent for a couple of weeks." He waited a moment, then turned around to climb the stairs, shaking his head. "She said Lonny told her she needed to be sent back to the factory for repairs."

I hadn't heard the last of it. A few days later, Lonny came downstairs and said, "Listen, hey Joey? When you take apart the hogs at the packinghouse, are there wires inside them? Transformers, stuff like that?"

"Am I supposed to laugh?" I asked him.

"Not actual wires, stupid, I mean——"

I interrupted him: "Don't call people 'stupid.' "

"All right, I mean is a hog a kind of machine, though?"

"It's got systems. But it's alive, you have to remember that."

"So what difference does that make?" Lonny said.

"It makes a difference. Which isn't what you told your mother the other day, I hear."

"My mother. Being alive doesn't make any difference."

"Yes, it does."

"What's this big difference, then?" he said.

"I'm not actually sure. Living things power their own systems, for example, and machines don't."

"I already thought of that," Lonny said scornfully.

"So good for you." I picked up my lake-picture. I didn't want to bother with him.

"The hogs have to be born to get charged," he said. "They have a battery cell. When it runs down, they're dead. It's just a difference in how they're manufactured, that's all."

"You haven't said anything by that. Where do they get their power? You don't know. What kind of power is it? You don't know."

"You don't know either," he challenged me.

"I know that the power in people is a whole lot different than the electricity in machines. It's cool instead of hot, for one thing. I suppose hogs are much closer to people in this, but I don't have any actual way to find out, since I'm not a hog."

"I want to see the packinghouse."

"You asked that when I first came here, and you know what your father said."

"So what, I'm older now, and I have a good reason."

"You mean besides enjoying all the blood?" I said. "One big bombing run?"

He refused to be nettled. "It's a scientific reason. To see."

"The blood's all you'll see. You think your father has a job to complain about? Besides, you can't answer questions like this just by seeing things, Lonny. If you want to know how living things work, you should look at yourself. Just watch over yourself. You might find out how pigs work and radios work, but if you don't know how Lonny Birlak works, what good are you going to be? How are you going to be happy?"

I figured I'd had the last word with that, but he ignored it. "I want to take the guided tour through the packinghouse," he said.

"You ask your father." The truth was that I didn't want to take the tour myself. I didn't want to know what I was involved in by working there, any more than I had to know. The idea that the hogs might have an energy like my own had never occurred to me before. At least, I thought, I wasn't eating their dead flesh any longer. "Your father's the boss around here," I said.

"Yeah, all right."

"And this time don't put words in my mouth."

"Yeah, all right."

He didn't mention it again for a couple of weeks, and I made the mistake of forgetting about it. Ned and June were busy instructing me about the details of the house and the routine of plant watering so that nothing would die or collapse during their few days on Lake Michigan. They were in a nervous fever. June told me that it would be their first weekend alone together since Lonny was a year old. Watching them load the car, I suddenly felt sorry for myself. But I consoled myself: Look, you're watching the culmination of the Birlak stunt. You're doing better.

Once June had finished with her last-minute instructions

and her make sure this and her make sure that and her hugging Lonny till he squirmed, and once Ned had gotten her out the door and into the car and they'd driven off, Lonny remarked mildly, "The tour's at ten o'clock, Joey."

"What tour?"

"Through the packinghouse. Tomorrow. It's your day off, isn't it?"

"Did you ask your father?"

"Mm-hm, yes I did."

"And what did he say?"

"He said okay if we went together."

Lonny was looking at me with a very innocent expression, and so I didn't actually believe him. But it was too late to check on him, unless I called up his parents at their motel that night, and I didn't want to bother them and make June nervous all over again. Besides, I thought a good sight of gore might shock the boy a little. I'd been irritated with him for twisting my systems theory the way he had, and I didn't like how he'd been trying to use me to get around his father. The idea that he might find something different from what he expected at the slaughterhouse pleased me.

The tour began in a bright clean room lined with dioramas setting forth the anatomy of the hog and the history of meat packing in America. There was a grocery corner with the products of the place and a display of pharmaceuticals containing animal derivatives. The display was pill bottles pouring from a red plastic pig's mouth. A small man with a high voice and a sharp face, dressed in a white medical coat, came in and lectured us: "The Hog: Beneficial to Man." His name was Crosby. I'd seen him from my seat on the job, leading tourists across the iron walkways overhead. There were about a dozen of us on the tour that day: three or four older couples on cross-country trips and a pair of bearded college kids from Fort Wayne who said they were in the neighborhood visiting their grandmother. "Any questions?" said Crosby. "Follow me, then. Please keep to the marked walkways. Do not run."

We tramped on the walkways from huge black room to huge black room, each given over to the dismantling of another part of the hog. There were quartering rooms and tanning rooms and lard-boiling rooms and gut-drying rooms. Lonny pretended to be taking it all in with cool interest, but I could see that his stomach was turning just a bit, along with the rest of us. Crosby kept soothing us by pointing out how clean and efficient the place was. "You know what those long white strips on the stretcher down there are, my young friend?" the tour guide said to Lonny. "Intestines. Guts. Miles of them. That's what makes the jacket on your breakfast sausage. Didn't know that, did you? I thought you didn't." This went on for close to an hour. "They say we use everything but the squeal. If you could think of a way we could use that, you could patent it and be a rich man," Crosby said. "Any ideas, anyone? How about it, my boy?" I didn't mind seeing Lonny without an answer for once. He was looking rather pale.

Suddenly there was the faint sound of squealing, and Crosby herded us into a waiting room full of green furniture and photographs of waterfalls. He gave a little speech about how the last part of the tour was a little strong for some people, and anyone who wanted to sit it out right here, please feel free to do so; the room was fully air-conditioned. The old ladies and the college kids decided they'd had enough touring for the day. The old guys were ready, though. "As for you, my friend," Crosby said to Lonny, "young people have to be fifteen years of age to see the slaughtering room, so I guess that means a parting of the ways. We have *Field and Stream* and *Popular Science* on the table there."

"Oh, no, thanks," Lonny told him. "I'm fifteen years old and three days. This is part of my birthday."

He must have planned it in advance. It was possible; he looked old for his thirteen and a half. The tour guide looked at me. I was feeling queasy, and I didn't want to fight over it. I also didn't want to admit to Lonny that I'd just as soon sit out the slaughtering room myself. I told myself angrily, fine, I hope it really upsets the kid. I said to Crosby, "It's like Lonny says."

The squealing of the hogs sounded halfway between the screaming of horses and the screaming of women. It blasted at us when Crosby opened the door to the slaughtering room. We had to cover our ears against the noise. It was another black room, slightly smaller than the others. We filed along a walkway twenty feet above the floor. Through a tall gate at the far end of the room, the fat brown hogs were being prodded into a chute one by one from the stockyards outside. The hogs flailed in a panic to climb the sides of the chute, but they couldn't get a grip with their hooves. As each one blundered out from the near end of the chute, two men, one on each side, reached down, wrestled with the hog a bit, then snapped a clamp on each of its hind heels, and the clamp suddenly swung the hog upwards to a moving chain eight feet above the floor. Hanging upside-down by its hind feet from the chain, the hog rode across the room, jerking and squirming till it seemed it would break its back. Its open screaming mouth flashed at us. Two shirtless brawny men stood just below us with long knives in their hands. As each bawling hog drew near, one of the two men snatched it by an ear, swung up his knife, and sliced the hog's throat half through. Blood jumped out in a wide rope and splattered over the slaughterers. Then, twitching and spurting, with its head flinging half off its moorings, the hog rode off through a door on its way to the dinner plate.

It made me sick to think that I had been taking a hand in this murdering. I wanted to get out of that packinghouse and never see the sight of it again and never see the sight of meat again. I completely forgot about keeping an eye on Lonny. Suddenly there was a commotion on the walkway. The tour guide pushed past me and let out a yell. Lonny was running back toward the door that we'd come in. One of the old men was stumbling on ahead of him, retching his guts out. Before Crosby could catch up to them, Lonny slipped in the old man's vomit, pitched forward under the railing of the walkway, and fell twenty feet down to the floor below, just behind the nearest slaughterer, in a wash of blood. The boy's face turned up to us, twisted in fear and pain, with his mouth wide open; we couldn't hear his yell over the hogs' screams. Crosby hurried down a ladder with me after him, and he shut off the power to the chain. When we reached Lonny, the slaughterer had already cut the boy's right trouser leg with his machete and was ripping it up to the crotch. The leg was bent in the middle of the thigh. But the skin wasn't broken. Lonny was sobbing with fright. The last hog twitched just above us on the halted chain, flinging blood on us. It was hanging stock still and staring by the time the ambulance drivers came in with the stretcher. Then at the hospital, the doctors kept Lonny waiting in the emergency room for three hours before they got around to him.

While we waited, I told Lonny about the hi-lo race and my own accident, so as to get his mind off the slaughtering room and to show him that luckily his broken leg wasn't very serious by comparison. He didn't want to hear about it. He didn't want to talk to me. He lay there chattering. I had to go down to the nursing station and yell; in order to get a blanket for him. I cursed myself for agreeing to take him to the packinghouse and especially into that last room. I'd wanted to get back at him. It was shameful. A kid that touchy, at that upsetting age, and I had to take advantage of him. I told myself he'd probably go back to his bombing runs with a vengeance now. I sat there watching Lonny and waiting for the surgeon, alternately badgering the nurses about the delay and cursing myself for still being a complete incompetent with people and always ending up by wrecking things and hurting people, despite all the progress I'd thought I'd made.

I'd left word by telephone at Ned and June's motel on Lake Michigan, and soon enough toward evening, after the doctors had straightened Lonny's leg out and put it in a cast, there was June half-running down the aisle of the hospital ward, with Ned charging in behind her. June was weeping and scared out of her wits. She ran up to the boy in the midst of telling him it was all Mommy's fault and she'd never leave her little Lonny ever again. I believe I felt worse about hearing that than about any of the rest of it. Ned was pacing up and down the aisle and yelling at me, "Well, what happened? They wouldn't tell me what happened."

I told him what had happened. "It was a clean fracture, Ned. He's going to be okay."

That set June to weeping again, which exasperated her husband. He cursed me, his face pale under his shadow of beard. "What did you take him to that place for?" he said. "Didn't I tell you to stay home and work on that radio?"

"The kid said you gave him permission, Ned. I should have called up and checked with you. It was a mistake."

Ned turned on Lonny. "You hear what Joey says? You're going to get it, mister, believe me, before this is over."

"Stop it, Ned, stop it," June was saying.

Lonny turned his head away from her and said quietly, "Joey said hogs are different from machines, and I said they weren't, so we went to have a look. You wouldn't understand, Mother."

June yelled at me, "How can you talk to a child about such things?"

"Take it easy, June," Ned said. "This is a hospital."

She went on in a quiet voice, "You came into our house, and we didn't care about where you'd been or what kind of trouble you'd been in, but when you start talking about all your disturbed ideas to my child——"

"All right, June, all right," Ned said.

She shouted at him, "You're the one who said there was something wrong with him, and you let my baby get mixed up with him——"

A nurse and three orderlies were pouring down the aisle at us. "It's all right," Ned told them. "We're taking care of this. Joey, will you——?" He nodded toward the door, and the two of us walked out the ward while June called after us, "You just get him out of my house, Ned Birlak."

In the hallway we stood against the wall, out of the way of traffic. "Listen, Joey." He looked at the floor. "Whatever she said, will you forget about it? Because I think you've been good for Lonny, you've been real good for him——" His voice trailed off; he was shaking his head and sweating.

"Look, I don't want to cause any more trouble," I said. "I feel terrible about this. As soon as my next paycheck comes in, which will be Tuesday, I'll clear out, okay? And she won't have to bother with me."

He had already interrupted me and was saying furiously, "Don't you listen to what she says——" He cursed her.

I tried to calm him down a bit by saying, "She was right, though, Ned. If I hadn't been happy to see the kid get disgusted, I wouldn't have let him into the place, probably."

"It's not your fault, Joey, and I'm not going to let her pin it on you." He went on after a moment more quietly: "Something had to happen. If it wasn't this, it would have been something else. She'd have found something. She'd have spoiled it somehow."

"She's going to slow down one of these days, Ned. The kid's going to grow up. She's going to let him go."

I'd touched the raw spot. He was shaking his head again and weeping. We didn't talk any more.

# 7

# TOM TERRY'S VALLEY

I stayed another ten days at the Birlaks' house. June spent most of her time with Lonny at the hospital, and so I hardly saw the boy at all. I didn't want to get in her way there. Ned came downstairs several times to talk to me. What had happened seemed to have helped him finally admit to himself that something had to be done about the problems in his life. I tried to find the right words to encourage him to look at himself.

"The woman needs help," he said one night. He had come home late from work, and we were eating together in the basement. June was still at the hospital with Lonny.

"How are you going to tell her that?" I asked him.

"I don't know. She won't listen to hardly anything I say to her right now."

"If a person doesn't believe he needs help," I said, "then he won't accept any. I know this from my own experience, see."

Ned gave me a sharp look, as if it had suddenly occurred to him that I might have a past he could compare with his own.

"You could suggest that you both go for help," I said. "As a married couple."

"Yeah, I don't know, though." He was frowning.

"You'd have to admit that you also need help, the same as her."

He didn't answer, and I didn't know if he'd accepted what I'd said. But later he told me he'd discussed things with June, and she'd agreed they could use someone to talk to.

Over the next few days, I thought about how I could bring up what I believed I'd learned to help him in a way that he could accept. "Everything you have in this house," I said to him one evening, "not just the plants, but all the feelings, are things you and June put together. Nobody else did it. If you built it, you can rebuild it. Why don't you start your nursery?"

He shook his head. "I told you why."

"You told me, but the reasons are reasons you and June made. You can unmake them as soon as you're ready." He didn't want to talk about it at first, but I coaxed him by trying to challenge all his reasons, which more or less came down to his being afraid to make a break and to his resenting his wife for not being willing to risk a financial loss. I told him she wanted him to start a nursery.

He snorted at that. "What makes you think that?" he said.

"She told me. She's just afraid to tell you, is all. She's afraid of you, Ned."

He changed the subject, but two or three nights later he was back with a sketch of the house and yard converted into a nursery, with a glassed-in front porch and the basement under lights and an expansion of his new greenhouse out back. His idea was to build it slowly while he kept his old job. He asked if I would stay a few more months and work full time on building it, but I wasn't much of a carpenter, and I didn't think my presence was anything June wanted. I encouraged him to go ahead with it, though, and he said maybe his brother's son, who was in college in Wisconsin, might come down for the summer. I never found out if he began it or if their lives became any easier. Once Lonny came home from the hospital and June was there in the evenings, it was time for me to go.

I was glad. I'd had more than enough of the slaughterhouse. I wanted to get back on my concentration schedule and maybe add to it; I wanted to be alone again. It gave me hope that I had been able to help the Birlaks a little, or at least that I'd been able to try to help them, but I knew that my goal of taking control of my feelings was still outside my grasp. Lonny never would have seen the slaughterhouse if I hadn't been angry with him. It was better that I stay clear of involvements with people until I knew I could be my own master or until I found the discipline that I still hoped for as my guide.

Soon before I left East Chicago, Margherita wrote to say that she was selling our house and had moved into an apartment with a divorced woman she had met in cosmetology school. "I can't afford the payments, Joey," she wrote, "and I don't believe you're ever coming back now. There's a state trooper who's been asking me out, and I've been seeing him some. He's a nice person, and he has a little girl. I have to make my own life." This shook me, but I got back into my hopeful mood after a few days. I signed the house papers and sent them back to her, and I told her to go ahead and do whatever she felt was best for her.

"I know a lot more now what the energy is," I said in the letter I wrote to her, "but I don't know why it came the way it did to change my life and your life and Vin's. I just know that it turned my eyes around one hundred eighty degrees so that I began to see what's inside of me. This is what I'm living for now, to keep looking and looking into my own mind. Don't ask me when the looking will be over, because I don't know if it will ever be over or if there is any one thing for me to find. It's not like looking for an earring that's lost in the upholstery; it's looking for my real self and for the truth about my life. This is what anyone is really after, and I'm not different from you, basically. It's just that you look for your life in the family and the neighborhood, and I had to leave so that I could learn how to look for mine inside my mind.

"Maybe you still think this sounds crazy—I guess you probably do—but I know now that it's the opposite of crazy.

Concentrating your mind and freeing up your energy from your body and feelings, which is what I do, makes a person feel very solid, very pulled together, because everything inside you is under your control. You feel happy. But when you lose your mind, it's the opposite. You don't know where you've gone, because your pieces are busted apart and scattered all over the room. You can't get your thoughts and feelings together at all. I know this from the time I lost my head in the kitchen at home, and I had a worse time in Maine after you left. You can take a wrong turn when you start working with your mind. This is why people need a discipline, like what Father Jeremy has at his monastery. I haven't found a discipline for myself yet, but I am being very careful now until I do find one. If I'd had a discipline when I started, we wouldn't have had the trouble we had. It wasn't right that there was no one to help us and explain things to us. It shouldn't be that most people don't understand about the mind or about the energy inside them. I don't understand yet either, but I want to understand. I'm going to keep on trying to understand, because that's the only way I'll ever be able to pay you and Vin and myself back for all the trouble I've been."

I left the Birlaks and for nearly a week drove west, across Illinois, across Iowa, into South Dakota. The plains that were brown and empty in the spring were now warm with crops, gold with the ripe winter wheat and green with the unripe corn. The cornstalks waved their tassels like cheerleaders in the wind. Where was I driving to, through all this gaiety? It suddenly occurred to me that I didn't know; I hadn't even thought about it. I let the car drift to a stop on the shoulder of the road. Why drive at all? I'd always felt that I should go west, but otherwise I had no idea where to find what I needed to find. The hope I'd felt in Quebec was still with me: I still believed there was a right place for me. But since I didn't know what kind of place it was, I was afraid of driving right past it, or past the next turn to it, if I went too fast. Besides, the longer I drove the Volkswagen, the sooner my cash would run out, and I'd be forced to take another job and drain myself on routine things.

I drove into the college town of Mitchell, in southeastern South Dakota, and put two want ads in the school paper, one to sell my car and one to buy a used sleeping bag and backpack and the rest of the gear the young travelers I picked up as hitchhikers always carried. I sent half of what I made on the car to Margherita, with a note that there'd be nothing more from me for a while.

Selling the car, the last important object that I owned, seemed like the final act of leaving my own class of people, and it frightened me for a while, even though I'd never gotten along with my own class of people. With my thumb out and a sleeping bag riding on my shoulders, I kept having thoughts about what Margherita would think or what my mother would think if they saw me on the road like this, looking like a hippie. Finally I gave in to my feelings and ordered a Marines-style haircut in a barbershop in a town that consisted of fourteen weather-beaten buildings dozing by the railroad tracks. In the midst of the haircut, I burst out laughing at myself, startling the old barber so much that he gave me a nasty nick on the ear.

It was the middle of June, ten years ago. I hitchhiked north on the gravel roads, following the harvest of the winter wheat. I slept beside bales of hay that were piled in irregular stacks as high as houses, and I concentrated on my picture of a lake till the late sun was gone; then I stared at the summer stars. I didn't choose my roads, but let the farmers take me wherever they were going in their air-conditioned Pontiacs or Buicks. Sometimes I just walked all day with the high wheat on either side of me, till it seemed the road was a dusty ship channel marking an old course through a golden sea.

One late afternoon I stood on the roof of an abandoned car and watched the wheat flow everywhere over the flat lands, with nothing to break the surface but a line of hedge that rose here and there like a green shoal. A combine was harvesting at the edge of the round horizon. I could just see the glint of the sun on the window of the cab. The little smoke of its diesel stack puffed like a freighter's stack against the sky. I walked in among the wheat. The ripe heads scratched my hands. Then the wind rose, and I watched it sweep across the surface of the wheat, bending down the top-heavy stalks as it came, making a deep golden trough of a wave that sped across the fields. The hiss of it whispered around me. Then the wind divided into crisscross gusts, and the single wave broke up into hundreds that scattered and collided as if in fright. The heads of grain knocked against each other with a clacking sound. But nothing was lost; nothing had changed. The wind died, the sun sank; the wheat stood in its place and was still. As I watched I knew it was this that I wanted for myself. I wanted to know the winds of life but at the same time not be uprooted from myself: to be awake but be still; like the wheat, to give but not to move.

In North Dakota, just above the South Dakota line, after I'd been walking and hitchhiking for about two weeks, one of those square grey International Harvester vans stopped for me in the morning. A stocky little man sat propped up on straw cushions behind the wheel. "Morning," was all he said as I got in. His looks immediately intrigued me: he obviously wasn't a farmer. He wasn't wearing a hat, and he had a square head too large for his body, with short stiff black hair shooting this way and that in spite of the hair oil that shone from it. The hair oil touched the air of the van with a greasy sweetness. The little man could have been fifty or seventy; wrinkles were gathered on the pale skin by his eyes and below his ears, but his hands were clear. He had soft and rather fat fingers with clean, neat nails, which made me wonder what he was doing in the country, especially in that cheap green suit a bit too small and in that pleated white shirt and a string tie, too, with a turquoise clasp in the shape of the double letters TT. I looked in the back of the van. It was piled to the roof with flat grey boxes. This was the answer. "Are you a salesman around here?" I said. "That is, if you don't mind my asking."

"Don't mind at all, young feller, don't mind at all." He reached back and tossed a grey box onto my lap without taking his eyes off the road or his foot off the accelerator. Folded up in the box was a pile of pinkish hosiery. "Ladies' things," he said, "toiletries, bath soap, hair oil, cosmetics, and eau de cologne." He leaned over to me confidentially. "Specialty playing cards. Picture magazines. George Terry's the name."

"Joey Celebrisi."

"What's that now?"

"Celebrisi. You can call me Joey."

"I might at that."

"You travel, is that it, Mr. Terry?"

"Indeed I do, my friend. In the summer. Eastern Dakotas, western Minnesota, eastern Manitoba. I travel the farms."

He had a high, sharp voice that filled the van with much more resonance than you'd expect from a man his size; and he rolled off his lists of places and goods with the drama and satisfaction of a caller in a bingo game. I wanted to hear more. To keep the conversation going, I explained that I was seeing a bit of the country after quitting a job in a packinghouse.

"Never went into those places," Mr. Terry said. "Smelt them."

"If you went into one like the one where I worked," I told him, "you'd have to stop eating meat to save your stomach."

"Would I, now? Is that a fact." And he began a series of little whines on intaken breath, with his square chest bouncing up to his chin at each whine. I realized he was laughing.

"Don't laugh," I told him, laughing myself at his laughter, and I described the hog-slaughtering process. I said the only decent alternative was cheese-and-tomato sandwiches and pea-nut butter—pizza if you could get it. "Otherwise you're eating dead bodies all the time. You're eating the casualties in a war."

I was feeling pretty fanatical on the subject by then, and since he didn't answer me right away, I was afraid I might have offended him. I was about to apologize when he said, more or less to himself, "Yes sir, that's real original. Real original." He shot me a sharp sideways look. "What'd you say your name was?"

For half an hour he sat there without speaking or moving,

but smiling a small private smile and now and then darting
sideways glances at me, like people will do when they're per-
fecting a joke they've just invented. I had the feeling that I
shouldn't interrupt him. He barreled along the gravel roads at
close to sixty, and a hurricane of dust blew up behind us, with
stones clacking and ringing on the chassis underneath. I
watched the shadow of the car sail beside us along the golden
fields. I half-forgot that Mr. Terry was there. Suddenly he
cracked out with his sharp voice: "My brother Tom, now. You
never knew him. Well——"

"No sir, I didn't."

He let the disturbance of my interruption settle, and then
he said, "Tom was like a father to me, as I was the child of my
parents' old age—may God rest the lot of them." He rattled over
a cattle grate and passed a farmer's Buick. "Now, Tom was a
vegetarian."

"Oh yeah, he was?"

"Indeed he was," Mr. Terry said.

"Well, of course, I'm not actually what you'd call a formal
kind of vegetarian, I'm just not eating meat ever again if I can
help it, but that's very interesting about your brother." Mr.
Terry didn't answer, so I added, "So how did he get started on
this, do you know?"

"I'm fixing to tell you about it, young man. That is, if you
want to hear the story."

"Sure; I'd be interested."

He waited a second. "Now maybe you didn't know, if you
haven't heard about Tom Terry before, but all his life, until the
time I'm telling you of, Tom was famous all across the Dakotas
for his rabbit stew. Even his missus stood aside when Tom took
it in his head to cook up a mess of rabbit, and *her* rabbit stew
won the bake-off at the state fair two years running, even
though the rules confined the entries to fruit pies——" Mr.
Terry interrupted himself. "This doesn't offend you, now."

"Oh, no. Go on, no problem," I said.

"But Tom's stew, my young friend; *Tom's* stew: well, I

never had a taste of it; he stopped making it before my time. I do know that on the day Tom broke his shotgun over his knee and said he'd killed his last rabbit, there was an insurrection in the valley of the Cannonball that might have gotten dangerous if Tom hadn't cooked up a new stew good and fast out of turnip and greens. They had to admit that the new stew was better. As for the recipes, he never let on about either one. All he'd say was, 'Eat up before the juice dries and the fork sticks to your plate.' You never could get anything out of Tom, except when he was pleased to tell you."

Mr. Terry didn't stop to explain why he was telling me this story about his brother or how I was supposed to take it. He sat behind the wheel, still as a stone except to dart a sideways look once or twice to see if I was listening. His high clear voice filled the van.

"Now, when Tom was still a fancier of rabbit, he'd just pull on his wading boots and step across his fields to the banks of the Cannonball River, lined with thickets of cottonwood trees. He'd barge into the current and wade upstream, hollering, splashing, yowling, bellowing, generally raising a vituperous racket, and singing bits of hymns at the top of his voice—he had a fairly large voice for his size of man. I'm not going to tell you of the time he challenged a Montana grizzly to a roaring contest and deafened the poor beast. He was so sorry afterwards that he took the bear to the ear doctor in Minneapolis. But that isn't part of this story. As you'd expect, the rabbits who were busy nibbling the seedpods at the tops of the cottonwood trees along the riverbank—the rabbits being particularly fond of the topmost seedpods, which have the softest cotton in them—this diet being the reason why rabbits have such particularly soft fur, even now, though they gave up their tree-living, cottonwood-pod-munching ways long ago—as you'd expect, when these cotton-picking rabbits heard Tom Terry's racket come hollering and splashing and yowling and roaring and vituperating up the river, they never failed to stop munching and to push aside the silver cottonwood leaves, each with his right hind foot, and they'd take a look below. You know how extraordinarily curious their nature naturally is; at least, it was. What did they see but a thirtyish, fortyish, fiftyish feller in dark blue coveralls with a red woollen shirt and a yellow straw hat; he had a big drooping moustache the color of his hat and little sharp eyes the color of his coveralls, and blam-blam-blam-blam-blam! Inside of five seconds he had five brace of rabbit plummeting through the air on the way to his rabbit pouch. He was a wizard with a shot-gun, Tom was. His mother told me once that the day he was two years old, he shot out the candles on his birthday cake with the corks of two vinegar bottles at a distance of fifty yards. She may have been exaggerating; I couldn't say."

Would I ever be able to talk to people about my own thoughts with the faith and confidence this salesman was telling his story with? Not to mention with people at home, even with the Birlaks I was testing the water with every word, but this man had launched breezily into his story without any ceremony or any assurances from me. He knew exactly what he wanted to say; he never paused once to find a phrase. He didn't care what judgment this hitchhiker with a backpack and a Marines-style haircut was going to pass on him. He'd stopped looking over to see if I was listening; he was listening to himself.

He went on: "Well, a dry year came to the valley of the Cannonball. The stunted wheat rattled in the fields. Tom Terry found himself hollering his way up the Cannonball River two and three times a week to fill the bellies of his family. You'll understand me when I tell you that the rabbit got steadily scarcer as a consequence, and every day old Tom had to wade farther up the river to fill his pouch. One dry afternoon, far up the river, he took a turn into a bend that he didn't recognize. He told me afterward he could have sworn the river ran straight all down that country. But there was the river curving, in the shelter of a tall grove of ancient cottonwood trees. Their silver-leaved branches met far above the shaded water. As Tom was drawing breath to begin his hollering, he distinctly heard some-one calling out his name behind him.

" 'Mr. Terry'?

"Tom looked around; he couldn't see anyone.

" 'Hallo, Mr. Terry?'

"There it was again, coming from somewhere above him—the high voice of a young girl or a young boy.

" 'Speaking,' boomed Tom, and he scanned the trees for the source of it. After a minute, he noticed a shaking and a rustling high up in a particularly tall and stately cottonwood that stood at the apex of the riverbend. Hopping down among the silver leaves from thick limb to thick limb was a large jet-black rabbit, with particular white hieroglyphical markings on his cheeks and his brow.

" 'That Mr. Terry there?' came the high, rather squeaky voice again. It was the rabbit's voice; there was no disputing it. The sound came from where the rabbit moved, and his mouth formed the words. The rabbit hopped to the ground and walked up the bank toward Tom, using just his two long black hind feet, kicking one foot up in front of the other. 'Mr. Tom Terry?' said the jet-black rabbit.

" 'Himself,' said Tom, from the middle of the river, with the current rushing by him. He was too dumbfounded to say more.

"The rabbit kick-walked up the bank till he was opposite to Tom, turned sideways to show the white markings around his right eye, and said in his high, rather squeaky voice: 'Fire away, sir.' "

The storyteller's chest jerked up to his chin in little whines of delight. "It's not that Tom had a slow mind, now," he continued. "I wouldn't want you to think that was why he stood there speechless, his arms hanging slack at his sides and his shotgun butt trailing in the water. It was just that he wasn't used to seeing jet-black rabbits with particular white hieroglyphical markings on their faces, or any other color of rabbit for that matter, except a brown sort of grey, or maybe a grey sort of brown, and he wasn't used to seeing rabbits hop down to the ground and kick-walk up the riverbank, and he wasn't used to hearing them talk English, either, especially dictionary English.

In fact he'd never seen or heard tell of any one of these things. But Tom wasn't the kind of man to show his consternation for long, if he could help it; it didn't sit right with his principles. Mrs. Tom used to say that when the tornado of '33 snatched up their house and let it down politely on the top of the Grant County courthouse, then, snatched the house up again and set it down home where it belonged, except slightly skewed around, Tom didn't even bother to get up from his dinner to look out at the sights flying by below. His knee trembled a bit on the way down, according to Mrs. Tom. But Tom denied it. 'I always did want the kitchen facing the barn, so I could hear the cows better while I was eating' was all he'd say about it.

"The rabbit stood patiently on the riverbank, without the faintest touch of trembling about its black nose. 'Well, Mr. Rabbit, sir,' old Tom said at last, pulling himself together and bowing politely—he told me afterward that this was how he guessed a man ought to talk to a talking rabbit. 'My mother used to say, "Tom, if you don't know who he is, then he's your better" ' is how he explained it to me.—'Well sir, Mr. Rabbit,' said Tom then, 'If you'll excuse me, I don't believe I can shoot you. Not like this, in cold blood; it ain't right.'

" 'I beg your pardon,' said the rabbit rather sharply. 'Is that how your mother taught you to insult strangers? I believe my blood is as warm as any other rabbit's you've shot down recently. I'll thank you to aim, sir.' The rabbit turned his profile again.

" 'No offense meant, Mr. Rabbit,' Tom said, stowing his gun under his arm. 'But I'm not going to do it. A man has his principles.' Compared to Tom when he had his mind made up, his plowmules were fickle.

" 'Indeed,' said the rabbit, in a very polite, interested sort of way. "Just what are these principles, Mr. Terry? If there's no offense in asking?'

"Tom wasn't a talking man, and he was getting a little impatient. 'You don't shoot game that can't defend itself, if you've got any self-respect, Mr. Rabbit,' he said severely, thinking maybe the rabbit should have known this without being told.

" 'I believe I'm beginning to understand now; this is extremely educational,' the rabbit said. 'If I don't try to defend myself, then you can't shoot me; but if I try to hide or run away because I don't want to die, then you can shoot me. Do I have it right?'

"I told you Tom had a stubborn mind; but I also said he didn't have a slow one. "Don't you go and try running off,' he told the rabbit, 'with the idea it would get me to shoot you, because it won't do you any good.' And he hurled his shotgun onto the riverbank opposite and crossed his arms on his chest.

" 'On the farm, now,' the rabbit said, seeming not to notice, and with an air of someone trying to get a thing clear in his mind, 'before you slaughter a calf, say, do you require it to run around the pen a time or two, perhaps? Or maybe butt you a little first—not in a way that might hurt either of you, of course?'

" 'Mr. Rabbit, I'm not a man for words,' said Tom, with the air of someone who'd had enough of a thing. 'I just know my ground when I see it. We'll have turnip.'

" 'In that case,' the jet-black rabbit said, 'I'll take my leave. I wouldn't want to be the one to jeopardize Tom Terry's reputation for keeping his word.' The rabbit turned around, kick-walked his way back along the bank to the tall and ancient cottonwood tree at the apex of the riverbend, hopped onto a low limb, hopped onto a higher limb, and was gone among the shimmer of silver leaves.

"Tom walked home that day without knowing he was doing it. 'The cool air under those trees put me into a kind of sleep,' he told me afterwards. It wasn't until he got home, and Mrs. Tom asked him why he was out in the garden digging turnips when it was time to cook up some rabbit, that he suddenly remembered what had happened. He told Mrs. Tom about it, and she asked him if he wasn't feeling well. She might have persuaded him he'd dreamed it all, too, if he hadn't noticed the next morning that the butt of his shotgun was warped. You remember I told you that he let it trail in the river when the jet-black rabbit first dumbfounded him by talking. 'I had to go back and find him,' Tom explained to me afterwards. 'Here I'd been wondering all my life why rabbits live in trees, and when I had a chance to find out, I forgot to ask. Besides, you never could tell: maybe the rabbit knew what the cows talk about in the barn at night. I was always wondering about that one, too.'

"So Tom trudged up the river again. But the bend with the grove of tall ancient cottonwood trees wasn't there to be found. Tom walked miles beyond where he thought the bend had been, and miles back again, but the river ran straight all down that country. He looked up and down the valley of the Cannon-ball for three days. At every particularly tall or stately cotton-wood, he stopped and called up the trunk, 'Mr. Rabbit, sir! If you're there, I would be mightily pleased for some polite and peaceable conversation!' Or he'd say, 'Mr. Rabbit, sir! I've been thinking over what you said! I don't have my shotgun with me, just take a look!' He'd hold up his hands to show they were empty. But no squeaky voice came in answer.

"From those three days Tom came back home a sore-throated and a weary-legged and a changed man. He never shot a living thing afterwards; he wouldn't have a gun in the house. 'I can't know who I might shoot,' he told his missus. 'It might be him.' At night you could sometimes hear Tom out in the barn, chatting with the cats and swapping stories with the cows. If you laughed about it, he tended to get testy. 'They'd talk to you, too, if they thought you'd listen,' he'd say. Nobody missed his rabbit stew. The fame of his savory turnip-and-greens stew spread far into Montana and east across the Minnesota line. Mrs. Tom said it was the dill she'd spied him sneaking in from the garden. But he wouldn't admit to it. 'I save on buckshot' was all he'd say, 'and I never felt better in my life.' "

The salesman stopped speaking. I wanted more, and I waited for him to go on; but he was silent. Finally I asked him, "So did your brother ever find the rabbit again?"

"Hm?" He hadn't heard me.

"That isn't all there is to the story, is it?"

George Terry seemed to remember himself. "That's all for the moment, young feller. But you say there's more to it, do you?"

"Well, I don't know, you're the one who's telling it. I certainly never heard it before."

This set him to laughing again. But he didn't answer me. He seemed lost in his thoughts.

To get him to talk again, I asked him if there were many people who traveled the farms as salesmen the way he did.

"Oh, there's still a few; up and down, over the line into Canada, I'd say quite a few. Not too many know the tall tales, though; not too many." His look turned inward; then he nodded firmly. "Now in my grandfather's time, before the radio came, and even in my father's time: I can tell you it was different then. All the best travelers brought the tales along with their wares. Some of them didn't even condescend to sell goods; no sir, they lived on their art. My uncle James Terry, now; he used to ride the Great Northern. I rode with him sometimes, back in the twenties. He'd work the winters as a stevedore on the St. Louis docks, and in June he'd quit and head for the farms. Paul Bunyan, Pecos Bill, Febold Feboldson, the saga of Brigham Young, all the tall tales of the plains: he knew them all. He'd strut up and down before the fire, or in the hay barn if there was a crowd, and he'd play every part, switching from one to the other quicker than the eye. People would pay, then. They won't now. Although I doubt you'll be asked to pay for your dinner tonight, if you're still riding with me."

I asked him if his uncle had told the Tom Terry stories. "I guess there are more than one?"

"There are sixty-one, not counting the White Thunder stories. You'd have to say there are sixty-two now. As for my Uncle James reciting Tom Terry, he couldn't. Tom's my own invention."

"No kidding? You don't get them from books?"

He beamed with pleasure at this. "No, I only tell my own.

My Grandfather Norton, who taught me how to tell the tales, now he could recite hundreds of them, *and* he did his own. Sioux stories, most of them. He had enormous red side whiskers. I told my first Tom story to him, when I was twelve." Mr. Terry was silent for a while, chewing his lip. "It's rare as hen's teeth these days," he said. "There's a fellow out of Cutbank, Montana; he's got his own set of stories about the copper mines. He's getting old now. He pumps gas for his pay."

I said after a minute, "How do people take to the idea of a talking rabbit that lives in a tree and such things nowadays, though? If you don't mind my asking?"

He turned around to me for the first time: he had a wide, clear face and grey eyes. "Why, I don't know, my friend. You're the first man to hear this one. You heard it being invented, didn't you know that? And how do you take to the idea of a talking rabbit that lives in a tree?"

"Well, sure, I guess——" I didn't know what to say.

He turned back to the road again, laughing his intaken laugh with delight. "Yes sir, you've inspired a new chapter of Tom; new and clean. I thought it would all be old ones this summer. It makes a man feel young."

We had been driving for nearly an hour without stopping at a farm; but suddenly Mr. Terry said, "Reach behind you, if you'll be so kind"—he flipped open a spiral notebook on the seat—"and fetch me one of those grey boxes of hose, with the number 5 on the label, and a number 3 box also, and a box with the yellow label, number 4, and a box with the brown label, number 14."

I rummaged among his boxes as he slowed the van and turned down a long driveway. The wheat raced past close by the fenders. Ahead, a square white house with a nearly flat red roof stood sheltered by a grove of slender trees. The van rattled across a creek on a wooden bridge; then the trees were overhead. A wind was hissing through their pale green leaves. Like shoals of darting fish, the leaves flashed their undersides of pale silver.

"Are those cottonwoods?" I asked Mr. Terry.

He looked. "That they are."

"What about your brother, then? Didn't he find the rabbit?"

"Hold your horses, young man. The lady's at the door." He dismounted from his van, carrying his boxes under his arm. He called out, "Morning, Mrs. Anderson."

A wide woman with curlers under her scarf stood in the shadow of the doorway. "Well, Mr. Terry, now I know it's summer. I've been looking out for you; yes I have."

"And how's the master? And Betty Lou?"

We spent the rest of the morning and all the afternoon barreling up driveways ten, twenty, twenty-five miles apart, to square white houses with red roofs that stood in the shelter of cottonwood trees, and he toted his boxes up the front steps to the women of the farms. They all knew him; he knew them all and the names of their husbands, their children, their parents, their grandchildren. They invited him in for coffee and cake, which he refused by reason of his waistline, and then they gossiped on the doorstep. "Young Fred Pearson, down by Orrin," he'd say, "has signed up for another hitch."

"Has he now."

"I had it from his mother just this morning."

"Well, I bet she's proud."

Whoever in southeastern North Dakota was married, hired, in hock, in the clear, trying a new crop, or gone to Minneapolis or Omaha, Mr. Terry picked it up like a dustmop and shook it out at the next stop, without missing so much as a name. At just the right moment in the ritual, there'd be a small pause and a motion of his arms, and the boxes would be open one by one. He knew what they always bought, and he had something new to tempt them with. He entered each sale in his spiral notebook afterward.

"Mr. Terry," I told him, "You aren't just a traveling salesman, you're a traveling social page."

He thought a minute. "I am, at that." He leaned over to me confidentially and advised me, "Don't tell Sears."

Between stops, he invented more of the story of the rabbit. He said that so many people came to hear of this man Tom Terry, who talked to animals instead of eating them—like the journalist who came up on the train from St. Louis to ask impertinent questions, and the fancy lawyers for a meat-packing house in Kansas City who went to federal court to stop Tom from cooking his turnip-and-greens stew—that Tom bolted himself up in the cow barn, saying he'd talked to his last human being. He stayed in the cow barn for two weeks; for three weeks; the harvest was coming; he wouldn't budge. Mrs. Tom finally had to call in White Thunder, the Sioux medicine man, who coaxed Tom out by an ingenious trick— it had something to do with making Tom believe that the cow barn had moved, as I remember. White Thunder was the hero of George Terry's second set of stories, and for my benefit there were side-references to numerous marvels. Afterwards there was a monumental week-long battle between Tom and his wife's cousin Febold, who was tired of turnip and wanted rabbit again. At the height of his battle, the jet-black rabbit returned and politely asked Febold to shoot him. I don't remember exactly how it ended, except that the rabbit won everybody over by discussing recipes. He had an especially delicious parsnip-and-carrot soup. Then he disappeared again. Mr. Terry went over the whole story two or three times. He said he wanted to get it straight and smooth in his mind. Although it changed with the retellings, to my ears it ran as smooth as water each time he spoke it, perfected immediately by the practice of fifty years.

All the warm afternoon, I listened in the van and then waited in the front yards of the farms, swinging back and forth in the old tires that hung by ropes from tree limbs, or feeding bits of bread to white ducks bustling around the duck ponds, or picking around the grandfather tractors that were rusting out their age behind machinery sheds. I dreamed through the heat in Tom Terry's world. I wanted to forget, for a while, my own uncertain real world, and Mr. Terry had the power to replace it with his own. Of course, soon enough I came back to myself;

but what about him? To him, I thought, his imaginary brother must be more alive than anyone else he knew: he had lived with Tom Terry not for an afternoon, like I had, but for a lifetime. Ordinary real life was a distraction to him; it was a detail. He bought and sold lingerie, but he invented a world, and his best delight was to give it away, with no conditions attached to the giving, with no questions asked.

Before he was even out of school as a boy, I thought, he must have decided that he didn't want to surrender himself to the routine he saw around him. He'd seized hold of himself, formed himself to his wish, and created his own life. He made me think of Father Jeremy and Brother Stephen; they all had set aside the ordinary habits and circumstances that most people believe are inevitable. Instead they had chosen a discipline, one that gave them the strength to live a different life that made sense to them. The monks' discipline was certainly the harder and the higher one, promising a deeper peace, because it brought order to their entire selves and not just to their imaginations. But the monks were still young men, still making their discipline their own, while the storyteller had practiced his discipline truly into his old age, and there was no struggle against the old habits now. His stories flowed from him like clear water. Walking in his imagined brother's valley was as simple for him as walking on the solid earth. He was a free man; he was the master of his life. Then who could shake him by not accepting the gift of his tales? By ridiculing him, who could diminish him?

Still, I wondered what he was getting himself in for when he told me he would launch his new story that evening before an audience of local people. He invited me along. "That is, if you don't mind hearing about Tom again."

"No, sir, I'd be interested."

"There'll be refinements, my friend; there'll be refinements."

Near dinnertime, he turned off the highway and drove down a mile of dirt road to a town of maybe thirty white houses.

Over them, like a stern old aunt who'd been too tall to get married, a grey wooden grain elevator stood fifteen stories high, with a small replica of itself perched like a hat on its peaked roof, to house the pulley machinery. There were a wooden Lutheran church in the town and a gas station with the kind of pump you wind up by hand to return the dial to zero. A single paved street ran beside the tracks, and facing the tracks and the grain elevator stood a line of half a dozen wooden commercial buildings, each with a peaked roof hidden by a rectangular false front. The largest was a two-story hotel called the Colorado Inn. Seeing it, I remembered the farm women asking Mr. Terry where he'd be staying that night; he had given them this name. We went across the lobby and through swinging slatted doors to the restaurant and bar, to be seated in the center of the room by the very large proprietor himself, who served us our dinner free. As night fell outside, the room began to fill with farmers and their wives, dressed for an evening out, in string ties, collared sport shirts, jeans, clean boots; in print blouses, pastel slacks, and open-toed shoes. Some came over and greeted the story teller, always as Mr. Terry. They ordered dinner or coffee or whiskey. The proprietor brought in more chairs. Then the room was quiet, and Mr. Terry told them the story of the talking rabbit who offered up his life to teach a man not to kill.

I watched them listen. They listened the way I had listened, to forget themselves. Soon enough they stopped shifting in their seats, crossing their legs, ordering drinks, smoking cigarettes. His high clear voice held them. It became the only sound in the room. They listened, not as if the tale was a children's story, but as if it was true, and as if its truth was more vital to hear than the truth about ordinary things. The golden valley he held in his mind was a valley in their own history. He invited them there, and in their minds they went. They forgot the work their minds ordinarily did; they forgot their bodies. When he had finished and they felt the absence of his voice, then their minds snapped home like an elastic band that had been stretched and released, and for a moment it hurt. I could see it in their faces. They looked up; they remembered they were sitting in the restaurant in the Colorado Inn.

But where had they been while Mr. Terry's voice held them? If I'd asked them the next day, they'd naturally have said that they'd been sitting right there in the hotel. They'd have said Tom Terry's farm in the valley of the Cannonball was only something in the mind, and where the mind goes, what the mind sees, these things are not real. Where the body is, they'd have said, what the eyes see: only that is real. But for three-quarters of an hour, they hadn't believed it. For that time they'd known what I myself had come to believe: that everything is contained in the vastness of the mind, and that we ourselves decide what is false there and what is real. If Mr. Terry's valley was unreal when it was in the farmers' minds, then what about the thoughts that were there in their minds in the morning? What about their feelings, their habits, their memories, their desires? You could say that some were good and some were evil, since some favored life, and some death, but none was any less an invention than any other, and all came forth from the bright energy of the true mind.

I went outside. Standing by the railroad tracks, I looked up past the silhouette of the grain elevator to the brilliant stars. Thick as lands, they filled the dark ocean of the warm night. I remembered from grammar school another children's story, about a Greek soldier who was sentenced by the gods to wander for eternity among the stars. I thought of him up there, rowing, maybe, across the black straits between those two bright star-islands, or resting at harbor in that constellation, crossing that diamond continent, then setting out again across that long sea, his sail bellied by the winds of space. There, was that his beacon? Who knew what distances there were in the night? Who could tell what distances there were in the mind, what continents in it and constellations, what sun might rise and flood it with light? I thought to that wanderer: If we travel together, brother, who will be the first to reach his destination—you the ends of space, or I the bottom of my mind?

# 8

# KAREN AND THE KING
# OF KALINGA

For a week I slowly rode north in George Terry's van. I had no real reason to stay with him, but there didn't seem to be any hurry yet to move on. His stories amused me, and it was a delight to travel with a master, even if his mastery was of another study than my own. I'd told him I was interested in mental concentration and that I was looking for someone to teach me a method for it. I'd even started to describe the energy, but he hadn't seemed to want to hear much about what interested me. His thoughts were all given to his own world.

He was happy to have a daytime listener, though; and from morning till evening, between the interruptions of his sales, the van rang with his stories. I asked him if he'd ever written any of them down.

"No sir, I haven't. No reason to. I believe I keep my memory fit enough. Now if I could find a young man to teach the stories to, so there'd be someone to remember Tom when I'm gone—I had my eye on my sister's boy, but he thought it was nothing but a lot of tomfoolery." His grey eyes shot a sideways look at me there in the passenger seat. "I imagine you'll be on your way soon enough."

"You have to have the storytelling skill, Mr. Terry," I said. "I don't have any skill in this."

"Well, you don't know till you try." He nodded quickly. "You get it into your bones, until they're made of it."

The idea of becoming George Terry's student mildly intrigued me, but I knew it would only be a way of avoiding my own task. Sometimes it was hard to admit to myself that a year had passed since the monsignor stunt and the vision of the light and yet I still didn't truly know what had happened to me or where I ought to go.

Late one afternoon, as I fretted because we were just one day from crossing the border into Canada—something I hadn't wanted to do, because it felt like a going back instead of forward—late that hot afternoon, after Mr. Terry had been silent for a while, I fell into an unsteady doze and dreamed that I was walking beside the Cannonball River. I was picking my way along the bank among the saplings and the knees of the cotton-woods' winding roots; there was no path. The heat of the day sank down through the still leaves. I was frustrated and sweating; I couldn't find the place I was looking for. Then I noticed a break in the trees up ahead and a dip in the bank that led to a few feet of sandy shore. I made my way to it, with the thought of trying to cool off for a moment, and as I leaned over to splash water on my face, another splash just beside me startled me. Four or five feet from me, a little girl was squatting on a rock in the shallows. The current rose over her bare feet to the hem of her long white dress. Her cheek rested on her knees, so that she watched me sideways, and the piled tresses of her long black hair, arranged in ringlets as if for church, drooped down toward the water. Her bare arms trailed beside her in the current. Water bubbled over the speckled pebbles she held in her hands. Her dark blue eyes studied me skeptically.

"Where are *you* going?" she said, in a voice unusually strong for a girl her age; she couldn't have been more than seven.

"I don't know," I told her. "I can't find the spot I was looking for."

She wrinkled up her nose a moment. "Well, you're wasting your time going *that* way."

"There isn't any path, though," I said.

"What's wrong with this one? It's the one *I* always take." Looking up, she raised a dripping arm from the water, and still holding her pebbles, she pointed past me up the bank. I looked around, and plainly a path of yellow earth cut the lip of the bank, shot straight through the opening in the trees, and plunged into the fields toward the low afternoon sun. I was surprised that I hadn't noticed it when I'd walked down to the water.

"Where does it go?" I asked her.

The sun lit her round face as she looked up the bank, and it seemed to me suddenly that she was far older than a child, far older even than my grandmother had been when she died— that a thousand years were remembered in her gazing eyes. She noticed me watching her and said, with an amused smile, "You'll recognize the place when you get there."

"How, though? Where is it?"

She watched me, smiling still, and then laid her cheek down on her knees again. She held out a small green stone between her thumb and forefinger. "Want a pebble?"

I took it and held it up, wet and sparkling in the sunlight. When I looked back to her, she was gone. I stood up and turned around toward the path, clutching the pebble tightly in my fist. I woke up. The pumps of a gas station outside the window of Mr. Terry's van surprised me. Someone was washing the windshield. I was clutching my left index finger tightly in my right hand.

I left Mr. Terry the next morning. I told him I still had to find the right thing to do.

"I thought you'd be going about now," he said, laughing his intaken laugh. "Happy landings, my friend." He wrote out his winter address in Omaha for me "in case you're ever passing through these parts again."

"I hope you find someone to learn the stories," I said.

"Don't you worry about Tom, now," he said, nodding quickly. "Tom's fine; Tom's all right." He left me as he crossed U.S. Route 2, the last east-west highway before the Canada line, and I watched his van roar off north, spitting gravel and dust behind.

Like the dream of the fish in West New York, the dream of the little girl gave me hope. I thought that there must be a part of my mind that knew better than my ordinary thoughts what I was meant to do and where it was best for me to go. Maybe it was this knowledge, or instinct, or perhaps it was a memory of times I had forgotten, as the fish had said, that had always been guiding me and that broke through in dreams. Perhaps I'd been paying too much attention to outside things, to people and scenery; as I hitchhiked west across the golden fields of northern North Dakota, I tried to listen within for the guide that had known, at least in the dream, where my path lay. Not long after crossing the state line into Montana, I noticed on the map a highway that ran southwest into Wyoming; just then I felt a sense of rightness in my body, a sudden removal of tension, and I felt distinctly that in this way I was being told, by some instinct within my own mind, to go southwest on that road.

The rides with truckers came easily. Southwest through Montana, the land rose from the lowland plains, and the dark earth of the Midwest gradually turned drier and more yellow. The fields of wheat were behind me, and beef cattle, then sheep, wandered on the crests of dry hills. Indians passed in battered station wagons and stood in dilapidated doorways, their dark faces staring, in my memory, from pictures in my grammar-school storybooks. I told myself to let the sights and people be and to listen within. I pulled the picture of the lake from my pack, and for the first time since I'd left East Chicago, I worked on my concentration during the daytime, as well as in the early morning and the evening.

I left my southbound ride in the town of Casper, in central Wyoming. It felt wrong to head south any longer. Although my money was low, I spent two days in an upstairs hotel room in the town, practicing concentration, trying to keep up my hope, holding onto the promise of the dream. The little girl's path had led west toward the afternoon sun. Yet it felt right to wait longer before going on. I tried to bring up as questions the different possibilities; then I waited with a still mind, to see if there would be a feeling of rightness in answer. Was I supposed to wait in Casper? Was I supposed to look for work? I couldn't tell. Nothing felt confirmed. I slowly walked west out of town, not hitchhiking, not wanting to commit myself.

A few miles beyond the last building, a brand-new pickup truck with its hood up was blocking the gravel shoulder. Walking around it, I came upon a little leather-faced old man wearing a beret and leaning over the engine. I had seen these berets in Casper on small dark men who sometimes spoke a strange language: they were Basques. They herded sheep on the high plains. The engine in the pickup truck smelled of burnt insulation. I pulled out the shorted circuit and told the old man I'd go back to town to get the parts and rewire it for him. He said the truck belonged to the ranch where he worked. "Just charge it, and don't hurry," he said. "No need to hurry." The breakdown probably meant the rest of the afternoon off for him. But I caught rides both ways, and I had the truck started again after a little more than an hour and a half.

The old sheepherder—Juan, his name was—complained that he'd been happier when he'd patrolled the range on horseback; the patrol was all done by pickup truck now. He'd come into Casper to the local hospital to have the stitches removed from the back of his leg, where a ram had gashed him with its horns a month before. "I was on foot, and I didn't get over the fence in time," he said. "A truck can't always get to places, that's the thing of it. Never would have happened with a horse by you." He took off his beret, wiped his head with his sleeve, and put the beret on again. "The rams are trouble this year. I guess it's the weather."

He asked me where I was headed, and when I said I didn't know, he offered to drive me out to his ranch. He said that the manager usually hired someone for a while to check through the vehicles and the machinery after the sheepshearing but that no one had been hired yet, though it was July then, and the shearing was well over. "Seems like you can fix things right enough," Juan said.

It made sense, especially since I needed the money; and perhaps this would be the delay that I'd felt was needed. I rode with the old sheepherder up forty miles of dirt road, across the dry, tan, broken lands. There were no houses. There were only small scattered mounds of tough grass, dark bushes, the jagged gouges of dry creek beds, and sudden high cliffs, alternately pink, yellow brown, and pastel blue; the colors wavered on the faces of the cliffs in ragged horizontal stripes. Sheep grazed in dry canyons, where water from the spring snowmelt survived in brown pools in the empty creeks. Juan said the ranch covered seventy-three thousand acres; the owners were a group of doctors in Los Angeles.

The road ended in a wide canyon. The ranch buildings were strewn out beside a live stream that was shaded with bent willows. Twenty-five sheepherders lived there, Juan said, though they were often out on the range for two weeks at a time. He took me into a small air-conditioned office to see the manager. Behind a desk, a fellow in his late twenties leaned back in his chair, touching a twirled, waxed moustache that made him look like an educated wild boar. A diploma from a business school in San Diego hung behind him on the paneled wall. He peppered me with questions about where I'd been and what I could fix, and then he hired me for three weeks.

Sheepherding is work for loners. The ranch was a company of silences. No one took an interest in anyone else's peculiarities. When I asked the cook to make extra bread for me and no meat, all she said was, "Extra bread. No meat." People who liked rules and family life, the kind of people I'd known back home, kept away from those empty lands. Outside of the canyon where the ranch headquarters lay, outside on the high plains, among the dry bushes and sudden winds and dust, the tumbleweed bowled like thoughts down a vast stillness. Above the monotonous land, it was the sky that changed. The social doings that ordinary people are always watchful of were replaced for the sheepherders by the sky's doings: piled thunderheads, mysterious lightning, roofs of ribbed clouds, infinite stars. They called it the weather, but they were afraid of it and half-worshiped it.

But in the sheepherders' quarters, where they gave me the bunk and dresser of the previous cook—an old man who had suddenly died two weeks before—there was unaccustomed talk: it was of the new cook, who was a young woman. The sheepherders' heads were spinning with her presence. They weren't used to an unmarried woman in their company, or to any woman at the ranch, except the manager's wife, who kept her distance in her house farther down the canyon. For months I'd kept to my rule of not staring at women, in order to keep clear of painful feelings, but it was impossible not to watch this woman, the new cook, who moved around the dining room with a cool and distant grace that seemed to come not from womanhood, but from something else one couldn't name. Perhaps she'd been in professional sports, I thought: a swimmer or a gymnast. She was around thirty, and above middle height, taller than me, with clear dark blue eyes and black hair she wore straight to her shoulders, or in a folded pile above her head when she was cooking. Her mild voice, pitched low for a woman, was very pleasant to everyone's ears, but she spoke little. No one knew where she had come from. Juan told me that a week after the old cook had died, when the unmanned kitchen was a turmoil of opened cans and burnt vegetables, she had walked into the ranch and straight through the frazzled manager's door, saying, "I can cook. You can hire me." He'd hired her without another word, except to tell her where the kitchen was; he'd even forgotten to ask her name. No one knew what it was until Juan was deputized by the other sheepherders, as being now the oldest, to go ask her. She laughed and told him it was Karen.

I worked mostly around the ranch buildings, where the shearing and branding machinery was and the vehicles were stored, so I often ran into her. Several times I noticed her in the dirt yard behind the kitchen, sitting bolt upright on a sleeping bag; her legs would be tightly folded up and her eyes closed, while her lips moved. She'd seem to be singing to herself. Her wide face would be at rest. It intrigued me. I had never seen anybody sit that way before. Was she chanting or praying? Her cool manner didn't invite approach, but I was too curious, and finally I went into the kitchen while she was cooking and asked her what she was doing sitting that way.

"I'm singing to myself," she said.

"Tell me a little about it. Are you praying?"

"Praying? No."

"I'm interested in these things," I told her. "I wouldn't discuss it with the sheepherders."

But she wouldn't be coaxed. "I have to cook," she said. I didn't intend to drop it, though, and the next evening, when I spotted Karen again in the kitchen yard, I just sat down near her and tried to fold up my legs the way she had hers. Her legs were braided, rather than just crossed: her left foot was resting on her right thigh, and then her right foot was pulled up over her left knee so that it rested on her left thigh. It was clearly impossible. With just my left foot pulled up over my right knee, my hip shouted in pain at me, and my left knee sprang up into the air. Karen sat there ignoring me while I struggled with it. A mild frown touched at her closed eyes; she was obviously trying to concentrate on whatever she was muttering to herself, despite the noise I was making, and probably despite the pain her legs must have been giving her. I remembered the fat little lady who forgot her arthritis while she knelt and recited Hail Marys in the chapel at Father Jeremy's monastery. But Karen had said she wasn't praying. For lack of anything else, I sat there reciting the Hail Mary. It seemed that when I sat bolt upright with a straight spine, the energy rose up faster in my body than usual.

A few minutes later, Karen was looking over at me. "What are you reciting?" she said.

"The Hail Mary. It's all I know."

Sun was in her eyes. She shaded them with her hand. "Mary's very nice to think about. Do you pray to her image?"

"No, I don't pray to anybody," I told her. "I don't actually want to think about anything when I'm trying to concentrate my mind, but it's not that easy. Usually I try to concentrate on a photograph I have of a lake."

"Now, that's something I've never heard of anybody doing," Karen said.

"I just hit on it. I don't know if it's right."

"Perhaps you ought to use words."

"What words?" I asked her.

"It doesn't matter what words just yet." She unfolded her legs. "Just try a sound."

"Try it how, though?"

"Just recite it. Recite it with your voice and also in your mind, and listen to it. Don't listen to anything else." She stood up. As she was turning away, she pointed to my awkward legs and said, "Try to drop your energy down toward your belly. It'll help your knees and ankles loosen up, for one thing."

I was stunned that she would use the word "energy" that way, and I wanted to pursue her into the kitchen to find out what she'd meant by it. But the kitchen door had already swung shut behind her. After a minute, I decided to wait and try out what she'd told me first: I didn't want to risk putting her off by pressing questions on her too quickly. I had no idea how much she might know.

It was clear right away that she knew something I didn't. As soon as I tried concentrating on the sound "ah," I saw that reciting and listening were a far better method of concentration than staring was. My eyes would get tired when I tried to concentrate by looking, and I'd have to rest them every ten minutes; but reciting a sound, I found I could work on concentration steadily for three-quarters of an hour without a break, although I couldn't sit bolt upright the way Karen did, even with just one leg folded, for more than a minute or two at first. I could see that the trick was to hold onto the recitation in the mind, not just in the voice, because otherwise it was very easy to drone on with the voice while the mind rattled off into thoughts of other things. The recitation itself was a kind of thought, if it was spoken in the mind's voice, and if I held to it and listened closely to it, it could drown out the trivial worried thoughts that always tramped across my concentration, such as whether they'd have the tractor parts I needed in town or whether there'd be something to my liking for dinner. The new method elated me, and I felt grateful to the inner guide that had led me to the sheep ranch and had not failed me.

During the next few days, the longer I pushed myself to try to listen to the sound, the more peaceful and awake I felt afterwards. I found that I could also recite during the daytime, while on the job—the work was mostly lubrication of the shearing and branding machinery, routine tune-ups of the pickup trucks, and a messy transmission job on the six-wheel-drive tractor. In the evenings, after I'd been reciting all day long, a pause in the recitation would leave a silence without thought that would last a long moment, then another, then another, and with each moment the energy would burn harder and its stillness would spread wider in my mind. The stillness would wash like calm water into the narrow harbor between one sound and the next, and for a moment between the headlands I could glimpse the sea. There, it was there I wanted to go, to set sail across the unmapped distances of my mind. But I couldn't leave the shore. I had to recite the sound again quickly, even though it divided me from the very stillness that it brought close, because if I stopped reciting, the ordinary thoughts crowded back like noisy beachcombers.

I experimented with what Karen might have meant by dropping my energy toward my belly. The energy's motion in my body had always been to rise up my spine; it had never occurred to me to try to send it down again. But I found it was as easy to will it down as to call it up, once my mind was calm. What Karen had said was true: my legs relaxed if I sent energy down to them, and they folded flat more quickly when I tried to sit upright. As I dropped the energy, its burning seemed to gather at my throat instead of in my head, and sometimes in my chest, just to the right of my heart. At one point I suddenly noticed that my mind's voice was reciting there, too, in my throat or chest, and not in my head at all. It was an odd sensation to feel my mind in the middle of my body, with my head floating above as just another limb. I was startled at first by the idea that my thoughts could be located in different places. Yet I'd felt for a long time that the true substance of my mind could spread beyond the boundaries of my skin. It seemed to be only because I was nailed to my feelings and clamped to my ordinary thoughts that my mind was normally confined to a single place inside my body.

Because Karen was so closemouthed, I tried to decide on the one question I most wanted to her to answer, in case she wasn't willing to answer any others. I went back into the kitchen and asked her if she knew of a sound to recite that would stop all the other sounds and then stop itself, so that there would be only stillness.

She looked up from the cutting table. "Why do you want to stop things?"

"It's not stopping them, exactly, it's stopping your connection with them. If I get free of thoughts and feelings and distractions when I'm concentrating, I feel a lot of energy freed up. I guess you know about this; isn't this what you were mentioning the other day?"

"Mm, I mentioned it." She went back to chopping vegetables, but at least she didn't ask me if I shouldn't be seeing a doctor. Instead she said, "What do you want to be still for?"

I decided to put my cards on the table. I couldn't be sure that she would understand what I meant, but the worst she could do was laugh at me. "All this machinery, see, all these systems of thoughts and feelings and all the ordinary things we do: I don't believe they're actually real. They're there, all right, but they're all invented. We're just making them up as we go along. They're also a lot of pain and trouble, and they keep us from being at peace. I believe there is a true mind that's empty and still and made of energy and light. I think I can feel it there on the other side of my thoughts when I practice concentration—your recitation method is very good for this. I think that living in the true mind is the only way I will ever be happy. What I want to do is get out of the machinery and find the true mind and never come back."

Karen had put down her chopping knife and was watching me across the table. "When you get there," she said, "what do you mean to do?"

I shook my head. "I don't think there's anything special to do there, except maybe to help other people understand how to get there themselves, so that they can be happy. I tried to do this a little at home, but I didn't understand anything, and it just got people annoyed with me."

"I don't expect people generally want to be informed that all their thoughts and feelings are false," Karen said. "Here, chop some carrots." She handed me a knife, adding mildly, "Do you really believe what you've told me, or is it just something you talk about because you don't have anything else to do?"

"I want to get out," I said with a little heat, "and I've been trying to get out for a long time. In a way I've been wanting out for my whole life, but I've never known how to do it."

"There's no reason to get irritated," she said, slicing potatoes into neat quarters across the table from me. "If you were really free the way you say you want to be, I could needle you for the rest of the afternoon, and you wouldn't feel the slightest bit of anger."

"Okay, you're right, I agree with that, but I need a method, Karen. I don't have any skill. I'm just floundering around in this thing."

"You could recite the Buddha's name," she said, "if you want to be still."

"The Buddha, who's the Buddha?" For some reason, the word made the hair stir on my head.

"The Buddha is just anyone who has completely become his own true mind," she said in her low-pitched voice. "You could also say that you're a Buddha and I'm a Buddha, because everyone has the same true mind, but it's only a potential for us until we've actually become it. It's not enough just to talk about it."

She had stunned me again, just as she had when she first mentioned the energy. Here she was, matter-of-factly talking about the true mind as if it was something that other people spoke about and knew about and not just a phrase that existed only in my own thoughts. I felt tight in my stomach; I didn't know what to say to her. I wondered if she would cut off the conversation then, as she had done before, but she said; "You can recite 'Namo Amita Buddha,' which is Sanskrit and means, 'I take my refuge in the Buddha of Infinite Light.' Amita Buddha realized his true mind long ago and vowed to help beings in this world. His name is what I recite. I'll show you." Raising her head, she sang her recitation in a clear voice that rang through the kitchen. From her mild and smiling face, energy streamed across the table and beat against me like an electric wind, just as it had streamed from the chanting fathers at Father Jeremy's monastery, only stronger; it ignited my own. She sang the seven syllables twice in a two-phrased tune:

Na-mo A — mi — ta ——— Bud-dha, Na-mo A — mi— ta Bud— dha.

"You sing it," she said.

Feeling weak and strange, I joined her, cleared my throat, joined her again. After a few recitations, she was suddenly silent, but she nodded at me to go on, and I sang in an unsteady voice until I knew the tune.

We said nothing for a while. She was gathering the cut vegetables into a steamer. "How do you know about this?" I asked her then.

She looked at me as if the answer to my question was obvious. "I study Buddhism," she said.

I remembered seeing television film clips of Buddhist monks in Vietnam; I had a vague image of men with shaven heads chanting and bowing in long robes.

"What do they say the true mind is, though, do they talk about this?"

She said after a minute, "Buddhism teaches people how to find the true mind right there within themselves. It says that everything we need is already inside us. That's why we practice recitation and other kinds of meditation: to hold our attention within, away from the false and onto the true. What the true is"—she paused as she lit the fire under the steamer—"you can't say what it is in terms of something else. It's itself; it's our being. It's what isn't born and doesn't die, and it's the same in everyone."

"Is this the energy?" I asked her.

She shook her head. "The energy is the power of your body and your feelings. It's a manifestation of the true mind. You can't experience the true mind the way you can experience the energy or anything else, because you yourself are the true mind. That's why you don't want to get too attached to your experiences. If you have unnecessary thoughts about what's happening to you or what's around you, then you've wandered off from the true. Just recite and keep pulling your hearing back to listen within."

She was silent again. I didn't think she wanted to talk more, and I was just as glad. I wanted to take the knowledge that had suddenly been given to me and embrace it, practice the song of it, and let it begin to fill my life. I walked back into the courtyard and stood in the sunlight, reciting as she had taught me and shaking joyfully.

During the next few days, I came to the kitchen yard after supper to sit in meditation nearby Karen in the evening light. She would sit upright, her legs braided in what she called the lotus position, for a full hour and a half without a single movement except for the silent recitation on her lips. If a mosquito came, she let it bite her. Once the manager stuck his head through the door from the kitchen and spoke to her several times; she didn't even open her eyes. "He just wanted to see what we were doing," she said afterwards. She didn't tell me very much more about Buddhism; she said very little to me at all. But she never objected to my sitting in the yard with her, despite the commotion I made shifting my legs and rubbing them, stretching them out and pulling them in again. Sometimes when the sitting period was over, she would turn aside to me before unfolding her legs and help me along. "If you sit in half-lotus,"—by which she meant only one foot pulled onto the opposite thigh—"put your left leg on top, since that's the leg that goes up first for full lotus." Another time she said, "You should get up earlier and sit more."

I felt slightly indignant. "I get up at five-thirty and sit for an hour and a half."

"It's summer; anybody can get up at five-thirty. Get up at four-thirty."

I did as she told me, and I found that the extra hour of recitation gave me more than enough energy to compensate for the lost hour of sleep. It also doubled the strength of the concentration that I took with me into the day's work.

All day long I sang the name of Amita Buddha, taking Karen's advice not to worry about who he was or where he was, because, she said, all the Buddhas are one substance with the true mind of all beings. When I recited his name, I was also singing of my own truth, of the best in myself and in everyone, of the harmony at the basis of the world. I remembered Brother Stephen's telling me of his astonished discovery that he was happy; I was not astonished, but realized slowly that I'd never guessed, in all my search for a method and a teaching, that finding them would give me such joy. I wouldn't have exchanged the one phrase "Namo Amita Buddha" for a mountain of rubies, a Caribbean island stocked with free women, a twenty years' supply of mushroom pizza, which I sorely missed, or the promise of eternal life. My concentration was far more firm than before. Holding one's thoughts on such a pure song, who could be defeated by the burning heat of the canyon or the almost impossible trickiness of the transmission job on the tractor? Even the most painful of my thoughts—the thought of having lost my son—quieted when I told it that in our fundamental nature he and I were not two and that now, perhaps, I would have something to give him one day in return for his having lost his father.

I let the energy go, not trying to call it up or send it down. I found that it flowed by itself in a current that made an incomplete circuit, up from the base of my spine, around the top of my head, back down the center of my face to my throat, and sometimes into my chest, but no farther. I asked Karen what might be blocking it.

"Probably an old emotion," she said.

I felt immediately that it was the residue of my unhappiness about losing Margherita and Vin. I started to tell Karen about it, but she didn't want to discuss it.

"Just have patience," she said. "Your skill will come if you are determined."

One thought did defeat my concentration whenever it arose, however, and that was often: the thought of her. I was full of fantasies about how to persuade the manager that I could still be useful at the ranch beyond the three weeks I had been hired for. I was sure that Karen knew far more than she had already taught me, and I wanted to stay around until I had learned it all. My thoughts of her as a teacher, though, were confused with my thoughts of her as a woman. I tried not to look at her more than necessary, because I didn't want to put her off or jeopardize my chances to learn from her, but at night I would sometimes catch my mind imagining events that justified in spirit, though not in fact, the coarse suggestions the sheepherders sometimes made about my spending time with her. But Karen was always collected within herself, and there was never a hint from her that our relationship could have the tone of man and woman. She turned aside every question I asked about her past or her plans. I persisted in spite of myself, until she said finally, "What do you need to know about me for? I thought you said you wanted to get out of the machinery."

I blushed red for the first time since I was a boy. "Yeah, you're right, Karen, I'm sorry." Afterwards I was glad that she had called me on it. In fact I didn't at all want to mess up my new progress and new peacefulness with thoughts of sex, which drained my energy and scattered my concentration just as much as anger did. I realized she probably would have spoken more and taught me more, and perhaps she would have told me about herself, if I hadn't been confused in my own mind about her. As it was, I never even learned her last name.

The sheepherders persisted in asking me about Karen. I told them that she was teaching me how to sit in meditation and that anything else was their own imagination. It was clear that in fact they believed me. They could see for themselves that Karen never departed from her cool grace, which I knew now came naturally from her firm hold on her recitation. But it wasn't what the sheepherders wanted to believe. They felt deprived that Karen was not playing what they saw to be the desirable role for a woman, if not for their enjoyment, then at least for someone's.

"How can you just sit there, man?" one of the younger sheepherders, whose name was Manuel, asked me more than once.

"It's what I like to do," I said.

It exasperated him; I, too, wasn't playing the proper role. Sometimes I had the feeling I was back in West New York, and I didn't know whether to be angry or to laugh.

The sheepherders took to walking into the kitchen yard in the evening in groups of two or three and standing over us, saying angrily: "What's this for, huh?" "What are you, nuts or something?" "Hey, Juan, you seen them yet? Take a look at this, he doesn't move!"

Their annoyance never became ugly. They never did more than shake my shoulders a few times, and Karen they never touched. They were not bad men. Still, I became a little afraid of them, and though I followed Karen's lead in not moving or speaking when they challenged us, I asked her why she didn't try to answer them.

"I don't think you can explain anything to people with words, Joey, unless they're ready to hear. You can only show them. Go ahead, though, try if you want, maybe I'm wrong."

I did try several times, in the bunkhouse in the evenings; I told them that sitting peacefully was very restful and invigorating and that reciting was in some ways like a prayer, though you weren't asking for anything. They were a little mollified, but they still couldn't see the sense in it.

"You're making a big mistake, that's all I can say," was Manuel's view of it.

One morning after I'd been working at the ranch about two weeks, the ram that had slashed Juan's thigh attacked another of the sheepherders on the range. Fortunately he leapt into his truck with no more than a ripped jacket; but his dog was gored. They were ready to shoot the dog, until Karen insisted on driving it into town in the truck where it lay. They stitched its guts together at the animal hospital.

"It'll be too skittish to be much use as a sheepdog now, even if it does come back," Juan said when Karen drove into the ranch again with the news that the dog would probably live.

She looked down at him quietly; she was a good six inches taller than him. "How can you be so uncompassionate?" she said. "I've noticed they feed you while you're on disability."

Juan walked away shaking his head.

The manager was on the telephone to the owners in Los Angeles. They couldn't decide what to do with the ram. He was a liability that would normally be sold for slaughter, but a good breeder in his strain was very hard to find, and he was worth several thousand dollars. Two of the sheepherders put the ram down with a tranquilizing gun and brought him shackled down off the range to the pens below the garage. He filled the canyon with his bellowing when he woke up.

A specialist flew in from Sheridan, in the north-central part of the state. He put the ram down again, pored over him, and ran some tests in town. He found nothing wrong. "Wait," he told the manager, who pulled at his moustache and stalked back to his house.

I walked down to the ram's pen with Karen that evening. When the ram saw us, he lowered his head and trotted over toward us, snorting and waving his ribbed spiral horns in figure eights. He stopped on the other side of the wooden fence and stared at us with hot yellow eyes. Karen looked at him for a while. "He's angry" was her diagnosis.

"Yeah, but why?" I asked her.

"I don't know."

His bellowing echoed after us along the canyon walls as we walked back along the driveway in the hot night. I remembered the hogs screaming in the slaughterhouse, and I told Karen about my job there, and about Lonny Birlak. I wanted to know what she thought about my debate with him whether animals have an energy like our own.

She said after a little while, "They, too, share in the true mind. That's one reason why the Buddhas teach us above all to have compassion and not to kill. We are all the same at the source. When you recite, you recite not just for yourself, but to give your light to other people and the world."

A few evenings later, Karen didn't join me at her usual meditation spot in the kitchen yard. The next night after supper, when she was missing again, I walked down to the ram's pen to look for her. One of the sheepherders had told me he'd seen her there in the early morning, "just sitting on the dirt and singing to the old grouch." As I followed the yellow driveway, thick with summer dust, beside the willows that bowed over the stream, I heard Karen's clear singing in the quiet evening. She was sitting in lotus position on the bare earth a few feet from the gate to the pen, reciting much more loudly than usual. Her eyes were closed. Just inside the gate the ram stood watching her and listening, then waving his head and snorting, then listening again. His rank stench was heavy on the humid air. He noticed me and trotted off around the circuit of his pen, bumping occasionally against the posts of the wooden fence, flipping his dirt-caked tail.

I sat down quietly, trying not to disturb either of them. I thought it best to recite silently, since it was her mild voice that the ram was used to. He was soon standing nearby again and listening. We sat by his gate for half an hour, for forty-five minutes; night fell. Suddenly there was a small thud and a sharp creak. I raised my eyes and saw in the dimness that the ram had butted his gate open. He was already halfway out of his pen. Karen was looking up with startled eyes, not at him, however, but at me. It was obvious she hadn't expected me there and hadn't heard me sit down. My first panicked thought was that some idiot sheepherder had forgotten to close the latch after bringing in feed. But then it struck me that Karen might have left the gate open deliberately. She was trying to tame him.

She said to me quietly, "Send him your light, and don't move." Then she closed her eyes and a little more softly began again to sing.

A hundred thoughts of cowardice and fright shot through my mind as the ram came trotting toward me. I thought of running and vaulting over the fence and shutting myself in the pen; I might make it, but where would that leave Karen? I thought of shouting for help; the sheepherders could come and shoot him. I thought again of running; if that excited him and he gored Karen, that was her fault for being so stupid as to risk her life to save his. But it was already too late. The ram had stopped a few feet in front of me. He was swinging his horns in small upward swipes. His strong breath blew against my face. The muscles of my chest and throat that faced him trembled. Hot fear leapt through my body like a shooting flame.

"Send him your light," Karen said again quietly. "Recite for him."

The ram looked around at her, then back and forth between us, snorting for a moment. What light could I send him? My energy was bound up in fright. I had dropped my recitation when I'd heard the gate open. I was ashamed in the midst of my fear. I'd sat through the sheepherders' taunting us, hadn't I? Yes, but they weren't going to kill us. No, one of them could have drawn a knife, you didn't know, but you still sat there. Yes, but this is a wild animal.

Suddenly, as the ram snorted a few inches from my face, the black-and-white rabbit in George Terry's story hopped into my mind. I heard him saying, in Mr. Terry's imitation of a squeaky voice, "Fire away, sir." In the midst of my panicked debate, the memory oddly delighted me. Having spent so many years doing stunts, how could I fail to recognize Karen's stunt? Fire away, ram! I hadn't even thought of what Mr. Terry's rabbit did as a stunt, but that's exactly what it had been, the fundamental, the true stunt: he had put aside his ordinary self for the sake of something true. Father Jeremy, Brother Stephen, George Terry himself and the rabbit of his story, and now Karen: they were all doing in their own way the true stunt that I had wanted to do, except that I'd never been able to find something that was worth letting myself go for. But saving the ram by taming him, and showing the sheepherders the power of recitation and nonviolence in the bargain—wasn't this a true stunt worthy of a risk? The ram still hasn't attacked me, anyway, I thought; he probably can't make any more sense of us than the sheepherders could.

"Fire away, ram," I murmured. I was smiling to myself. The ram was still standing in front of me, watching me. I closed my eyes and recited the Buddha's name. In my mind I gave the ram my body to attack if he wanted it. I felt the giving as a release, as a gladness. I turned my hearing inward to my recitation, and as I listened, a gate in my chest locked by tension seemed to fly open and to let some nameless sorrow go. My feeling of being a separate body slowly dissolved at every point on my skin, then at every point inside me. The energy welled up from within. Like cool water it flowed in every direction out across the borders of my skin, down into the ground, and into the air. I tried to focus it toward the ram. I recited for him, because he could not.

Minutes passed. I heard him make a sniffling sound, near where Karen was sitting. My eyes flew open without my intending it. The ram was standing in front of her with his head down. In a minute he lifted it with a sideways rotation of his jaw: he was chewing. Caught in the moonlight was a lump of sugar in Karen's open hand. The ram dipped his head down again and clamped the sugar in his lips, and as he chewed it, Karen plunged her hand into the yellow-white fleece behind his ears and scratched him. He flipped his ears back and forth. Still reciting, she stood up after a minute, opened the gate, and tossed another lump into the pen. She slapped him gently on the flank, and he trotted back inside.

"I didn't know he was ready for a second person," she said cheerfully as she closed the gate and latched it. "He's only been out twice now. In fact, I think I'll invite the manager down tomorrow. It just might get him to stay the execution."

"You mean to prepare him for what he's going to see, I hope?"

She laughed lightly. "Oh, yes. He can stay in his truck."

I stretched my legs out. I had never kept them pulled in without moving them for nearly so long before. They were both completely asleep.

The next night I recited with Karen again by the ram's pen. Not long after we'd sat down, the four-door pickup truck, driven by the manager and packed with five or six of the sheepherders, stopped beyond us on the driveway. In his pen the ram raised his head and snorted at the truck, but the thought of the sugar lumps was too strong for him, and in a few minutes he butted the gate open and trotted out over to Karen. He sat on his knees and chewed on the sugar and on the carrots she had brought him for dessert. Finally Manuel, saying, "This is too much, man," jumped out of the truck and walked over to the ram to pat him on the shoulder. The ram waved his horns at him but didn't get up from his meal. Karen and Manuel led him back to his pen together.

My three weeks at the ranch were over. More and more there grew in me a dread of losing Karen's guidance and wandering again in my own guesswork. Finally I went into the kitchen when she was making bread and told her frankly what I was feeling.

"I need more teaching, Karen, a lot more. I'm still a total idiot. My job is up, but I want to keep learning from you."

She shook her head. "I am not the one to teach you."

"Who is, then? Where am I to find the person?"

She divided up the dough for the pans. "What you need is a place where you can study Buddhism and live it. Then you will make progress, I think."

"Where is this place, do you know one? Is this where you were?"

"There are some places in San Francisco you could try," she said.

"Which one, though?"

"You'll recognize it."

Her evasiveness was making me half-frantic. "Come on, Karen, do you really have to keep this from me?"

"After facing up to our friend down the canyon the other night, you still don't have faith in the Buddhas, or in yourself either?" she asked me.

I stood there biting my lip. As I watched Karen pat out the dough in the pans, the little girl in the Cannonball River in my dream appeared in my memory. She had said the same thing: "You'll recognize the place when you get there." I thought Karen was probably right: I should believe in my own instinct; but it was hard to let go when it seemed that Karen could give me certainty.

"I guess I don't have faith in anyone yet, Karen, though the idea appeals to me."

"You will, when you've recited long enough," she said.

"Anyway, I suppose I'll be here for another few weeks. You could call me if something goes wrong."

I had never seen her even partly relent before. "Okay, Karen, that'd be good. Thanks."

'Don't thank me," she said, squatting before the oven with her back to me. "Just stop worrying about yourself."

Juan was driving into town the next day. The manager told me I might as well go, and he gave me my check. As we were about to drive down the canyon, Karen came out of the kitchen, waving her arm and wearing a delighted smile.

"News," she called out. She walked up to Juan's truck. "The King of Kalinga has his reprieve."

The King of Kalinga was what Karen had named the ram, after a fierce-tempered character with a large harem who had attacked Shakyamuni Buddha with his sword but later had become his disciple. Shakyamuni Buddha, she'd told me, was the Buddha who brought the teaching to India for this age of this world.

"They're taking the king back to his range this afternoon," Karen said. She slapped the panel of Juan's truck. "Do well, Joey."

"If you come to San Francisco, I'll see you. You'll probably recognize the place."

She laughed and walked off. Juan waited till she was beyond the range of the dust of his truck before he started down the yellow driveway. I didn't see her again for four years, but later she became a bhikshuni—a Buddhist nun—and she is here now.

# 9

# GOLD MOUNTAIN

An old couple hauling a trailer to Yellowstone picked me up outside of Casper. We rode west across Wyoming through the morning. The dry and empty highlands rose into green forests and then to the grey fortresses of the Rocky Mountains, whose peaks were still white with the last unmelted snows. The next day, a chain-smoking black trucker carrying apples to the Port of Oakland stopped for me near Pocatello, Idaho. We followed the Snake River southwest and crossed the Nevada desert in the hot night. My thoughts were full of hope. I wanted to end my looking and spinning around and wandering. I wanted to find a resting place, a place to let go of everything that kept me from my true mind. The trucker was taking me there. He was rattling at seventy-five miles an hour along the arrow of the desert highway, but I couldn't see why he wasn't going ninety.

At dawn, another wall of mountains dismayed me by standing grey and sharp in front of us. Its steep glaciers burned in the rising sun. "Didn't I already cross the Rockies?" I asked the trucker.

"Where have you been all your life?" he asked, coughing and laughing. "These are the Sierras."

I had never heard of them. We climbed slowly up another delay of dry highlands, yellow and bare but for clots of spiny bushes and cactuses jerry-built of round green plates. The trucker shook his gearshift down and down, and roaring in bottom gear we inched into the clouds. Suddenly we were gliding, then hurtling downward in shadow through forests of firs and red-barked pines. Five thousand feet below, dim and blue, lay what I thought was the ocean—"Hey, is that the Pacific?"—till the trucker recovered from his wheezing and laughing and told me it was California.

The mountains descended to brown empty hills, and the hills to the Sacramento Valley, as flat as the Great Plains. The highway hurried between fields of beans, tomatoes, and fruit trees planted in patches a half-mile square, in what might have been a vegetable garden on a planet of giants. The lines of red earth flashed at us between the planted rows. Here and there, earth dikes snaked through flooded fields of green grass: rice, the trucker said. Sometimes near, sometimes far down among the flat fields, clumps of men and women in white shirts and straw hats were bent over at the waist, picking in the heat. Small towns built of neon signs and flaking stucco shot past. Then the valley rose, and yet another range of round hills, lion-colored and studded with green live oaks, opened to accept us. The heavy road forced its path among them; cities lay on their slopes. The trucker dropped me at the Oakland bus station, and in an hour I was sailing over a long bridge across a bay to the white towers of San Francisco.

I went straight to a phone booth to look up Buddhist temples in the phone book. Despite what Karen had promised, I had a sudden fear I would find nothing, but instead there was a list of more than a dozen. Before I could begin wondering how I could choose among the names, a feeling of rightness settled on one of them, with the same removal of tension from my body that I had felt before in North Dakota and Wyoming. It was the only monastery in the listing. I remembered the peace of Father Jeremy's valley. If I can find such a valley where the road leads to the true mind, I thought, then I don't need to look any farther.

The lady in the ticket booth at the bus station gave me directions. I went outside. A chill fog lay on the city. I walked south down Mission Street, where white wooden houses, with patterned decorations dripping from their eaves, floated in the mist between printing plants and Mexican grocery stores. I shivered in the cold, wondering if the monks would speak English and if they would let me in.

The monastery was a rectangular three-story building of red brick, with the doors and window trim painted gold. Above the entrance hung a sign with carved red letters: Gold Mountain Monastery. I rang and waited. Perhaps no one will answer, I thought. Maybe they're in retreat; maybe they don't accept outsiders, the same as at Father Jeremy's place. But after a few moments, a monk opened the door so that I could pass by him into the vestibule. He was an American. His head was shaved, and over a long robe he wore a brown sash that covered the left shoulder but not the right. He nodded toward a registry on the counter. I signed my name. Having read it, he looked at me keenly for a full half-minute.

"Why have you come?" he said.

"I want to study Buddhism. Can people do that here?"

"Have you studied before?" he asked me.

"Just a little is all. Someone taught me how to recite the Buddha's name. I'm looking for a place to learn more about it."

He nodded. "That is taught here, but we're having a Chan session right now. Have you ever practiced Chan?"

"No, what's Chan?"

"You can come in and try it if you like," he said.

He turned and pushed open a glass door covered with white translucent paper. I followed him. Behind us, out on the city street, radios sang, engines revved, men shouted; inside, beyond the doors, there was total stillness. Along the two sides of a long, high-ceilinged, cool white hall, forty people sat on benches in lotus position the way Karen had sat, upright with

their legs drawn in and their hands folded in their laps. They
didn't seem to be reciting; their lips were still. Most of them
were Americans. At the near end of the hall where I was, they
were all laypeople, dressed in ordinary clothes, men on the
benches on the right side and women on the left side; farther
down, beyond them, sat people in robes and brown sashes,
monks beyond the laymen, and beyond the laywomen, as I
guessed, nuns. At the far end of the hall, high upon an altar in
bright light, three golden statues sat in meditation, each upon
the carved petals of a flower. Carved flames were gathered
around their heads. I felt very curious to go look at them more
closely, but I noticed that the monk who had shown me in was
standing next to me. He was pointing to an empty space on the
bench among the laymen. I nodded, and he went himself toward the front of the hall to sit down.

The bench creaked loudly against the silence as I sat on it.
No one looked around at my noise. Some of the people's faces
were slightly tense, as if against the pain in their folded legs, or
perhaps in a struggle to hold their concentration; others were
intent but relaxed, with the faintest of smiles on their lips. It
was clear that they knew something about concentration, because the hall was crammed with their energy. It pressed against
my skin like a cool and mild electric shock. When one of the
monks passed silently along the benches on some errand, an
added breeze of it pushed against me as he came and drew off as
he walked past. What was this "Chan" method? Had Karen
known about it? Was this monastery the place she had meant?
Maybe I should ask the monk who'd let me in if he knew her. I
didn't know her last name, though. Everyone was silent. No
one moved. I was going to have to wait with my questions. I
recited silently and told myself to take Karen's advice that I still
needed to learn patience.

Soon my left ankle struck up its usual complaints, and my
right calf underneath it began to cramp and go numb, but I
didn't think it would be right to disturb the stillness of the hall
by taking my legs down and rubbing them. My stomach embar-

rassed me by growling; I hadn't taken time to get breakfast on my way there. I started looking at my watch and wondering how long these silent people would sit without moving. I noticed one, then another of the laypeople near me shift their legs out of the lotus position, and I was about to shift my own legs, when suddenly a sweet bell rang once in the hall. People began to stir, unbending their legs, putting on cloth shoes, then leaning forward, waiting. Again the bell rang, and everyone stood. A wooden block was struck twice, and swinging their arms they began walking briskly in single file around the hall.

We walked quickly for twenty minutes. No one spoke. There was only the sound of slippered footsteps and the swish of robes. Some people looked around them, perhaps newcomers like myself; others kept their eyes on the floor, keeping up their meditation as they walked. Each time we passed around the high altar, I looked at the three golden statues seated above us on their flower pedestals. Their hands were held up, each differently, in gestures of teaching or explanation. On their faces was the same faint smile I had seen on the lips of some of the meditators. The statues seemed to be of beings who were totally awake and totally at ease, seated in meditation without distraction, wandering thought, or pain, as if they were models for us in the hall. Their carved clothing was the monk's sash and simple robe. I guessed that they were probably not meant to be statues of gods, because they didn't have the kind of elegance and jeweled majesty that I thought a god would have to have; and Karen had told me that Buddhists recognized the existence of gods but did not worship them. Nor were they full of emotion, like the statues in church that poured out upon the worshipers the agony of Christ, the grief of the Virgin, and the ecstasy of the saints. Instead, the wide, clear, golden faces of the statues in the hall were at peace. They were the faces of people, but of people who had been transformed, who had liberated themselves from both grief and ecstasy, from agitation and exhaustion, from love and hate. They were at rest in the simple kindness of joy.

After we had walked for about fifteen minutes, a young monk approached the altar, lit a long stick of incense, held it up to his forehead briefly, and stood it in a large potbellied censer with three bent legs that rested on the altar among vases of flowers. The white smoke wandered upward in a zigzag stream. Then the monk stood before a square yellow stool, with palms together, and suddenly he bowed down so that his knees, elbows, hands, and forehead rested on the stool. He turned up his palms beside his head in a kind of offering. Was it to the statues, or to what they represented, that he was bowing so humbly? After I had walked in line behind the altar and had come round again, there he was bowing a second time, and a third, and then last a half-bow at the waist. No one paid attention to him. The thought spoke in my head: You should be bowing. Why, though? It struck me only then that they were statues of Buddhas.

"Run!" the monk who had bowed called out in a clear voice, and everyone broke into a jog. After we had made one circuit of the hall, he struck the wooden block once, and everyone stopped short; then we walked back to our places on the benches. I assumed there would be another period of sitting, and I pulled up my legs; they seemed to fall into place a little easier than before. I recited and looked down the hall at the statues. Seated there, they spoke silently of the perfection of the true mind. That there could be such statues made me glad. If there were other people who could conceive of becoming the true mind clearly enough to make a statue of it, then it was not ridiculous of me to conceive of my becoming it. Watching the statues, my recitation took on more strength, and the Buddha's name fell like a bright stone through the rushing water of my hopeful thoughts to the still place beneath.

Someone began speaking in the silence. He was sitting upright on a small square bench just beside the high altar: yet another American monk, perhaps around thirty-five, with a wide forehead and heavy black eyebrows that grew out every which way. I had a momentary feeling that I'd seen him before, although I knew I had not. His dark eyes watched intently a single spot in front of him as he spoke.

"This is the second day of our seven-day Chan session," he said. "Most people are settling into the schedule and putting aside from their minds the affairs that occupy their daily lives. For those of you who are here for the first time or who haven't done a Chan session before, let me remind you that no one is allowed to leave the hall during the sitting periods for any reason except monastery business and that no talking is allowed in the hall at any time. Even outside the hall, talk as little as possible while you are here this week; the best would be if you didn't talk at all. Talking spends your energy, and a Chan session is an opportunity to build your energy. Moreover, if you talk you'll probably be talking about your likes and dislikes, your desires and attachments, the stuff of the self that covers your true mind, just the self that you've come here to look into and let go."

Good, I thought; this is the kind of language I want to hear. I noticed that the other people in the hall were keeping to their meditation posture, without looking at the speaker, and I dropped my eyes and tried to listen with a quiet mind as he went on: "What is this self? Who is this person I have so actively, so doggedly been for so many years? To investigate that question is the practice of Chan. The word 'Chan,' which is derived from the Sanskrit, means 'consideration in stillness.' Firmly, with a determined hand, we channel the current of all our thoughts into the consideration of one question: 'Who am I?' Here at Gold Mountain Monastery, when we are not holding a Chan session, many of us recite the name of Amita Buddha as our practice, and we have just completed a seven-day Buddha recitation session. Now we are doing Chan, and so we can ask, 'Who is it who's been reciting the Buddha's name?' In the Chan School, 'Who's reciting the Buddha's name?' has long been the traditional way to ask the question 'Who am I?'; this fosters the combination of both methods—recitation and Chan—in one life of practice. Perseverance in the two methods together has enlightened the minds of many Masters. 'Who recites the Buddha's name?' That is to say, 'Who is this person who reveres the Buddhas and takes them as his guide?' 'Whose voice is it that recites?' 'Whose mind is it?' The Chan question can be turned in any direction, however. If a particular thought disturbs your concentration, or if your attention is disrupted by a stimulus from outside, you can refocus the question to shine there: 'Who is it whose back aches?' 'Who is annoyed by that sound in the street?' 'Who is it who's thinking of home?'

   " '*I* am thinking of home,' you answer. Yes, but who then are you? 'I'm myself,' you say. 'I'm the one right here who's thinking of home.' Then are you merely the things you are thinking and doing? Are you anything other than your thoughts and desires? Are they founded on anything lasting and real, or is each one based on something else, which is again based on yet another thing, so that all are simply a structure of impermanent circumstances? If the street is quiet and there are no thoughts of home, what is left? 'My body,' you say. 'My friends, my beliefs, my memories.' But shine 'Who?' on every one of them; without each one, would you still be here? 'Beyond everything I take to be mine but which is not fundamental to myself, who am I?' If you press that question and press it yet harder, the thought may suddenly dawn: Perhaps behind the curtain of all these habits and feelings and thoughts, nothing is there. Perhaps my self is just a collection of accidents. If there is anything fundamental beyond it, I do not know what it could be. This gathering sense that the ordinary self is not real is called the Chan doubt. When your 'Who' questioning has reached this point of doubt, your meditation can be said to have begun."

   The monk paused for a moment, then continued: "Does that mean that in the final analysis there is nothing at all? Yes, that is what the Buddha taught. But this nothingness is not the nothingness of blank emptiness. It is the emptiness of light. When I say 'light,' I am not using a metaphor. It is an actual light that is brighter than the brightest day of this world. It is the fundamental substance of the universe and our true identity, which does not die. In Buddhism we call it the true nature, or the true mind, or the Buddha nature. It is the original presence, and this body and this ordinary consciousness with its ego are intruders. Its state is happiness. Yet we have forgotten it. We are like a people of a land where there is no weather but storms, and they do not know there is a sun. But the sun has not gone out; it is simply clouded over. Ask the Chan question 'Who?' or recite the Buddha's name just once, and the cloud cover will begin to thin. Recite or ask 'Who?' for a seven-day session, then every day of the year, to quiet, purify, and concentrate your mind as you go about your business in the world, and you will feel your bright true nature welling up inside you. Sometimes there may be a brief rent in the clouds so that for a moment your eyes are dazzled with light."

He was silent for so long that I thought he had finished speaking, but then he said, "Whether we recite the Buddha's name or investigate the Chan question, the work is to concentrate the mind. When you singlemindedly recite 'Namo Amita Buddha,' that one pure thought of homage rises like a great sound wave to drive before it the noise of all the other thoughts. You subdue the selfish songs of your scattered mind with a single line of praise. The Chan method is different. The 'Who' question is not something to recite. It is not a sound, but a sword. During the Chan session we drop every detail of monastery life—except for the hall proctor, who represents us, we don't even bow to the Buddhas—so that every thought can be devoted to using the 'Who' question to slice away our attachment to our false selves. The Chan meditator is the temple guardian at the doors to his mind, and whenever a thought approaches, or whenever a stimulus comes knocking from outside to summon his attention, he raises the sword of his Chan doubt to cut the intruder down. 'If I don't believe that my false-thinking self is real, who can it be who is distracted by this thought? If the self is false, who can be disturbed by this sensation?' Slowly the thoughts will cease to arise, and the sights and sounds will no longer disturb us. Then the mind will be at rest, and the true nature will appear, like a sky that is free of clouds for ten thousand miles. Strike up your spirits, then, and take up your sword!"

With that he stopped speaking. He straightened up and half-closed his eyes and there was a rustling of clothes and a creaking of benches as people adjusted their meditation postures. Then the wooden block was struck three times in slow succession, and stillness settled on the hall.

While he was still talking, I had already begun trying his method. Who's listening to this monk? Who's sitting here in a Buddhist monastery in San Francisco? Who's Celebrisi? Long before, during the stunts, in another age of my life, I'd already begun asking myself that question. In a way I'd felt the Chan doubt, without knowing its name, since I was a boy. Why else had I left West New York but because I believed nothing in my life there was real?

I thought about what the monk had said about the difference between recitation and Chan. Karen's method was to drown the false self out with a joyous thought of the true, but she had never raised the point that the joyous thought itself was false; it was only another thought, though a special one, manufactured by the false mind. Who, in fact, was it who recited? Whose voice was it? Whose mind? Who was this person who used the recitation sound as a road to find the true? I thought this must be what the monk had meant. If one asked "Who?" bluntly enough, there could be no answer. In the last analysis, when everything that seemed to be an answer had failed, it was clear that no one real was there. The Chan question seemed to point directly like a finger to the emptiness beneath everything, including even the thought of emptiness.

Yet that, too, brought its own kind of quiet delight. For a long time I had felt the unceasing babble of my thoughts as something painful, like the radios that sometimes bawled through the open windows of the Chan hall from cars passing in the street. By pointing to the stillness beyond the thoughts, the "Who" question created a kind of separation between the thoughts and myself. The monk had described the question as a sword that cut the thoughts away; I experienced it as a kind of stairs. As I asked, Who is it who recites the Buddha's name? there was sometimes a distinct feeling of shift in my body, as the place of my awareness, the place where I asked "Who?", seemed to step aside and upward as if on a stair. My thoughts would be moving past below.

I remember noticing a thought about Vin, for example. In my mind we were walking around the hall of the monastery. Immediately I wanted to step down from the stair into the thought and begin talking to him about the place. Who is it thinking of him, though? I asked myself. My mind resisted the question. I wanted to think my thought; it was mine. Who wants it, though? Who's Celebrisi? If Celebrisi is a falsehood, what is this thought for? Slowly there was a parting, a pulling as if against a magnet, and then I had snapped free. The thought was gone. Who is it who's left, then? From the street an air horn blasted, and the black trucker who had driven me over the Sierras was there, wheezing and laughing, pulling me down into the thought of him. Who's thinking of him? Who? The pull of the thought passed, and I seemed to step up a second stair. As I concentrated on doubting the thoughts and staying above them, energy rushed in. Its rising force helped to hold me on the stairs.

The bell surprised me when it rang. I had been sitting for almost a half an hour in half-lotus position without noticing any pain in my legs at all. The sensations of my body below were lost in the energy. My own and the energy of the other meditators in the hall around me seemed to flow back and forth, intermingled across the boundary of my skin. I didn't want to get up. I felt wonderfully comfortable, as if for the first time in my life I had found the proper place for my legs and hands and arms.

The wooden block sounded for walking, but instead of circling around the room, the meditators filed through a yellow side door to another white hall, set with a row of long tables on either side. Taking up round bowls from their places, the monks on the right and the nuns on the left passed along separate tables laid out with dishes of rice and cooked vegetables. We laypeople followed them. There were also beans, fruit, nuts, and bread, but no meat. As I loaded up my plate, my hunger pulled me down the stairs so that my thoughts could mingle with the salty steam. I sat down and began eating quickly. After a few minutes I looked around and noticed that most people were eating slowly and deliberately, obviously trying to hold onto their "Who" questions in the face of a strong challenge. I tried asking who was hungry, but the hunger overpowered me, and I couldn't concentrate on the method. Throughout the meal, no one spoke. I sat at my place drinking tea—there was no coffee—letting my thoughts wander for a little while, resting in the peace of the place.

All through the afternoon, as the hall warmed with the sun through the high windows, on through the evening and far into the night, we sat and walked, and sat and walked, and sat and walked in silence. With every hour the burden of my thoughts became heavier and the stairs of the "Who" question harder to climb. At length the distraction of the ache in my ankles and shoulder blades defeated me. As my concentration weakened, the energy drained out of me, and there was nothing to shield me from the pain. By late afternoon I could hardly sit cross-legged at all. A few others around me seemed to be having trouble sitting still, but most of the people sat quietly till the bell rang, and when a supper of rice and vegetables was ready around six o'clock, only a few people came into the dining room to eat it; the rest stayed seated in the hall.

I can't measure up to these people, I thought; this is just going too far. That sit before lunch this morning was just beginner's luck. As the evening deepened, only the sight of the young monk bowing three times by the altar was able to raise my spirits enough so that I would try again to ask the Chan question. His bowing and rising seemed somehow perfect to me, in a single quiet motion again and again subduing himself and returning, subduing himself and returning. But once we'd sat down again and my thoughts of him had faded, I would soon enough be slumped over, half-dozing there and hoping for an end to it.

At last at midnight, there was no call for a run at the end of the walk. At the striking of the wooden block, the women left the hall by the front door, heading, I guessed, for another building, and the men went through another door behind the altar to climb some stairs. Even then a few monks stayed sitting in the hall. One of the laymen showed me a room on the third floor. He had a two-day growth of black beard and bright eyes that didn't look the slightest bit tired. I immediately fell asleep, and it seemd that I was immediately awakened by the same layman. It was actually twenty to three by my watch; I had slept two and a half hours. Outside the corridor, a monk was beating a thick octagonal board with a mallet. Knock, knock, knock-knock: the clean sound echoed in the silence. Men were walking quickly toward the bathroom, rubbing their heads or buckling their clothes. I can't take this, I thought as I followed them; these people play just too much for keeps. I'm going home.

The thought startled me. Who could possibly want to go home? In answer, a stream of complaints emptied into my mind. I challenged them: Who just wants to sleep? Who can't go without coffee? The complaints slightly disgusted me; if coffee and sleep were all I wanted, what had I bothered to leave West New York for? Whose body is this, anyway? I asked, and for a moment it didn't seem to be entirely my face that I was washing. Whose face is this? Suddenly the point of my awareness stepped up a stair, and into the chasm between the question and the complaining thoughts, a cool current of energy rushed in. My head cleared. I went back down to the hall, where people were already walking.

I held onto the "Who" question and stayed mostly on the stairs through the first sit and even sat in half-lotus for twenty-five minutes before giving up and letting my aching legs down. During the second sit, I fell asleep without knowing it, slumped over in my place until someone shook me awake; it struck me that the person I had heard snoring was myself. Throughout the long morning and the long afternoon, throughout that day and the next and into a third, I mounted the stairs of my meditation, fell down into my thoughts, struggled back up, and tumbled down again.

It surprised me at first how much vigilance was needed to keep the thoughts at a distance. After a while I realized that I hadn't been forced to hear all my thoughts when I was reciting the Buddha's name, because the sound of the recitation could overpower them; but the "Who" question revealed them. There below, company by company, the thoughts marched like an inexhaustible siege army onto the field of my mind. They were of hunger, thirst, and pain from sitting; of how that grey-haired laywoman sat enviably, maddeningly straight and unmoving across the hall; of the irritating small sniff the man next to me insisted on making when he breathed. They were of the people I had known: Lonny, George Terry, Brother Stephen, Father Jeremy, Karen, my friends back home, my father and mother, Margherita, and Vin. Whatever I regretted, whatever felt incomplete in what I had been to them and they to me, came forth onto the field to declare itself and call my attention down to be captured and taken away. It didn't want to hear that it was of the past and that the past was gone. It didn't want to be asked who it was; it knew, though I did not believe it. Many times I would suddenly realize that my mind had been wandering far along the path of some winding regret and that the fort of my meditation had been abandoned.

Again and again the impulse to leave the hall and get on a bus to New York swept through my thoughts. It took me by surprise; months had passed since the wish to go home had troubled me. Yet there I was in my mind's eye walking with Vin or sitting at the dinner table with Margherita or making the canasta party laugh. It was a fragment of a person living inside me, good old Joey, built of habits and desires that I'd turned my back on; I'd thought he had died. But he had only been biding time in the back of my mind, waiting for his chance to be master again. Panic that the Chan practice and the Buddha's name would pull me free of him for good had flushed him out of the shadows.

When his voice was there in my mind telling me to go home, I argued with him that what he wanted could never be recovered. Margherita had already written me that she was seeing someone else; she probably was planning to send me the divorce papers as soon as she had a new address for me. I knew she wouldn't want to stay single for long. But my arguments only increased the panic in my thoughts. If she was planning to get married again, they said, you have to go home right now, before it happens, and get her back. Do you want Vin to have another father and forget about you, so he doesn't even recognize you? You have to get out of this place. Don't wait for the end of the sit, don't worry about disturbing these people, you don't owe them anything. Get out of here right now, right this minute.

Then I would hold on tightly to the bench and recite the Buddha's name. I would gaze at the golden statues above the altar and think of what I hoped, of what the statues seemed to promise, that at last I would be able to break free and let Celebrisi go. Whatever he might say, I knew I was glad that Margherita had found someone else—glad for her, because it was what she wanted, and glad for myself, because it took away the heaviest of the obligations that had followed me ever since I had left West New York. If she married a good husband who agreed with her view of things and who'd be a good stepfather to Vin, then I was free of her, and I could forgive her. Then what need would I have to hold onto Celebrisi any longer?

Between the recitations, I would begin to ask, "Who?" again. Who is this reciting? Who's Celebrisi? Slowly I would remember that I didn't know and that I had never known. Celebrisi had been an invention, a disturbance on the sea of the true mind; he had been a dream. Who was holding onto him, then? Let him go. When that was my thought, good old Joey and his memories lost their power, and with a single question

"Who?" I would let them dissolve with a feeling of happiness. Then around me and within me I could feel only the energy burning in stillness. How could I not believe what the monk had said, that the emptiness of the true mind was made of light? Hadn't I seen it transform the buildings of Jackson Street at the end of the monsignor stunt? Though I'd never seen it since, hadn't I felt it shining there a thousand times, invisible beneath the darkness of my mind's eye?

The unreasonable schedule of the Chan session, twenty-one hours of sitting and walking, sitting and walking, made sense to me now. No one in his right mind would keep such a pace if he believed that his body and his desires and ordinary thoughts were the real substance of his life. Every step was a denial of them. My body ached as if it had been beaten, and my mind was exhausted. The walled path of the schedule was itself a "Who" challenge that forced the meditator, at every thought, to choose whether he wanted to rest and forget and let his old self conquer him or whether he still had the courage to let his old self go. Even when I hadn't been thinking of home, I looked at the door to the street more than once and decided I just might go through it during the next walk and not come back. It wasn't for sure, I thought, that this was the place that was right for me. I'd been looking for a long time, and I could keep on looking. It wasn't for sure that I needed to press the fight so relentlessly hard.

Some of the monks and nuns had taken turns giving instruction during the short sit before lunch and also for a period in the evening. On the fourth morning, the black-browed monk who had spoken on the day of my arrival returned to the bench beside the altar. He began by asking if anyone had a question. I had been feeling impatient and also afraid that the hour would come when my memories or my exhaustion would defeat me and drive me away without my wanting it. I asked the monk, "How long does it generally take for this Chan method to work and get you into your true mind, can I ask this?"

He looked down the row of benches and studied me. "What's your name?" he said.

"Celebrisi."

"And your first name?"

"Joey."

"When did you come here?"

"Well, just three or four days ago, but I've been trying to look for it for a pretty long time now."

I thought maybe I shouldn't have spoken up, since I was so new there, but he said, "Who is it who's looking for it?"

The question startled me. It had never occurred to me to doubt the thought that doubted the rest of the thoughts. "There has to be someone who wants to get out, though, doesn't there?" I asked him.

"Will that someone take his impatience with him into Buddhahood?" the monk asked me. He waited a moment for an answer, but since the answer was obvious, he went on, "If you don't plan to take your impatience with you, why are you holding onto it now?"

I didn't know what to say to him; his logic had silenced me.

"Did I put this false idea into your head: 'Here this person has been telling me how wonderful the Buddha nature is, so I'm going after it and grabbing it right away, because then I certainly won't have any more problems, and that's going to feel marvelous.' Something like that?"

"Something like that," I said. "You didn't put it there, though. I've been thinking it for a long time."

He laughed lightly. "In fact, it will feel marvelous. But who will feel it? Do you expect you can keep your self around so that it can have a good time being enlightened? No, this is not what the Buddha taught. Enlightenment requires letting the self go. You can't expect the true mind to relieve you of your afflictions. The true mind is not a god that takes your problems away. If there were a god who could do that, he would already have done it. Even the Buddhas can't keep our afflictions from us. We ourselves manufacture them in our false selves, and on our own initiative we think about them and attach ourselves to them and suffer from them. We ourselves must do the work of letting them go. When we have done the work, then our true minds, which are beyond affliction, will appear naturally, without our asking."

His dark eyes looked away from me and up at the golden statues behind him. "The three Buddhas whose images are seated above the altar—Shakyamuni Buddha in the center, who was our teacher in this world; Amita Buddha at his right, the Buddha of the Pure Land of the West, whose name we recite; and Medicine Master Buddha, the healing Buddha of the East—all taught the same truth: that all beings already have the Buddha nature and that only the thoughts and attachments of their false selves keep them from realizing it. What they taught was a summation of their own experience and the experience of countless other Buddhas who came before and after them. They, too, were people who had to let go of their old selves before their true natures could appear. Only then did they become the Buddhas that we all can become."

The monk was watching me again. "You yourself must have suspected there was something true beyond the false, to have been looking for it for so long, as you say. But if you know the true is there, why do you persist in seeking for it? Simply pull aside the shade of the mind that seeks. If you strengthen the mind that seeks by grasping for enlightenment, you are making your enlightenment impossible. The seeking mind is the source of your suffering. The Buddhas know contentment and joy because they seek for nothing: not for food, or sleep, or love, or wealth, or fame, or the true mind either. Therefore the path they teach is not to seek the true mind, but to end seeking. Let go of your desires, and suddenly you will be at your destination. When will that time come, though? It could be tomorrow; it could be ten thousand lifetimes away. It depends on what you do.

" 'If we're not to seek anything, what are we to do?' you may ask. 'Just sit here and wait?' No, the Buddha didn't teach us not to do anything; far from it. He told us not to seek while doing, to have no self while doing, to act without attachment to action. When you do something, ask yourself: 'Am I doing this for my own benefit, or for the benefit of other people?' If it's for yourself, then you know you are reinforcing the false self and postponing your realization of the true. If you are acting to help others, then ask yourself: 'Do I expect something in return, perhaps thanks or a good name?' If you do, then you still are not passing the test.

" 'That's hard,' you say. Of course it's hard. If it were easy, we would all have become Buddhas long ago. What are we to do, then, until we do become Buddhas? Simply act like a Buddha acts, as best we can. We become a Buddha not by wishing to be one or seeking to be one, but by practicing being one. We know that a Buddha does not kill, steal, lie, indulge in sexual misconduct, or take intoxicants, because these are selfish acts, and a Buddha is incapable of selfishness, because he has transcended his self and knows that he is one with all beings. Therefore we follow these five compassionate precepts. If we do not, how can we claim to be following the Buddha's path? A Buddha's mind is like a clear sky, unclouded by a single thought or feeling of the false and separate self; therefore we practice meditation to quiet and purify our minds. We purify our minds and purify our conduct; we study the wisdom of the Buddha's teaching; we benefit others and forget ourselves. How then can we fail to realize our true minds at last? Don't worry about how long it will take. Your worry does nothing but postpone it. Place your feet firmly on the path and walk it every day. There is nothing else you need to do."

He stopped speaking, adjusted his robe, and sat straight, and so I guessed he didn't expect me to respond to him. That was just as well, because I wouldn't have known what to answer. He had pulled the rug of my thinking out from under me. All these months I had been trying to give up every other desire for this one desire to enter the truth beyond desire, and I had never seen the contradiction in it, though it was obvious once he had pointed it out to me. This part of myself that wanted a new life: what made me imagine that it alone was true? I had never even looked at it, because it had been doing my looking. No wonder the old Celebrisi's memories were almost strong enough to defeat me; no wonder the Celebrisi who was seeking the new had never been able to find it. I had thought the new was separate from the old and would replace it, but at bottom they were the same self. Their tug-of-war was between two arms of the same body.

Who was Celebrisi, then, new and old? Who is this person who from the first moment he heard it liked reciting the Buddha's name? Who am I? I saw that I hadn't truly asked the "Who" question before at all, because I hadn't directed it at the full breadth of myself. If I was false, who was here? Was there anyone to ask who was here?

Suddenly it struck me that there was no one here. With the beginnings of fear, I looked around in my mind: I could find no one. Even the one who saw that there was no one was also no one. The one who saw that, too, was no one. Each step of the stairs vanished beneath me, and it struck me that there were no stairs above me, either; I had invented them. I was afraid. I felt I had to hold onto something. If it wasn't good old Joey, and if it wasn't the part of me that sought the true mind, who was it going to be? There had to be someone; I couldn't stand the idea of a blank nothing. It would be like the emptiness of the woods, and I couldn't face that emptiness ever again.

The sweet bell rang in the hall. The hall's here, I thought. These people are here, and I don't believe any wrong emptiness can come to this place. They all recite the Buddha's name here. I myself began to recite. The sound of the recitation flowed into the empty vessel of my mind. I remembered the monk's words: "You become a Buddha by practicing being one." We were walking around the hall, and I saw again the golden Buddhas above the altar. The young monk was bowing before them. I left the line and stood a few feet behind him. I bowed awkwardly, not knowing exactly where to put my hands and knees. As I bowed again, and then again, my mind calmed, and the thought came that the monk was right: I didn't need to look now. I was here. Karen and all my other teachers and my own inner guide in my dreams had brought me to this hall. The monk had already started to teach me the Buddhas' discipline; I had already begun to practice it. That was what I could hold onto; their discipline would guide me down the path of letting Celebrisi go. Making it my own would be my true stunt. If I ever saw Vin again, that's what I would have to teach him. Where else could I possibly need to go? I bowed, and in my heart I asked the Buddhas to help me learn to follow their path, live their pure life, and replace my false thoughts with their name.

I was alone there. The others had gone into the dining room. Suddenly I noticed that there seemed to be something wrong with my vision, as if someone was shining a lamp into my eyes. I couldn't see the Buddha images above me. I stopped bowing. I wasn't sure exactly where I was. In my own voice, the Buddha's name resounded around me. In a moment my eyes adjusted, and I saw that all the hall was blazing quietly with light.